# True Death

Books by Dale E. Lehman

## Howard County Mysteries

*The Fibonacci Murders*
*True Death*
*Ice on the Bay*
*A Day for Bones*

## Bernard and Melody Capers

*Weasel Words*
*Rooftop Sonata*

## Science Fiction

*Space Operatic*
*The Belt*
*Penitence*

## Short Story Collections

*The Realm of Tiny Giants*
*Found by the Road*
*Manifest Secrets*

# TRUE DEATH

a howard county mystery

## DALE E. LEHMAN

Chase, Maryland

True Death
Dale E. Lehman



Cover design by Proi
https://99designs.com/profiles/proi

Cover image copyright © Bowie15|Dreamstime.com
Hand sketch feather sketch copyright © Anton Kubalik|Dreamstime.com
Three feathers copyright © Dzhamilia Ermakova|Dreamstime.com
Winged angel copyright © Rolffimages|Dreamstime.com

Book design by Kathleen Lehman
Text set in 12-pt. Calluna

Published by Serpent Cliff, an imprint of One Voice Press, 2016
Published by Red Tales, 2019
Essex, Maryland
United States of America
https://www.DaleELehman.com

ISBN: 978-1-940135-57-1
ebook: 978-1-940135-58-8

*For my parents, who raised me right. Any errors that
remain are entirely my own.*

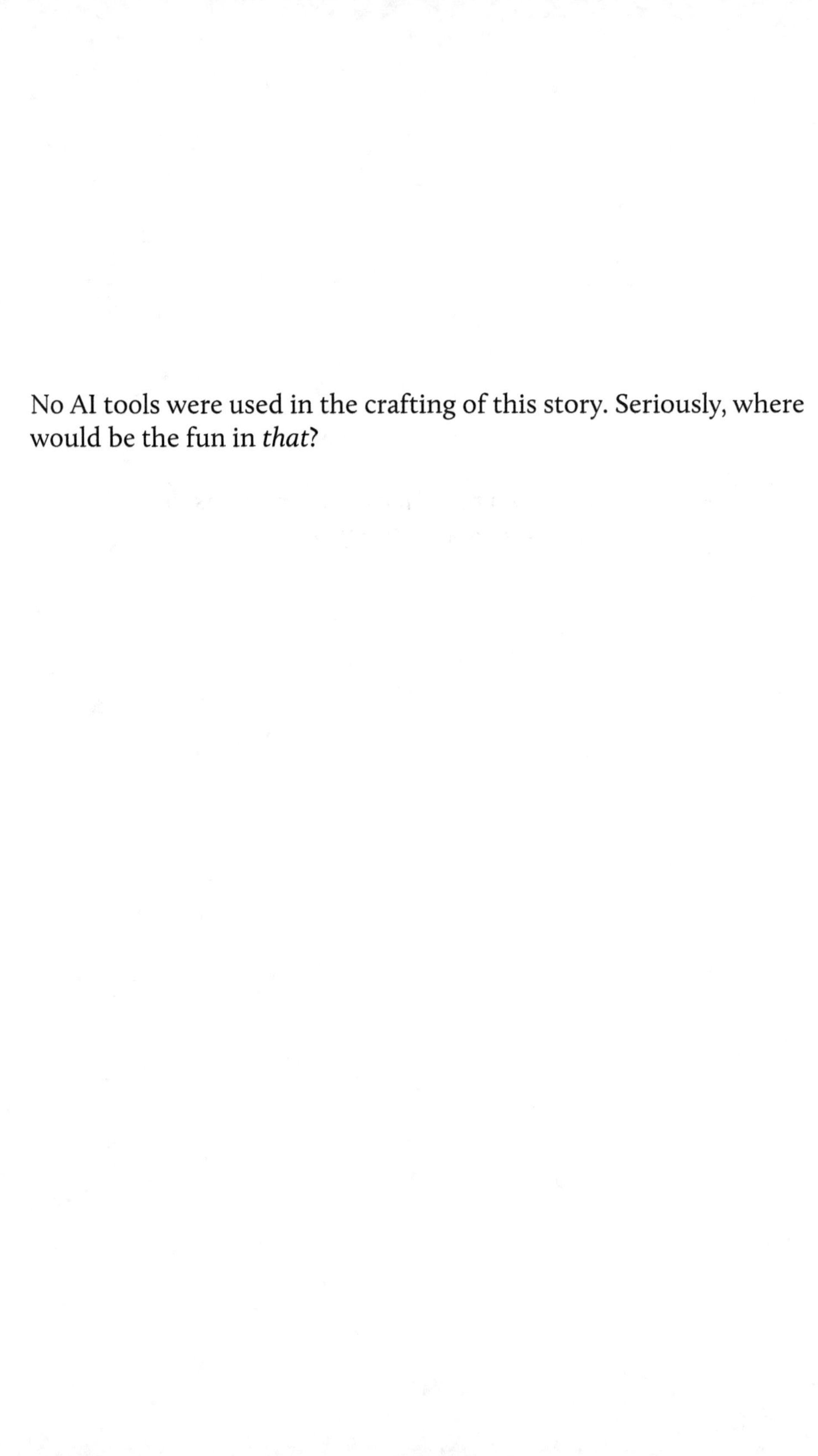

No AI tools were used in the crafting of this story. Seriously, where would be the fun in *that*?

## Acknowledgements

Many people came together to bring this book from imagination to publication. Foremost is my editor and wife, Kathleen Lehman, who deserves a medal for her extraordinary efforts. The rest of my family also has my deepest gratitude for their support and suggestions along the way. I'd also like to offer a special thank you to my wife's cousin Stella Laffleur, who championed *The Fibonacci Murders* but who passed away before the present work was published. And last but certainly not least, over thirty friends, family members, and total strangers contributed to a Kickstarter project for this book. Every one of them has my deepest gratitude. The following people were particularly generous and so deserve special recognition as patrons of this book:

Andrea, Bill, & Bridget Bullock
Claire and Stewart Mathison
Matthew and Melissa Ward
with Samara & Gabriel Greear
and Rose & Eve Ward

**Thank you one and all!**

## About the Setting

The places are real: Howard County, Maryland; Lockport, New York; Southglenn, Colorado. Some details of these locales were changed to suit the story, while other setting elements were made up from whole cloth. I assure you, shoddy research didn't enter into it. At least not on that score. I won't guarantee perfection in all other areas...

# O SON OF JUSTICE!

*Whither can a lover go but to the land of his beloved? and what seeker findeth rest away from his heart's desire? To the true lover reunion is life, and separation is death. His breast is void of patience and his heart hath no peace. A myriad lives he would forsake to hasten to the abode of his beloved.*

—Bahá'u'lláh, *The Hidden Words*, Persian 4

# Chapter I

The run cut into the base of the mountain, twisting and turning with the land, bubbling past old farms, past pine and spruce and deciduous trees waking from winter slumber, gurgling beneath small bridges on gravel roads, down past a mansion built by some retired executive looking to get away from it all, down through the gap between the mountain and its neighbor, down to join with the river just south of Centerville. A paved road kept the water company, winding through the mountains alongside it. Where the run entered the gap, splashing over a series of rock steps, an unpaved track slipped southward into the trees, climbed the slope, and ended at a small, run-down shack.

On the porch, a man in a scarred old bentwood rocker creaked back and forth, back and forth, his blue eyes directed at the treetops yet not focused on them. Few ever saw those eyes, but those who did frequently remarked how old they seemed compared to the body that hosted them. Vietnam veterans said he must have seen serious action in Afghanistan or Iraq; his eyes were *that* kind. Others speculated he had lost a wife or a child, or both. Not that anyone knew. He rarely came to Centerville, and then only to buy food. He arrived like a shadow, conducted his business, spoke to no one, and left like a faint breeze falling still. Whatever tragedy had befallen him, it seemed to have drained most of the life from him.

Had he talked to anyone, had anyone uttered such speculation, he would have shaken his head. He was, in fact, already dead.

Its official name was a mouthful: Baltimore-Washington International Thurgood Marshall Airport. The Supreme Court Justice's name had been appended in 2005, but most people referred to it simply as BWI or, if feeling formal, BWI Marshall. Typically ranking somewhere in the mid-twenties on the list of busiest U.S. airports, the terminals never felt all that busy to Phil Walters. His travels had taken him through more frenetic airports as well as quieter ones, but on the whole he liked BWI best. It felt roomy without sprawling, and ticked along efficiently.

This morning, Saturday, April second, the concourse seemed a bit subdued. Walters would have expected more travelers on a weekend, but their absence made it easier to spot the man he had come to find. Just over there at the kiosk, printing out the ticket for his flight to Denver, Detective Lieutenant Rick Peller had a tired look about him. His right shoulder sagged under the weight of his black carry-on, and when he turned Walters could see that his eyelids were drooping. The lieutenant stood just under six feet tall and looked fit for a man his age—about fifty, Walters guessed. His dark hair, thinning a bit and showing a touch of gray at the temples, was neatly combed with a part on the left. Peller studied his ticket as he began the walk to the gate, but he hadn't gone five paces before he stopped and cast a glance at Walters. He then pocketed the ticket, shoved the strap of his carry-on farther up his shoulder, and stood gazing out the huge windows to the parking garage beyond.

Walters bit his lip. It appeared Peller was waiting for him. How the detective had known escaped him, but there was no sense in playing games.

"Good morning, Lieutenant," Walters said as he approached. "Might I have a word?"

"I suppose," Peller said without enthusiasm.

Walters extended his hand. "Phil Walters."

Peller hesitated then accepted the handshake. "You already seem to know me." His eyes played over Walters for a moment, then he indicated a row of plastic chairs nearby. The two sat. "Let me guess. You're a reporter."

"A writer," Walters replied.

"Ah. You're writing a book on the Fibonacci murders."

Walters couldn't help but laugh. He supposed the whole thing was too obvious. Why else would a total stranger be approaching Peller just now?

"I'm sorry, but I can't help you. I'm leaving on vacation. My flight will be boarding in about half an hour, and unless you have a ticket, security won't let you follow."

"Actually, I wanted to propose a collaboration." Seeing Peller start to shake his head, Walters added quickly, "You don't have to answer now, but here's the thing. When incidents like this happen, all the major publishers scramble to contract books with insider bylines. They were on it well before you caught Freiberg. And let me tell you, there is a great deal of money to be made here. This is a story millions of people want to read."

Peller unshouldered his carry-on and set it on the seat next to him. He gazed down at his black sneakers and seemed to be pondering the offer. Walters held his breath in anticipation.

"I'm afraid," Peller said at last, "that I'm the wrong person for this. You should talk to Captain Morris."

The writer slumped and exhaled. "I already did. She said I should talk to you."

Peller cracked a smile. "Don't feel bad. You're in the same boat as ever other writer on this one."

"You've been approached by someone else?"

"Twice. I gave them the same answer. I can't do this. For several reasons." He stood and picked up his bag, adding, "None of which you'd understand. Good bye, Mr. Walters. I'm sorry."

Walters watched Peller as he made slowly for security and passed through on his way to his flight. The writer still had two more contacts to make, but it didn't look promising. The whole team, he suspected, was working from the same playbook. Yet something else was up with Peller. Walters would have bet on it.

That detective, he was hiding something.

⟨⟩

"Eric! Hey, Eric, wait up!"

Detective Sergeant Eric Dumas stopped in mid-stride and planted both feet on the carpet. He'd made it halfway from the door of his second-floor apartment to the stairwell before his neighbor Ozzie White realized he was passing by. White's hearing was uncanny. He seemed to be able to distinguish Dumas' footsteps from everyone else's, even through a closed door. At least, that was the only explanation Dumas could think of for the sheer number of times White had stopped him in the hall.

Dumas turned and smiled politely. "What's up, Ozzie?"

"I really got something for you this time. Man, you gotta see this one." He rushed over and held out a sheet of printer paper. "She's got an *incredible* pair of..."

"Ozzie, stop. I told you, I'm not interested in blind dates, especially not when they're arranged over the internet by you posing as me. I mean, come on."

White shook the paper at him. "Just have a look. You won't regret it."

With a sigh, Dumas took the proffered printout and looked at the photo. The light in the hall was so dim he could barely see the young lady's face or make out what she was wearing, although Ozzie hadn't been lying about her curvaceousness.

"Interested?"

Dumas gazed at his neighbor, who at the moment reminded him of nothing so much as a dog panting hopefully for its master's approval. "She's very beautiful," he said. "But I'd rather you let me find my own woman." He handed the paper back. Crestfallen, White accepted it. Dumas could feel those pleading eyes following him all the way to the stairwell.

Just as he stepped down the first step, White called after him: "But you never find one!"

Dumas descended the stairs at a modest clip, stopped to retrieve his mail, and left the building. He found White alternately amusing and irritating. The two of them were about the same age, but Ozzie's interests were far more worldly than Dumas'. He worked as an assistant manager at a cell phone store and always had the latest gadgets to play with. Over the four and a half years Dumas had known him, White had had a succession of nine girlfriends—some live-in, some not—and had pursued several times as many get-rich-quick schemes, none of which panned out. He seemed concerned, if not actually scandalized, by Dumas' lack of female companionship. Once when Corina Montufar had stopped by, White had come bounding down the hall to meet her, and was sorely disappointed when the much-anticipated girlfriend turned out to be just a colleague.

Dumas smiled at the memory as he got into his light grey Subaru and started the engine. Montufar, he thought, wouldn't be a bad match for him, although he was pretty sure she wouldn't appreciate the suggestion. *And that right there*, nudged a voice in the back of his brain, *is why you don't have a girlfriend. You'd always be comparing her to Corina.*

He told the voice in the back of his brain to shut up. He shuffled quickly through the mail, mostly credit card offers and coupons for stores he wouldn't shop again until Christmas, and tossed it on the seat. As the envelopes fanned across the upholstery he realized that one item wasn't junk. He fished it out and stared at the return address.

Ethan Dumas. Plano, Texas.

Uncle Ethan.

He turned off the engine and stared at the envelope as though it had been overnighted from Pluto. A knot growing in his stomach, he gingerly opened the envelope and pulled out the sheet of stationery within. He held it for several minutes, still folded, while half-formed thoughts swirled through his mind.

Twelve years ago, Uncle Ethan had told him in no uncertain terms that the family didn't want him around anymore. Since then, Dumas hadn't been in contact with any of them: not a letter, not a phone call, not an email.

Dumas' hands shook as he unfolded the paper and read:

*Dear Eric,*

*I heard about the murders out there and got to thinking. It's probably well past time we buried the hatchet. Philip is dead, killed three years ago in Juarez. Your aunt's been seriously depressed since then. Other things I can't bear to think about have happened along the way.*

*You may not believe it, but I probably did you a favor. Now it's time to come home. Give me a call.*
*Sincerely,*
*Uncle Ethan*

Dumas read it a second time. *Just like that?* he thought. *You shove me out the door and then twelve years later order me back?*

He crunched the letter into a ball and threw it onto the floor of the car.

∽

Eduardo Montufar didn't look too bad for a man who'd had skull and pelvis fractured in a car wreck three and a half weeks ago. Fortunately his injuries hadn't been as bad as they might have been, and he was able to leave the hospital just five days after the accident. He was now able to move around using a walker so long as he avoided putting weight on his left leg, and as usual his optimism sustained not only himself but his entire family.

His sister Corina, though, didn't like what was coming out of his mouth today. She struggled to keep the smile on her face as he said, "Summer is coming. I'm looking forward to playing some...some..." He made a swinging motion with his right arm. "Baseball."

The words themselves sounded fine, but they seemed to come out a bit too slowly—or was that just her imagination? At any rate, he shouldn't have had to fish for the name of his favorite sport.

Eduardo was lying on the sofa in the living room of his modest ranch-style house. A subdued clatter came from the kitchen where his wife Sylvia was busy making dinner; from the backyard came the laughter of their children, Jimmie and Susannah. Montufar tried to relax and soak up the comfortable sounds of the children playing and of onions being expertly chopped on a wooden cutting board. She could almost slip back to her own childhood, almost forget her worries.

Almost.

"In another month," Eduardo mused, his gaze slipping from her face to the world outside the window. The sun shone brightly on houses and cars and trees. "I should be ready to..." He waved again, this time toward the window. "You know."

"Just promise me you'll listen to the doctors," she said, again forcing a smile.

"Like I have a choice. Ella pleads, the doctor commands, and you give me that cop glare." He mimicked his sister's sternest face.

Montufar laughed, but stopped short as a movement outside the window snagged her attention. A short, sandy-haired fellow had just sprung from a red sports car and shoved the door shut. Now he stood motionless, staring at the house as though checking for booby traps.

Eduardo scratched his cheek. "Friend of yours?"

"Never saw him before."

Finally making his decision, the man approached the door at a determined pace and knocked. Eduardo nodded at his sister, who rose and answered.

"I'm sorry to disturb you," the man told her. "I'm looking for Detective Sergeant Montufar."

"And you would be?"

The man held out a business card he'd been concealing in his palm. "Phil Walters. I'm a writer."

Montufar took the card and studied it. It was simple and elegant, with the writer's photo occupying the upper left corner and his name, phone, and email address opposite.

"Looks like you found me," she said.

"I don't mean to impose, but could I have a word?"

"Being a writer," Montufar replied, deadpan, "I hope you have more than one." As Walters laughed, she stepped aside and motioned him in. "I suppose you know this is my brother's house."

"Yes, and I'm sorry if I'm intruding, but I'm in a bit of a jam and I was hoping you might help me."

Montufar led him in and introduced Eduardo, who smiled broadly and shook the writer's hand. She resumed her place and motioned Walters to a recliner. Sitting on the edge of the seat, he pitched his project: a first-person account of the investigation into the Fibonacci murders with her byline given pride of place and earning her a handsome cut of the royalties.

"I'm flattered that you would think of me, but I really don't feel qualified," she said when he had finished. "Captain Morris would be a better choice, or Lieutenant Peller. Although, he's just left on vacation."

"Yes, I know," Walters said, his voice wavering between irritation and exhaustion. "Why is it none of you people will go for this?"

Montufar leaned back and stared at the ceiling. She knew she was hedging, but she didn't think she could explain, and indeed there were things she couldn't in good conscience tell him. Inevitably, the military angle had been played up in the press, prompting certain elements to remind the department about a billion times about the "negative impact on national security" if the full story got out. They had agreed among themselves to pretend they had no clue what had plunged Lucas Freiberg into murderous insanity. It wasn't entirely obfuscation; in all honesty, they only knew part of the story anyway.

"It's complicated," was all she said.

Eduardo had watched silently, his eyes moving from one to the other as they conversed. When neither seemed to know what to add, he offered his own observation. "It's too soon."

Walters turned a surprised look on him. "I'm sorry?"

"You don't know what Corina and the others went through. They have a lot of emotion and stress to work through. It's only been..." He held up three fingers and studied them. "Three weeks, I think."

Walters just stared.

Eduardo shrugged apologetically. "I was in an accident. I may have lost count."

"My publisher wants this story three weeks *ago*," Walters said. "It's not too soon. It's nearly too late!"

Montufar rose. "I'm sorry, Mr. Walters. I've given you my answer. Now my brother needs his rest."

Walters looked at his feet, then nodded and stood. "All right. But you're throwing away a pile of cash. You know that, don't you?"

"There's more to life than money," Eduardo said before Montufar could reply. "'No servant can serve two masters. He will either hate one and love the other, or be devoted to one and despise the other. You cannot serve God and mammon.'"

Walters paused at the door. "I don't think your sister's soul is at stake here. I just want to help her tell an important story."

Montufar didn't say anything further but simply held the door until Walters had passed through and was well on his way. Then she quietly closed it and returned to her brother's side. Taking his hand, she stroked his fingers. "You're a lot brighter than you look," she chided.

He lay back and closed his eyes. With a childlike smile, he said, "I know."

# Chapter 2

The scream of the jet's engines and the voices of the other passengers smothered Peller. Seated by the window, an elderly couple quietly conversing next to him, he felt out of sorts, as though the world had been tilted sideways and everything familiar had slid out of reach. In part, he was sure, this was the psychological aftermath of the Fibonacci case, but in part it was trepidation over what lay ahead. He and his son Jason hadn't fully worked through his wife Sandra's death. In her absence, a silence had fallen between them, stifling Peller. There were things his son should know, that he should have told him, but he himself found them difficult to understand or accept, so they remained unspoken. He closed his eyes, wishing he could sleep.

"Twenty years, isn't it?" the man next to him asked.

"No," the man's wife said. "Nineteen. You're thinking of Chuck and Cassie."

"Why would I be thinking of them? They're Bob's family."

"Cassie's your niece."

"You know what I mean."

"Nineteen, anyway. But you don't even remember how long we've been married or how old *I* am."

"I got that part down," the man said with a laugh. "You're twenty-nine and we've been married forever."

Peller opened his eyes and looked out the window at the Midwestern farmland drifting by: a muted quilt of greens and browns, half-finished on the frame, seamed by the thin lines of roads, dotted now and again with a white square of town; top and batting and tick seemingly pinned together to the north by a massive collection of giant wind turbines.

*Looks like home*, Sandra whispered in the recesses of his mind.

*Home*, he silently replied. *It does indeed.*

Although for them home had been Lockport, New York, not the Midwest, and wind turbines had only been futurist dreams. Peller had grown up in town, Sandra on a farm seven miles southeast, just south of Dysinger. While he took a job with the Lockport police department and was attending the academy in Buffalo, Sandra went to Cornell and studied agronomy. She moved to an apartment in Lockport and got a job with the Greenway Cooperative, which specialized in organic farm products and, eventually, heirloom seed. The two might never have met except for a strange accident.

Peller had been patrolling the north end of town one morning, driving north on Mill Street just before it made its northwest bend. Traffic was typically light; there was only one car behind him at the time and nobody in the oncoming lane. Suddenly, he sensed a blur of white coming fast out of the woods to the left. Turning his head, he was surprised to see a large Dalmatian running flat-out. It came right up alongside his car, very nearly pacing him. Unnerved, Peller eased up on the accelerator. The dog, never breaking stride, raced on and, without warning, cut in front of him.

Peller hit the brakes. The car behind plowed into him and pushed him forward into the dog.

Cursing himself, he jumped out of the car and took a step forward before his mind caught up with events: his first priority was the other driver. He turned to see a young woman getting out of a gray Mazda. The hood of her car had buckled. Green fluid seeped out from under the vehicle and spread across the dark pavement.

"Are you okay, ma'am?" he called to her.

"Yes, I'm fine," she snapped. "Where's the dog?"

Peller went to find out. The Dalmatian, a male, was lying on its left side, panting rapidly. A bit of blood was seeping from its lower ribcage. On the whole it looked in better shape than he would have expected, although he knew it might have suffered internal injuries.

The woman rushed to kneel beside the dog. Stroking his head, she murmured, "Good boy. You'll be all right. We'll take care of you." She looked up at Peller, eyes pleading.

He was momentarily distracted by her face, a soft heart-shaped face framed by wavy dark brown hair. He could have gazed at her forever, but he forced himself to focus on the job at hand. "I don't know. I'm not sure we should move him ourselves. There's a veterinary clinic about three miles up route 78. I'll put a call in to them."

The woman nodded, and Peller returned to the squad car to report. Five minutes later, a blue Dodge pickup arrived. A woman wearing a white coat jumped out almost before the vehicle stopped. She was followed hastily by a young man wearing navy blue scrubs. The doctor—Mary Evans, according to the stitching on the left breast pocket of her scrubs— peered into the Dalmatian's eyes and checked his heartbeat while the man retrieved a stretcher from the bed of the truck. Peller helped him move the dog onto the stretcher, and once the animal was secure they placed him in the truck bed.

"I'll be there shortly," he told the veterinarian. As they left with their patient, Peller turned his attention to the woman. "There's the small matter of you running into my squad car," he said, and winked.

"Entirely your fault," she replied, not amused.

"Guilty. But you're not going anywhere in that." He nodded at her smashed car. "There's more coolant on the road than in your engine. I'll call a tow truck for you."

She waited while he arranged it.

"I'll need to see your license."

"Why?"

He shrugged. "Have to do the paperwork."

He watched her return to her car for her purse. She was, he thought, quite pretty in her jeans and red plaid shirt, her hair shifting about her neck and shoulders in the light breeze. It was too bad they had to meet under these circumstances.

She returned with her license and handed it to him but didn't release it. "You'll be honest about what happened, I hope?"

He took hold of the edge of her license and looked at it. "Sandra Fielding," he read aloud. "I will, Ms. Fielding. My dad would turn me over his knee if I didn't."

Sandra looked him over head to toe and smirked. "I doubt he could," she said and finally let go.

Peller gave her a smile, then took down her information and recorded the accident details. The tow truck arrived as he was finishing up. Once Sandra's car was hooked up, the driver asked if she wanted a ride to the garage.

"Actually," she said, turning to Peller, "I'd like to check on the dog. Would you mind?"

"Not at all."

The drive to the veterinary hospital was mercifully short. He couldn't think of a thing to say to her, and she didn't seem interested in talking anyway. She stared out the side window, either not noticing or ignoring his occasional glances at her.

The animal hospital didn't look like much on the outside, just a brick and glass storefront that could have been any small shop, but the waiting room was a bright place with orange and yellow seating, cheerful dog and cat photos on the walls, and a smiling receptionist who had been told to expect the police. She led them into the leftmost of the four exam rooms, told them the doctor would be in shortly, and quietly shut the door.

Peller took in the exam room with a quick glance: the stainless steel table, the cabinet with various medical supplies arranged on top, the informational brochures on fleas, worms, and other common pet maladies in a holder on the wall. A second door, no doubt leading to the surgery, was at the back of the room. Sandra sat in one of the two plastic chairs along the wall. Peller elected to remain standing.

"I hope he's all right," she said quietly.

"He's in good hands." Peller hoped he was right. He hadn't owned a pet since childhood and had never visited this clinic.

Dr. Evans came through the back door carrying a couple of x-rays. "He's one lucky dog," she said, clipping the films to the light-box. "Nothing's broken, although you can see here one of his ribs is cracked." She pointed.

Peller nodded, although he wasn't sure he was seeing what the doctor saw. He found most medical images cryptic. Sandra rose and stood beside him studying the pictures as though she were a doctor herself. Peller found the seriousness of her face endearing, and perhaps a touch amusing.

"He got one heckuva road rash," Dr. Evans continued, "but other than that, nothing too serious. He doesn't have any tags. Do you know who he belongs to?"

"Afraid not," Peller said. "He ran out of the woods. Nobody came looking for him while we were there."

The doctor shook her head sadly. "We'll put the word out, but if nobody claims him we'll have to find him a home or send him to a shelter." She raised her eyebrows at Peller, then at Sandra.

"I'm afraid I can't take on a dog right now," Peller said. "Not one of that size, anyway."

Sandra shook her head. "I live in an apartment that doesn't allow pets. Poor guy. Can I see him?"

Peller thought she wanted to claim the dog in spite of the rules. Her sadness was almost painful. "I'll ask around if no owner comes forward. Maybe one of the guys on the force would have room for him."

"That would be wonderful," Dr. Evans replied. "I don't want to move him too much right now, but you two can come back for a few minutes."

She led them into the back, a large area lined with cages, some occupied, some empty. An orange tabby stretched out an inquisitive paw as they passed. The Dalmatian, his wound dressed, was resting in the largest of the cages. It perked up when it saw Sandra. Dr. Evans opened the cage so Sandra could pet the animal.

"Good boy," she said. "You're looking better already!"

The dog wagged its tail and nuzzled Sandra's arm.

"You get lots of rest. We'll find your family for you."

Peller and Dr. Evans both smiled at her.

Once Sandra managed to tear herself away from the patient, she and Peller thanked the doctor and returned to the squad car. Peller looked up at the sky, mostly clear with a scattering of small cumulus clouds. "You'll need a lift somewhere, I suppose."

"Is that a professional offer or a personal one?"

Peller felt a flush of embarrassment.

She gave him a coy smile. "Actually, I was on my way to work."

"Where is work?" he asked, glad she had given him an out.

"Greenway. Up Mill Street."

"I know it. Let's go."

Once in the car, they lapsed into the same uncomfortable silence as before until they arrived at Greenway, a bland warehouse fronted by a store. He parked at the main entrance. Sandra got out but before closing the door leaned in and said, "I might need a ride home. I get off at five."

"So do I," Peller replied, surprised at how quickly he'd effectively offered to pick her up.

"Dinner?"

"Well..."

"My treat. My place, in fact. It won't be fancy, but..." She shrugged.

"I'd love to."

She smiled, closed the car door, hurried to the store entrance, and vanished inside. Peller watched her the whole way.

"Wow," he told himself.

Eric Dumas returned to his apartment laden with shopping bags filled with groceries and new clothing. It was going to take him three trips from the car to get it all upstairs, one of several things he didn't particularly like about apartment life, but he couldn't see spending money on a house just for himself. For now, he could put up with the inconveniences.

His hands full and his head still rattled by thoughts of Uncle Ethan, he mounted the stairs and moved quietly down the hall, hoping to avoid any more of Ozzie White's harebrained schemes. As it happened, Ozzie wasn't lying in wait for him this time, but there was a fellow knocking at his door, a shortish man with light hair. The man turned as Dumas approached. "Detective Sergeant Dumas?"

"In person."

"My name's Phil Walters. I'm a writer."

"In search of a book, presumably."

"Indeed. Could I have a few moments of your time?"

Dumas shifted bags from his right hand to his left and fished his keys out of his pocket. "I could use a distraction," he said, unlocking the door. "Come on in."

The apartment had two bedrooms, one of which Dumas had transformed into a library. The front door opened directly onto the living room. At the back, a dining area huddled by a sliding glass door, flanked by the kitchen. Dumas had furnished the living room simply: a couple of comfortable but inexpensive forest-green chairs, a sofa of similar style, and a modest flat-screen television. He motioned Walters to a seat, deposited his bags on the dining table, and joined his guest.

"I won't waste your time," Walters said. "I've been approached by my publisher to do a book on the Fibonacci murders. They want an insider's story. If you'll work with me, you'll get the primary byline and a big chunk of the royalties. Books like these have enormous potential. People are eager to get the full scoop."

"And you think I'm the right person to tell the story?" Dumas asked. He thought he already knew the answer, so wasn't surprised by the response.

"Frankly, you're one of four people who could tell it. The other three all refused."

"So I'm your last hope?"

"If necessary, I can research and write the book without your help, but it wouldn't be the same."

Dumas leaned back and regarded Walters with some curiosity. "How could you research it if the key players won't talk about it?"

"Someone will talk. Someone always does. But you're right, details would be missed."

"How much money are we talking?"

"We're talking bestseller. At minimum, I'd guess a couple hundred thousand, split between us. Likely more. And that's not counting subsidiary rights. It would be a great subject for a film."

"Enough to keep me in police work, anyway," Dumas said with a laugh.

Walters smiled. "Exactly."

"Assuming I were interested in money."

"Who isn't?"

"Food isn't free, but to be honest, wealth doesn't motivate me."

"What does?"

Dumas didn't answer right away. He wasn't sure he could explain it to someone like Walters—or much of anyone, really—but the question deserved an answer. So he said, "The journey."

Walters waited patiently for more.

"Life is a sort of quest, you see."

"I do," Walters said. "I once spent a year in a Zen monastery up in New York."

Dumas hadn't expected that. Intrigued, he leaned forward and rested his chin on his folded hands. "Really! With what result?"

"Chiefly a book. But if the journey is the thing, the result doesn't matter. Or does it?"

"Of course it does. Each result sets the stage for the next phase of the journey."

Walters studied Dumas, his expression serious, like a committed student absorbing a lesson from a master. The thought made Dumas uncomfortable; he was certainly no master.

Finally the writer ventured, "The ultimate goal is truth."

Dumas nodded. "One never quite gets there, but one can always draw closer to it."

"Which brings me back to my proposal. Why not tell the truth about these murders?"

Leaning back, Dumas exhaled heavily. He should have known better. But he was willing to play along. "You think someone isn't telling the truth?"

For a moment, Walters seemed unsure of himself. He shifted uncomfortably and looked out the back door. Not that there was much to see, Dumas knew, aside from another apartment building.

"I think someone regards something about this case as too sensitive for public airing. I'm not saying anyone is lying, but someone is definitely hiding something."

Intrigued, Dumas asked, "Who would that be?"

Walters shrugged. "Maybe all of you, but especially Lieutenant Peller. I got the feeling that he really didn't want to talk about something."

"Several things," Dumas said, and Walters looked up, surprised. "But most of them have nothing to do with the case. He lost his wife a few years ago, and his family is still trying to come to terms with her death. If you got a feeling from him, it was likely because of that, not because of anything connected to the murders."

"He was certainly evasive about the murders."

"I'll be happy to tell you one thing about that case," Dumas said, "but only one. For the rest, you're on your own."

Walters leaned forward. Dumas figured this was the most the writer had gotten out of anyone so far, and as the old saying went, beggars couldn't be choosers. "Tell me," Walters said.

"It was hell on all of us."

The writer waited, but Dumas said nothing further, so finally he asked, "That's it?"

"If you'd been where we were, you wouldn't say that. Can you imagine what it's like for a cop in a place like Howard County, a place where murder is mercifully rare, to suddenly find bodies piling up on his doorstep? And not knowing how to stop it?"

"But you did stop it."

"We got lucky." He shook his head and ran his hand through is hair. "Twenty people died, and that was lucky. Think about that."

Walters appeared to be giving it consideration, but then he changed course. "About Peller's wife. How did she die?"

"A traffic accident," Dumas said absently. "A hit-and-run. We never found the other driver. You want to talk about hell, that was the worst. For all of us, really, but especially for Rick."

"You knew her, didn't you?"

"Yes, I knew her. She was one amazing woman."

"A loss like that with no closure. Yes, I see now."

Dumas nodded, but he found the look on Walters' face disconcerting. It wasn't sympathy. It was calculation.

"Someone should help him find that closure," the writer said. Then he stood and offered his hand to Dumas. "I've taken up enough of your time."

Dumas rose and shook the writer's hand. "No problem," he said, and saw Walters out. But that look of calculation haunted him for hours.

# Chapter 3

The blue-eyed man rose from his bentwood rocker, stretched without enthusiasm, and padded into the shack. Although the day was bright enough, inside it was dark. The few windows, opaque with years of grime, admitted little light, and although the cabin had electricity, the man didn't use it for lighting, only to keep food cold and run the oil heating system in winter.

The cabin only had two rooms: a larger one in front which served as both living area and kitchen, and a smaller bedroom in the back with a bathroom off to the side. He went to the kitchen now, made a peanut butter sandwich, and drew a glass of water. He sat at the small wood table and ate.

He thought of her.

He always thought of her.

He wished he could stop, but he couldn't, no more than he could forgive himself for what he had done to her. And for what he had done to himself.

The battery-powered clock on the wall chimed noon.

He wished he could turn back the clock.

The clock ticked on.

Two weeks before, Denver had shaken off an abnormally hard winter. Now the airport registered a temperature of sixty-eight under a clear blue sky, conditions Peller found just right for the start of a vacation. The whole family met him in a massive group hug as he exited the concourse: Jason and Belinda, eight-year-old Susie, and six-year-old Andrew. Then Peller swept up his grandkids, one in each arm, and they peppered his cheeks with kisses. People flowed around them, some smiling at them, others marching past without a glance, minds set on their destinations.

Jason looked a lot like his father: a touch taller at exactly six feet, dark brown hair parted on the right, hazel eyes that seemed to take in everything but revealed very little. His smile, though, was his mother's. Dressed in jeans and a plaid shirt, he made Peller think again of Sandra, and for once the memory of her carried with it no sadness. She lived on here, now, in their son, and to his surprise he found the thought comforting.

Belinda stepped forward and lifted Andrew from Peller's arms. "Let's let Grandpa breathe," she said gently. A good four inches shorter than her husband, she had dressed more elegantly in an ankle-length floral skirt and a lightweight blue sweater. Her hair was a pale brown with gold streaks here and there. She wore it pulled back in a ponytail.

Peller set Susie down on her feet and took her hand. "I deduce you're all happy to see me," he said with a wink at the kids.

"You're all they've talked about for the past week," Jason said. "Let's get your luggage."

Small talk dominated until, bags in hand, they stepped outside the terminal. Peller had never visited Denver before and was momentarily awed by the dark blue wall of the Rocky Mountains, topped with gleaming white, in the near distance.

"I wouldn't mind having that view from my back yard," he said.

"It's definitely one of our selling points," Jason agreed. "We'll take you up there tomorrow."

The children bombarded him with stories from school while they walked to the car and drove to their three-bedroom ranch home in Southglenn. The street looked quiet to Peller, a gently curving row of similar homes, the yards landscaped with small trees and beds of annuals and perennials exploding with color in the spring warmth. Jason and Belinda's place was pale blue with a two-car garage on the left and a stone chimney on the right. Even before setting foot inside, Peller somehow knew he would feel at home here, a thought in the face of which his earlier unease seemed to evaporate.

The sensation was familiar; he'd known it once before, decades before.

"It's not much," Sandra told him as she unlocked the door. "And a bit of a mess, I'm afraid."

"So that's your plan," Peller replied. "You're going to put me to work cleaning."

"Curses, foiled again." She pushed the door open, stepped into the dim foyer, flipped a light switch, and led the way.

Before entering, Peller somehow knew he was going to feel at home here, and he wasn't disappointed. Although the living space wasn't large, Sandra had managed to arrange a simple collection of inexpensive furniture in a way that made it feel roomy. Perhaps it was the lighting: a floor lamp here, a table lamp there, a mirror on the wall catching the light and throwing it back. She led him to the dining area where a light wood table waited and offered him a chair.

"Be right with you," she said and went down the hall to her room.

The kitchen flanking the dining room was quite small. Everything could be reached just by turning around. He thought that convenient but suspected Sandra found it claustrophobic. There were some unwashed dishes piled in the sink, but aside from that he couldn't see much reason for her to say the place was a mess. A tan suede jacket was draped over the back of the sofa and a few books and magazines were strewn on an end table. There might have been a bit too much dust about the place for her tastes, he supposed, but he wouldn't have noticed it had he not been looking for some elusive sign that something was amiss.

He rose and went to look at the reading material: current copies of *National Geographic*, *People*, and *Mother Earth News*, a romance novel with a fairly steamy cover, Rachel Carson's *Silent*

*Spring*, and something that looked political by an author whose name Peller didn't recognize. It seemed an odd collection.

While he was wondering what the literature said about Sandra, he was startled by a rattling at the door. His training brought him to full alert: was someone trying to force entry? As he began to move forward to check on it, a woman outside shouted something, either in anger or annoyance.

Before he had taken more than two steps, the door flew open to reveal a slight blonde woman, her arms full of paper bags, keys dangling from her fingers. She gave the door a rough kick and rushed inside, only to stop short when she saw Peller standing there in his police uniform. The door bounced off the wall and hit her, but she didn't move.

Confused, Peller just stared, fairly sure he was scaring her but not knowing what to say.

"What's going on?" she finally squeaked. "Is something wrong?"

"No," he said, feeling stupid. "Everything's fine."

"Where's Sandra? What are you doing in my apartment?" She looked around as though the answers might be lying somewhere in plain sight.

"Well," Peller said. He shrugged. "She invited me for dinner." And then his brain engaged. "Wait a minute. *Your* apartment?"

"Yes, my apartment." Apparently deciding there was no danger, the woman quickly crossed the room and set her bags on the table. "Ours, anyway. Sandra and I are roommates."

"She didn't mention a roommate."

Sandra returned, wearing a knee length rose-colored dress. "You're just in time, June," she said to the other woman. "I'm making dinner tonight."

"You didn't mention a roommate," Peller told her.

"No," she replied with a sweet smile. "I didn't. Sit down. I'll have it ready soon."

June looked Peller over carefully, then followed Sandra into the kitchen, where there was barely enough room for the two of them. "You also didn't mention you had a date," she said. "But if he has a brother, I'll overlook that."

"Do you have a brother?" Sandra called to him.

"He's in the army at the moment," Peller replied, trying not to sound as rattled as he felt. "Down in Virginia."

"Just my luck," June said.

Peller watched the women working in the kitchen, unable to see what they were making but noticing that their movements were uncannily synchronized. In spite of the cramped quarters, they never got in each other's way. "You two aren't sisters, are you?" he asked.

Sandra laughed and looked back at him. "Don't tell me you think we look alike."

"You move alike."

"He's watching us move," June said. "Typical male."

Peller felt a flush of heat. "Typical cop," he protested.

"Uh-huh."

"Don't tease him," Sandra said. "He's nervous enough as it is." She whispered something to June and they both giggled.

Peller was grateful when they brought the food to the table but a bit surprised at the fare: stovetop macaroni and cheese, tuna, and a plate of sliced tomatoes and black olives, accompanied by a pitcher of iced tea. Although Sandra had told him it wouldn't be fancy, he'd been expecting a bit more.

Once the women were seated, Sandra folded her hands in her lap, closed her eyes, and bowed her head. Peller followed her cue, but she said nothing. He glanced up and noticed that June was simply looking out the window.

"Well," Sandra said, looking up, "let's eat."

They passed the food around. "So how did you two meet?" June asked.

"She ran into my cruiser," Peller said.

"Because he slammed on the brakes right in front of me," Sandra added.

Peller shrugged. "Because of the dog. Which I hit because she ran into me."

"Which wouldn't have gotten in front of you if you hadn't let it."

June looked from one to the other while they traded accusations. "Sounds like a match made in heaven," she said.

Peller couldn't help but laugh. "We've only begun to smash things up."

Sandra gave him an exasperated look, then joined the laughter. "Maybe we'd better find something less destructive to do," she said, shaking her head.

Peller was about to agree, until he saw June arch her eyebrows suggestively. Instead, he put on his business face and asked, "Do you have less destructive hobbies, ma'am?"

Sandra blinked at him, either surprised or doing a very good job of feigning it.

"Score one for the cop," June laughed. "Actually, very few of her hobbies involve mayhem. She wants to save the planet."

Peller wasn't surprised, having seen how much she had cared about the Dalmatian. "An environmentalist?"

Sandra nodded. "You could say that. I grew up on a farm and don't like where agribusiness is heading."

"Thus Greenway," Peller said.

"Right. We offer an alternative."

June gave Peller a coy look. "And what do *you* offer?"

"Well." He took a sip of his iced tea to hide his unease. "An alternative to chaos, I guess."

"Ah," June said, still eyeing him playfully. "You protect and *serve.*"

Sandra rolled her eyes. "June..."

"Sandra," June parroted. "If you're going to hang out with him, he's going to have to get used to me."

"Or I could just take her to a lot of restaurants and movies," Peller said.

June laughed and slapped playfully at his arm. "I like you." She turned to Sandra and said, whispering loud enough for Peller to hear. "He's a keeper."

But Sandra ignored her. She narrowed her eyes at Peller and asked, "What, on a policeman's pay?"

On the afternoon of Sunday, April third, Charles Moore stopped for a late lunch at a local restaurant in Elkridge on U.S. Route 1 just south of the Harbor Tunnel Throughway. A forty-six-year-old electrician, he had just come from his parents' house a few miles to the north in Halethorpe and was on his way to visit a lady friend in Columbia. A studious-looking fellow with moderately dark skin, a lean frame, and a pair of wire-rimmed glasses, he had carried into the restaurant a book on the robotic exploration of Mars. Everything else he'd brought along—some tools of his trade, a jacket, a couple of music CDs, his cell phone, and a laptop computer—had been left in his brand new Chevy pickup.

The book, his wallet, and the clothes on his back were thus the only things not stolen while he ate.

# Chapter 4

It was a warm day in the Baltimore environs, with the temperature reaching the mid-sixties by early afternoon, a light breeze, and lots of sun. A good day for tending the flowerbeds, Penny Lowell thought, so she was doing just that, dressed in jeans and a chambray shirt. She lived in a red brick rowhouse, the westernmost unit in a building of four. It was one of a number of nearly identical buildings tucked inside a slight bend in Interstate 695, the Baltimore Beltway, in Catonsville, to the west of the city. It wasn't the quietest location owing to the nearby rush of traffic, but it was pleasant enough and conveniently located to the Spring Grove Hospital Center, where she worked as a psychiatric nurse.

At the moment she was kneeling on the ground, digging weeds out of a bed of pink and white petunias and tossing them into a plastic yard waste bag. She paused and smiled at the sandy-haired man who was kneeling beside her, also digging weeds. "Glad you came out?" she asked.

Phil Walters returned her smile and nodded. "It's a nice day," he said.

"Too nice to be chasing after cops."

"If we weren't out here, I could be chasing after you." He nudged her arm with his elbow.

"Work before pleasure," she said.

"Is that a maxim or a promise?"

"Of course."

He resumed digging. "Then we'd better make short work of this."

Lowell grinned at him and returned to her work. Before long she was lost in other thoughts, ranging from the list of things she wanted to get done this spring to a planned trip to visit her parents in Harrisburg, Pennsylvania, next month to her partner's frustrated efforts to enlist a Howard County detective to work on his book with him. Walters had done well for himself, writing for a number of regional and national publications as well as having three moderately successful books published, but this project could take his career to the next level. The only obstacle: nobody wanted to work with him. He'd pitched the project to all of the key players and struck out every time.

Except...

"What about the mathematician?" she asked.

Walters glanced at her. "What about him?"

"Have you talked to him yet?"

He shifted his weight back on his calves and looked up at the sky. "No. I'm not sure he'd know enough."

"Are you kidding? He's the one who figured it out!"

"That's the social media chatter, but I suspect the reality was rather different."

Lowell tossed a couple of weeds into the bag and brushed dirt from her hands. For someone so smart, she thought, Phil sometimes could be incredibly dense. "Why do you think the cops don't want to talk about the case? Because they didn't solve it. It's an embarrassment to them. This mathematician..."

"Tomio Kaneko," Walters supplied.

"Right. He may well know more than any of them."

Setting aside his trowel, Walters shook his head. "I talked to Bernie Richards at the *Sun*. They wanted to do a piece on him, but Kaneko wouldn't talk. Said he didn't want publicity."

"You don't have to give him a byline. You could put, 'As told by an anonymous insider.' Something like that."

"Maybe." He sounded unconvinced.

"Come on, you're way more persuasive than Bernie Richards." She winked at him.

With a laugh, Walters brushed off his hands and stood, then helped Lowell to her feet. He put his arms around her waist drew her close. "I doubt what works on you will work on an old mathematician."

"I should hope not." She kissed him lightly on the lips.

"Actually, I want to track down what happened to Peller's wife. Maybe if I can help him, he'll be willing to return the favor."

"That would take too long. Besides, if the police never figured it out, what makes you think you can?"

"Because I don't have to build a legal case. I can play hunches that the cops wouldn't bother with."

"Like what?"

"Like what if the pickup that hit and killed Sandra Peller was stolen?"

Lowell pulled back, but not completely out of his embrace, and looked at him like she thought he was nuts. Which she did. "Why would you think that?"

"I did a bit of digging already. The circumstances of the accident were odd. It also occurs to me that if the truck was stolen, someone other than the driver might have put two and two together. Auto theft is big business. A lot of people are involved."

He pulled her close again, and she rested her head on his shoulder. "But Walter, if that's what happened, someone isn't going to want anyone to find out. It could be dangerous."

He nodded, but said nothing.

She raised her head and looked into his eyes. "That can wait. First find out if this Kaneko guy can help you. If not, then you have a plan B."

He studied her face and ran a finger along her cheek. "Maybe you're right."

"Of course I am. How about we go inside for a bit?"

Walters looked down at the flower bed. "We haven't finished weeding."

"Pleasure before work."

He raised an eyebrow in passable imitation of a *Star Trek* Vulcan. "That's not what you said before."

Extricating herself from his embrace, she took his hand and pulled him toward the door. "Woman's prerogative," she said.

The day in Denver began with an early breakfast of bacon and eggs, cinnamon rolls, orange juice, and coffee. Immediately after, the Peller clan drove north along the mountains and then west into Rocky Mountain National Park, where the kids gleefully dragged their grandfather up and down trails, around scenic overlooks, and into snowball fights. The highest stretches of road were still closed due to the winter's heavy snowfall, but they were able to reach an overlook at nine thousand six hundred feet, the highest altitude at which Peller had ever stood. He marveled at the views of pine-covered mountains and the occasional flash of brilliant blue when a Stellar's jay flew by.

"Your mother would have loved it here," he told Jason as they looked over the valley far below.

Jason nodded but said nothing. Peller felt as though a heavy curtain had suddenly been dropped between them. Before he could think of what to say next, the children ran up with news of some exciting discovery and dragged their father off to see it. When they were gone, Belinda remarked, "He never talks about her."

Peller gazed at the peaks across the divide. "They were very close. Even as a teenager, when he was pulling away."

"Still. It can't be good for him to keep it all bottled up inside him."

"Takes after his old man. I don't talk much about her, either."

"You should," she admonished gently. "She was worth talking about."

Peller glanced at her, surprised by the comment, although he wasn't sure why. People had always said things like that about Sandra.

The kids returned, each hauling their father by a hand.

"What was that all about?" Peller asked.

"They spotted a red fox back in the woods," Jason said. "I don't think anyone else saw it. Their eyes are as sharp as yours."

"You're all in the deep end of the gene pool," Belinda said with a laugh.

They arrived home late after stopping on the way for dinner at a mom-and-pop restaurant. By then the kids had dropped off into an exhausted sleep. Jason and Belinda tucked them into bed, and the adults gathered around the kitchen table to sip mugs of hot spiced tea. Silence hung heavily over the table until finally Belinda set down her drink and addressed her father-in-law. "Something's on your mind."

He shifted uncomfortably, and Jason glanced at him as though sensing what was coming. "Dad's just tired," he said. "He's had a long couple of days."

"And he's not young like you two," Peller said. He tried to smile but felt it turning into a grimace.

"Oh, come on," Belinda prompted. When Jason started to object, she raised her eyebrows pointedly. Peller was reminded of his wife warning a young, misbehaving Jason. His son leaned back, folded his arms over his chest, and looked away.

"Well." Peller tried to organize his thoughts as though he'd been called upon to make an impromptu speech. Probably not the right approach, he thought, yet he didn't know how else to get through this. And he did have to get through it somehow; it was part of the reason he had made the trip. "I've been thinking a lot about your mom lately. How we met, things like that."

Belinda smiled and raised her cup again. "She loved to tell how you made her crash into your squad car."

He returned her smile, spontaneous and genuine this time. "Yeah, she never let me live that down." But then the memory of her death encroached, and he realized for the first time how ironic fate had been. "We met because of a car crash," he mused, "and she died in a car crash. Strange." He wondered why he'd never made that connection before. Could it be that he'd suppressed the thought? How many other fragments of the past had concealed themselves in the depths of his mind?

While Peller spoke, Jason had shifted in his chair. Turned away from both father and wife, his untouched tea near his elbow, he eyed the wall with disfavor.

Peller rotated his mug, studying the ascending swirls of steam. "There's something I never told you two about that day. Something I should have, but I never knew how to explain it."

Jason turned on Peller, his face bordering on hostile. "It was an accident. What's there to tell?"

"It was a hit-and-run."

Belinda rocked back in her chair, her eyes wide. After a moment Jason cleared his throat and leaned forward. "Did they find the other driver?"

Peller shook his head. "You'll recall it happened out near the county fairgrounds, just past West Friendship. She was on her way to an agricultural expo. There were only three witnesses to the accident. Two of them were driving the same direction as Mom and were far enough back to stop. The other was a mail carrier going the other direction who'd stopped to stuff mail into a box. He looked back when he heard the squealing tires."

He gazed into his cup and shook his head before continuing, "So none of them saw much. The only coherent information investigators got was that a dark blue pickup sped onto the road from a farm lane, struck Mom's car, and took off westbound. It happened fast, and nobody was close enough to get the license number or describe the driver. We're not even sure what make the truck was. The mail carrier thought it was a Chevy, but the closer of the two drivers thought it was a Ford. The other driver had no idea."

"How could they miss a thing like that?" Jason demanded.

Peller shrugged. "Maybe the logo was missing from the vehicle. Or maybe they were all in shock. That happens. Witnesses to traumatic events miss details or can't remember them later."

Jason pushed his chair back and stood. For a moment he looked like a lost traveler, then he paced to the opposite end of the table and back, his fists clenched, his eyes focused on his shoes. "So he's still out there."

"He, or she. Whoever did it was obviously in good enough condition to drive off, although they may have been injured, too."

"You checked with the hospitals, I suppose?"

"Of course. Nothing turned up."

"Christ." Dropping back into his chair, Jason asked, "You're still looking, though, right?"

Peller spread his hands in a gesture of helplessness. "No point anymore."

"No point!" Jason leaped to his feet again, his voice rising in pitch. "What the hell does *that* mean?"

"The statute of limitations on vehicular homicide in Maryland is three years. Even if we found them, they couldn't be prosecuted."

Belinda took Jason's hand and pulled him back down into his seat. Fiercely, she asked, "Are you telling me that someone can kill a person in Maryland and if they're not caught in three years they can just walk away?"

"Vehicular homicide isn't murder. It's an accident, even if it's the result of traffic violations."

Jason wrapped his hands around his mug and closed his eyes. Peller could see his inner struggle to conquer his anger. "But why would you give up? Maybe officially you couldn't do anything, but you have access to everything you need." His eyes snapped open and he glared at his father as though challenging him to a duel. "You want to find them, don't you?"

"Jason, you—" Belinda began, but Peller interrupted.

"Fair question." Did he, he wondered? Well, obviously, yes. He certainly wanted to know who had killed his wife, certainly wanted to call them to account. But where Sandra was concerned, the line between justice and revenge seemed to vanish. As much as he wanted justice, he mistrusted his own judgement. "I don't know," he finally replied. "I think it might end badly."

"How can it be any worse than it is?" Jason demanded.

"I don't think—" Belinda said quietly, "I don't think that the truth ever can end badly." She rose from the table, laying her hand on her husband's shoulder for a moment, then went to the counter to fetch the teapot. "More, anyone?" she asked, but didn't wait for an answer to refresh their drinks, simply poured the hot beverage into the cooling mugs.

"It's not the truth I fear," Peller said. "It's myself."

Jason clasped his hands on the table, studying them as he might have done as a teenager trying to avoid difficult advice. "I'm sorry, Dad. I had no right to say that."

"It's all right. I should have told you this a long time ago. I'm not sure why I didn't."

Belinda reseated herself and took a drink of her tea. "That's an easy answer. You didn't want to drag it out for us. It was painful enough as it was. You knew the answers wouldn't be easy, or might never be found. You wanted to spare us. That's what every father does, isn't it?"

Peller didn't know if that was the reason or not. Four years had passed, and he wasn't too sure what he'd been thinking at the time. But it sounded as plausible as anything else. "Did I spare you?"

"For the most part." Belinda looked to Jason. "Wouldn't you say?"

Jason shrugged. "Maybe. I don't know. I don't think about it much anymore. I can't, not if I'm going to be able to do what's important now. What about you, Dad?"

Peller wrapped his hands around his mug, soaking up the warmth. "Rather the same. Life does go on. I have to do my job. I was never much on socializing. That was your mother's department. But I still talk to a few people on a regular basis. Colleagues. Jerry Souter."

Jason laughed, a genuinely amused sound. "Jerry's still around, is he?"

Peller raised his cup in mock salute. "Jerry will probably outlive me."

Belinda was shaking her head. "But you must think about her, I'm sure."

"Of course," Peller agreed. "And I talk to her with some frequency."

Jason's eyebrows shot up. "Talk to her?"

That, Peller thought, was going to be impossible to explain, so he didn't try. "Well. It feels like it sometimes."

Belinda put a hand on his shoulder. "I don't see why not. She'll always be a part of you."

Peller patted her hand. "That's the only thing that makes it tolerable."

⮑

When his cell phone chirped just after four-thirty and Dumas saw it was Montufar calling, his first thought was that some catastrophe had struck. Nerves, he told himself. The past month had felt like a video game in which everything was shooting at him, falling on him, and dropping out from under him at the same time. This could only be more of the same.

When he answered, Montufar hesitated before asking, "Are you okay?"

"Sure, why?"

"You sound like a rattlesnake has its fangs on your neck."

"Does it?"

"I wouldn't know. I've never known anyone in that position—literally, anyway." He could imagine her laughter. "I just called to see if you would like to join us at Eduardo's for dinner."

Surprised, Dumas replied, "Well, sure. I'd love to. What's the occasion?"

"No occasion. He just thought you'd enjoy some company."

He smiled. "Oh, so the invitation is from your brother, not from you, eh?"

Although he was joking and tried to make it sound that way, he could have sworn he heard her blush through the phone.

"What time do you want me to come by?" he asked.

"Anytime," Montufar said, a bit too quickly. "Sylvia said she'll have food on the table around six."

He got the address from her and said he'd be there in about forty minutes. After hanging up, he held the phone in his hand for a minute, gazing at it, wondering at her reaction, wondering if it was real or just his imagination. She always seemed to keep men at a distance, but then mostly he'd seen her in professional settings. She wasn't lacking in warmth for her friends, but every time he'd seen a man try to attract her attention she'd deftly turned him aside, usually with a clever remark that could pass for either humor or insult. He'd never seen her embarrassed by an advance.

Dumas thought he understood her: she wanted people to see her as a detective first and a woman second. Social progress notwithstanding, it could be tough being a female cop. He respected her and honored her wishes, as he understood them, by keeping their relationship businesslike when required, friendly the rest of the time, and nothing further.

*But that's not always enough, is it?* that voice in the back of his mind whispered.

*Eduardo invited me to dinner*, he insisted, *not Corina.*

*Oh, sure.*

Gripping his phone like a weapon, he marched into the bedroom to change into something a bit more formal: a pair of navy blue slacks and a light blue striped button-down shirt. He toyed with the idea of bringing a present for his hostess, maybe some flowers, but thought better of it. He could just imagine what Montufar would think then. She'd probably tell him his reservation had been cancelled. So he simply took himself, arriving almost exactly when he'd told her he would.

He parked on the street. Standing in the doorway, wearing a white dress with a red and green floral pattern, Montufar greeted him with a smile as he came up the walk. She was the brightest thing on the whole street—spring incarnate. Mother Nature.

"Good God, Eric," he muttered to himself, "you need help."

"What?" she asked.

He arrived at the door. "Nothing. I'm just having one of those days."

She gave him puzzled look, but didn't ask. "Come on in."

He followed her and took in the living room with a quick glance. A room of modest proportions, it was furnished with a comfortable tan sofa on which Eduardo was lying, a couple of matching chairs, some dark wood end tables, and a medium-sized flat screen TV. Today's *Baltimore Sun* lay disarranged on one of the end tables. A crucifix hung on the wall above the sofa. Prints of tropical beaches and forested mountains decorated the other walls. Dumas wondered if those were pictures of the family's ancestral homeland.

Eduardo pulled himself up from the sofa and, using his walker, approached slowly.

"Don't get up on my account," Dumas protested.

"Nonsense, I'm strong as a horse." Eduardo laughed and stuck out a hand.

Dumas took it and found to his surprise that Eduardo wasn't lying about his strength. He squeezed heartily and didn't let go for a rather long time. When he finally did, he said, "It's good to see you again. Maybe next time you come by, I won't need this…" He slapped the walker congenially. "This dumb thing."

"You've come a long way since I saw you in the hospital," Dumas replied.

"A long way, yes. But I wish I could remember what happened. That's the funny thing about an accident. You see it coming in slow motion, then it's over and you can't remember anything but the slow motion part."

Dumas had never been in an accident, but he thought he understood. Before he could reply, Montufar interjected, "You don't want to know. The pain you were in when you woke up was bad enough."

Eduardo eased himself back to the sofa and sat carefully. "I can remember some of it, though. Whatever it was, it was big. A truck? SUV? Don't know. But it was coming right for me. Why am I still alive?"

"Because it hit the back half of your vehicle, not the driver's door."

A woman's voice came from behind them. "Because God knows we need you here." Dumas and Montufar turned to find Eduardo's wife Sylvia entering from the dining room. Dumas thought her a striking woman rather than a pretty one—very nearly as tall as her husband, with dark eyes that commanded attention.

She smiled at Dumas and came over to shake his hand. "And you are Eric," she said. "Welcome! We're happy you could come." She was wearing a long beige skirt with a ruffled hem and a loose-fitting blouse covered with images of frolicking cats. She fairly swirled as she moved.

"Happy to be here," he told her.

"I should think so," she laughed; then, tossing a wink at Montufar, she returned to the kitchen to continue her dinner preparations.

Montufar rolled her eyes. Eduardo just grinned at her.

"Let's sit down," she said, choosing a chair close to her brother.

Eduardo waited until they were settled in, then rose and turned the walker toward the dining room. "I have to check something," he said. "You two talk." Dumas watched him work his way out, then listened as he clumped down an unseen hall.

"He seems to be coming along well."

"Fairly well, yes," Montufar said, glancing back as if to check on him. "But I'm concerned. Sometimes I think his speech has been affected. He can't seem to find the right word. I wonder if he might have suffered some sort of brain damage."

"Has his doctor said anything about it?"

"Not so far."

"Probably nothing to worry about, then."

She nodded absently and looked out the front window.

"What about you?" Dumas asked her. "Are you holding up okay?"

She threw him a glance that was either irritated or just supposed to look that way. "Of course. Why wouldn't I be?"

"I don't know. He's your brother. You just seem preoccupied."

"Is that a professional observation, Detective Sergeant?"

Dumas laughed. "It is, Detective Sergeant."

Absently she tucked her legs up under her and gazed at him, her head tilted towards the back of the chair. It was a stunning image, he thought. He felt like taking out his smartphone and snapping a photo of her, but he didn't think she'd appreciate it. "You're on edge, too, aren't you?" she asked.

Dumas shrugged.

"Come on, Eric. You know I can tell."

He did know. He decided to hazard asking, "Was Eduardo really the one who invited me?"

"Yes."

"Why?"

"He likes you."

"Oh."

"And he's a meddling idiot. He thinks you'd be a good match for me." She smiled mock-sweetly.

Dumas found his hands looking for something to do. He wished he had a half dollar in his pocket so he could practice a few magic effects, but he had left his coins at home. "You disagree?"

He'd said it before he realized it, and it apparently crossed a line. Montufar unfolded herself and sat upright, almost formally, and gave the opposite wall a frown that looked more perplexed than anything. But she didn't have a comeback.

"Sorry," Dumas muttered. In the silence that hung between them, he wished he could take the question back. Then again, if she did feel some potential chemistry between them, why should she pretend otherwise? As that writer, Phil Walters, had said, the goal was truth. Some people, perhaps most people, often couldn't handle truth, but he liked to think he could, and he certainly had always thought Montufar could.

"I like the sounds of food being prepared," she said suddenly. "It takes me back to my childhood. Simpler times. Happy times. How about you?"

He listened to what she had been hearing. A timer rang insistently. The oven door opened and closed. Someone was running water in the sink; the timer sounded again; a voice spoke unintelligibly and a burst of laughter followed. The aromas of cooked beef, herbs, and cinnamon drifted through the half-opened door. He would have given his right hand to have been surrounded by the warmth and comfort apparent in Sylvia's kitchen. "My childhood was anything but simple," he told her, "and some of it wasn't very happy."

"Really? But you're such an upbeat guy."

Dumas shrugged. "I overcame it, mostly."

Montufar waited in silence, perhaps sensing that it wasn't the time to pry. Dumas met her eyes and found them sympathetic but not demanding. Another thing to admire about her, and to intensify the awkwardness. He felt compelled to tell her, "I got a letter today."

If she thought it an odd change of subject, her expression didn't betray her. "From who?"

"From my uncle. Uncle Ethan. He wants me to come home."

She seemed momentarily unable to speak.

"Texas," he replied to her unvoiced question. He felt his heart pounding in his chest and wondered why he should be so worked up over this. It was ancient history, over and done with and good riddance.

"Are you going?"

"Of course not. He threw me out of the house and told me to get lost. I've been away for twelve years with no contact with any of them. He can go to hell."

She let out a long breath. "I don't blame you for being angry."

"I'm *not* angry," he said, then realized he was almost shouting. There was a sudden lull in the sounds from the kitchen. "Okay," he said, subdued. "I'm angry. Who wouldn't be?"

"What about your parents?"

"Dad ran off when I was six. I never saw him again. My mom and sister Helen and I moved in with Ethan and his family after that. When I was fifteen, Mom took Helen and split. Ethan told me she'd gotten a letter from my dad and was going to meet him. They never came back, either. I don't know what happened to them."

Montufar put a hand to her mouth. "Eric, I'm so sorry. I had no idea."

He shrugged. "Nobody does. You're the first person I've told. Literally. The first person."

World-weariness, curiosity, and concern mixed in her voice. "I probably shouldn't ask, but why did he kick you out?"

Dumas slumped in the chair. "Because I sent his son—my cousin Phillip—to jail."

"What had he done?"

"He was a pusher. Crack, mostly. A small potatoes operation, but he made enough money off of it."

"Did your uncle know?"

"He may have suspected, but he didn't want to know. Even if he had, he wouldn't have ratted out his own son. I used to think Phillip could have killed someone right in front of us and Uncle Ethan would've pretended not to notice."

"You were on the force when this happened?"

Dumas nodded. "I was a rookie and still living with them. I thought I was protecting the family. Phillip was getting involved with a violent crowd. I didn't want it to follow him back to us. He had two younger sisters—they were something like seventeen and thirteen at the time. I wasn't about to let something happen to them if I could prevent it."

"You did the right thing, Eric."

"I wonder if it mattered, though, aside from getting me out of there."

Sylvia poked her head into the room. "Dinner's ready," she said.

Montufar nodded at her. "We'll be there in a minute."

"All right," Sylvia said with a grin, "but if it's cold when you get there, you can do the microwaving." She vanished into the kitchen again.

Montufar rose from her chair, but instead of following Sylvia she turned to regard the image of the crucified Christ. Dumas stood and watched, wondering what to make of her action. Finally she said, very quietly, "It always matters that we do the right thing."

He couldn't find an answer, but the silence spoke profoundly.

Then she turned, smiled, and said, "Come on. Dinner's waiting for us."

# Chapter 5

Officer Kevin Graham, standing on western verge of Carroll Mill Road just south of its intersection with Benson Branch Road, gazed through a break in the trees across about sixty yards of close-cropped lawn to the edge of a lake. He wasn't sure if it was a natural lake or a filled borrow pit or what. It was about as wide as it was distant from him but much longer, with a dogleg right in the distance. A couple of big, pricey houses stood along its northern edge. Trees surrounded most of the rest of the shore.

Graham's attention was on the tire tracks ripped into the lawn running down to the water, where a bright green pickup truck sat half-submerged. There was no indication of an accident, and the tire tracks were so straight that someone must have purposely driven it down there. But had they overshot the land, or had they meant to sink the truck and failed?

He looked toward the houses. It was just before eleven o'clock on Monday morning, April fourth, and nobody was out and about. Shaking his head, he started down to the water, keeping well to the right side of the tire tracks.

Graham was a big man, a dark-skinned native of Jamaica who kept himself in top condition in spite of advancing age. Had anyone been watching, they would have been impressed as he strode along. Although moving at a good pace, he kept a sharp eye out for anything unusual on the ground. He found nothing—no dropped objects, no signs of passing feet, nothing at all—until he got to the water. There, a scramble of footprints marred the muddy bank. Someone had walked from one side of the truck to the other and back again, possibly several times.

But the footprints were not what caught his eye. There was blood smeared on the truck's passenger door, on the ground beneath it, and mixed in with the water and the mud. Lots of blood.

⌒

About forty-five minutes before Graham came upon the truck, Officers Zach Savas and Peter Kinsley had been patrolling Centennial Lane south of U.S. Route 40 west of Ellicot City when a call came in: an armed robbery with shots fired at Guilio's, a jewelry store on Route 40 not a mile from their location.

Lights flashing and siren wailing, the duo arrived at the store within a minute and a half. Guilio's proved to be the first store in a small strip mall built at a right angle to the street. Set within a façade of reddish and off-white brick, eight glass storefronts faced a half-full parking lot: Guilio's, a greeting card store, a cell phone store, a pharmacy, a dentist's office, a trendy foods store, a deli, and a wine shop. Strangely, all seemed quiet as the squad car turned into the parking lot. There was nobody outside, no cars moving, no sign of an armed assailant or a victim.

As Savas, at not-quite-forty years of age the older of the duo, pulled the squad to a stop in front of the jewelry store, Kinsley pointed out his window. "Looks like blood on the pavement." They were out of the car in an instant. Savas quickly took in the surroundings while Kinsley approached the stain. "It's fresh," he said. "Still wet."

"You get the feeling we're being watched?" Savas asked, then came to his partner's side.

"No," Kinsley replied.

"Me, neither." Savas studied the blood, noting that it was all in a confined space about two feet across. "Looks bad. Maybe the victim managed to get inside?"

Kinsley shook his head. "No blood trail."

"Thank God!" a woman's voice called. The officers looked up to find a fiftyish woman in an absurdly tight red dress almost running out of Guilio's.

"Are you hurt, ma'am?" Savas asked.

"No, I was inside. There's a woman..." She pointed toward the store.

"The victim?"

"Yes, she's inside. She's very upset."

"How badly was she hurt?"

Not waiting for the answer, Kinsley sprinted into the store.

"She isn't hurt, just real scared."

"There were gunshots, weren't there?"

The woman looked confused. "Yes, just one."

"So who got shot?"

She shook her head. Sirens wailed in the distance, rapidly growing louder.

"Ma'am, there's blood on the pavement here." He pointed and she looked, eyes suddenly empty. "I need to find the victim. They need help."

"She said he was dead."

"I'm sorry?"

"The woman who was robbed. She said he was dead." She pointed at the blood as though a corpse were sprawled in it.

"What's your name, ma'am?"

An ambulance pulled into the parking lot and stopped behind the squad car, followed closely by three more squads converging from both directions.

"Paula Hess," the woman told him. "I'm the manager on duty."

"Okay, Ms. Hess. Why don't you go back inside. Sit down if you need to. I'll be in shortly."

She nodded as Savas turned to brief the newly-arrived officers. "We have a robbery victim inside Guilio's and a shooting victim who's vanished. Sounds like just one shot was fired, but it obviously hit its mark."

They all pondered the blood. "Think he walked off?" one of the others asked. "Didn't want to talk to us?"

"Maybe, but if he was bleeding that badly, why didn't he leave a trail?" He waved his hand around to indicate the broader parking lot. "You guys check the other stores, but watch where you step and look for other signs of blood. I'll call for a crime scene unit."

As the officers dispersed, Savas puzzled over the blood once more. Maybe, he thought, the victim had been shot next to his car, had managed to get in and drive away. That would explain the lack of blood anywhere else. But the robbery victim thought he'd been killed, and dead men don't drive. Even if she'd been mistaken, the wound must have been serious. Could he have been in any condition to drive?

He called in for the crime scene unit, and then went into the jewelry store to see if Kinsley had found any answers.

By the time Corina Montufar and her protégé Detective Theresa Swan arrived at Giulio's, the crime scene unit was going to work. The responding officers had visited every store in the building plus the pizza restaurant on the next lot over and several of the shops on the opposite side of the street. A single gunshot had been heard by any number of people, but nobody had actually seen the attack and no shooting victim could be found. Indeed, nobody could swear to seeing anyone leaving the scene of the crime, because nobody had been quite sure where the gunshot had come from.

The officers were widening their canvass just in case the victim was nearby. Also, several of them were checking out a thick stand of woods behind the shopping center. It was possible he'd ended up back there. The EMTs were still at the scene, standing by. Montufar noted the pair, a young man and a woman who was probably a few years his senior, leaning on the back of their ambulance, engrossed in some discussion.

The blood on the pavement had been cordoned off and was being photographed as the detectives approached and studied it. Montufar asked if any other traces had been found. None had.

They entered Guilio's, where Paula Hess had gotten a grip and resumed her duties inasmuch as she could with police swirling through and around her store. Taking in the manager's choice of clothing and cosmetics, Montufar concluded that Hess was trying to look twenty rather than fifty-something. True, she had come close, but nobody that age could ever quite pull off such a drastic transformation. The image was likely the important thing, though, when one was selling beauty and glamour. A younger woman was staffing the counter, a tall redhead who had imitated the boss's style (or was it the other way around?) with the advantages of true youth and a better hand with makeup.

Montufar introduced herself and Detective Swan. "Was anything stolen in here?"

"No," Hess told her. "He never came inside. He might have been waiting for someone to come out with a purchase."

Montufar glanced toward the back of the store, where she could just barely hear someone sobbing. "I take it the victim is back there."

Hess nodded. "The officers asked if they could get her settled back there while they waited for you. I said it was okay."

"Did you catch her name?"

"No, sorry."

"That's all right. Was she injured?"

"No, just shaken up."

"All right. Detective Swan has a few more questions for you. I'll be in back if either of you need me."

Montufar hurried toward the back. On her way she heard Swan ask, "Did you see what happened outside?"

"Not at first," the manager answered. "I was looking over some paperwork when I heard the shot."

In the manager's office, Montufar found the victim huddled in an office chair gone scruffy with age and hard use. A middle-aged patrolman seated in a second chair offered her a Styrofoam cup of coffee, while a second officer stood to one side at rigid attention. Their nameplates identified them as officers Savas (the older) and Kinsley (the younger). Montufar wondered if Kinsley's stance was for the victim's benefit or for hers. There would be something like a breakroom back here somewhere, she supposed, but it wasn't obvious where. All she could see was a dinged metal desk supporting the obligatory computer, an assortment of office furniture, and the currently-occupied chairs.

The sobbing victim had a heart-shaped face, the pallor of which set her raven hair in stark relief. What had once been an elaborate mask of makeup now ran down her face in mingled streaks of color. Montufar thought she looked like a zombie Jackie Kennedy in a B-flick. She was wearing a dress with a floral pattern, lots of whites and yellows as befitted the springtime, and strappy yellow shoes with respectable heels.

The officer with the coffee stood as Montufar approached. She cautiously tried the vacated chair, which acquiesced with a creaky wheeze. "It's okay," she said. "We're here to help you. I'm Detective Sergeant Corina Montufar. Are you okay? You didn't get hurt, did you?"

The woman appeared on the verge of hysteria. Shaking her head, she whispered, "He killed that man."

"What man?"

"The one who tried to help me. He killed him. I saw it."

"What's your name?"

"Ruth. Ruth Hudson." She shuddered. "It's my fault. It's all my fault. I couldn't stop him."

"It's not your fault, Ruth," Montufar said gently. Why hadn't anyone gotten medical attention for this woman? Montufar was a cop, not a doctor, but even she could see that a cup of coffee wasn't what Ruth Hudson needed. It occurred to her that Ruth might be confused enough to think someone had been killed when nothing of the sort had happened. "Some scumbag tried to rob you. He's the bad guy, not you." Turning to the Officer Kinsley, she said quietly, "Ask the EMTs to come in."

He nodded and dashed out of the room as if grateful for the excuse.

Montufar turned her attention back to the victim, who was speaking again in a whispery murmur. "It was my fault. It was. I screamed."

"Of course you did. You were scared. I'd have screamed, too." Which, Montufar knew, she absolutely would not have done. But if she could get any information from Hudson before the paramedics came in, she needed to keep her talking.

"I don't know who he was. The robber stopped me just as I stepped into the parking lot. He had a gun and told me to hand over my bag. I'd just bought a pearl necklace." She looked around the office as if trying to figure out where she'd put the purchase. "Then this other guy came running up from nowhere and tried to grab him. There was a shot. I didn't see it, I just heard it." Hudson sucked in a breath. "He was a hero."

Montufar wondered if the hero had realized a gun was involved. She'd known it both ways: the hero who rushes blindly in, and the hero who thinks he's impervious to bullets. But that was irrelevant now. "Why do you think he was dead?" she asked. Since dead men didn't get up and walk away, Montufar was pretty sure he'd been alive. But it might help to know why Hudson had assumed otherwise.

The other buried her face in her hands and started sobbing again.

Montufar reached over to gently touch her arm. "Ruth?"

Hudson hauled a large white purse up from the floor and rummaged in it for some tissues. With shaking hands she wiped her eyes, then stared at the cosmetics-stained wads. "The robber shot him in the heart. Right here." She tapped herself directly over her heart. "He fell and didn't move."

That sure sounded like dead. "But there's no body."

"The robber took him."

Montufar leaned back, stunned. "The robber took him?"

Hudson nodded and dabbed at her eyes again. "There was a pickup truck, a green one, next to us. The body was lying on the ground, bleeding. The robber opened the passenger door, picked him up, and shoved him in. Then he ran around to the driver's side, jumped in, and blew out of the parking lot. I could hear the tires squealing."

*Why would he do that?* Montufar wanted to ask, but she held her tongue. She looked at Patrolman Savas who shrugged, adding a shake of the head for emphasis. Apparently he found it just as novel. Montufar could think of only two explanations: either the perpetrator was desperate to get an unintended victim somewhere for treatment before he died, or he was terrified of leaving a dead body at the scene of the crime. Either way, panic must have motivated him.

The EMTs appeared in the doorway with Kinsley right behind, and Montufar nodded to them.

"Okay," she said slowly. "I've asked the paramedics to take care of you, Ruth, but if you can answer a couple more questions it would really help. Did you happen to recognize the make of the truck? Just that much would give us something to go on."

Ruth frowned in concentration. "The logo on the front. It was a Chevy."

The female paramedic moved quietly to Hudson's side. Hudson looked up blankly at her.

"Hi, Ms. Hudson, I'm Ashley," she said, slipping a stethoscope from her pocket. "The policeman here said you witnessed a shooting a little while ago. Can I take a look, and make sure you're all right?" Hudson didn't react.

While the EMT checked Hudson over, Montufar turned to Savas and Kinsley. "It's a good bet the guy's dead," she said quietly, "but we'd better get on this pronto, just in case."

"Will do," Savas acknowledged. As one, they exited.

Montufar turned back to the witness. "I know it's a long shot, but did you happen to see the license?"

Hudson shook her head.

"Can you describe the thief?"

With effort, she managed, "Black, but not real dark. Tall, hefty. He must have been strong to get the other man into the truck. He had a beard, a kind of bushy one. That's all I remember."

"We'll need to move her to the hospital," the EMT interjected. "Do you have any more questions?"

"That's good enough," Montufar assured her. She patted Hudson's hands, then rose and returned to the storefront, where Detective Swan was jotting some notes. Paula Hess had returned to her own paperwork but couldn't seem to keep her eyes off the police for more than five seconds at a time. Her assistant was unlocking the case for an elderly woman who had come in. The customer was smiling and chatting amiably as though the swarm of police was entirely normal.

Swan looked up as Montufar approached.

"Anything?"

"Not much. The attack seemed to have occurred off to the left." She pointed. "So she didn't see anything except the perp jumping into his vehicle, a bright green pickup truck, and flying out of the parking lot like a bat out of hell."

"'Bat out of hell.' Her exact words?"

"Yep."

"Can she tell us anything about the truck other than its color?"

Swan shook her head. "It happened so fast, she didn't see all of it until it went by."

Montufar nodded. "Pity, but it fits with what Ruth—the victim—told me." She filled Swan in on the details.

"That's crazy," Swan said. "Why would he do that?"

"I'm not sure, but we need to find that truck. I'm going to check in with the captain. You let the officers know that the body is gone, so they can call off the search of the woods."

Following Swan outside, Montufar pulled out her cell phone and placed the call. While waiting for an answer, she wandered to the end of the strip mall and looked westward along route 40. Storm clouds were rolling up from the horizon.

Dumas arrived at the scene of the abandoned pickup moments after the crime scene crew had begun its work. He found Officer Kevin Graham leaning against his squad car, just popping a stick of spearmint gum into his mouth. "Kevin," he said with a nod. "What've we got?"

"Strange happenings again, Eric," Graham replied gravely. "I don't like it. You can see where the truck tore up the grass. Looks like it was driven straight into the water. Someone walked all around it, and there's blood down there. A lot. Something bad happened."

"Like someone in the truck was hurt?"

"Maybe." But he shook his head.

"You're thinking someone died."

Graham chewed his gum and didn't reply.

"Well, let's see what we can see," Dumas said, and started down.

He hadn't gone twenty feet before Graham called suddenly, "Eric." He turned and waited. "Where did they go?"

"What do you mean?"

Waving him on, Graham said, "Go look, then ask yourself."

Less puzzled than on edge, Dumas continued toward the truck, careful to stay out of the crime scene unit's way as they photographed and sampled and checked the vehicle's interior for fingerprints, fibers, and useful detritus. He noted the footprints, all about the same healthy size, moving back and forth around the truck. Although the tangle seemingly went both directions and overlapped at many points, he thought he could see what had happened. The driver had gotten out, walked around the bed to the passenger door, did something there, returned to the driver's side, moved again to the passenger's side, and finally went to the rear of the vehicle. From there, he could easily have walked off in the grass, leaving little sign of his passing.

The blood was another matter. It covered the passenger door in a wash of red that dripped to the ground. Dumas' eyes followed the trail to the water's edge, where a fitful wave lapped at it like the tongue of an indifferent cat. The pale shore of the bank was churned into ruddy brown mud above the waterline. Between the truck and the mud, a broken smear of red traced out a nearly straight path.

"Is there blood in the cab?" he called to a technician who was collecting a sample from the door.

"All over the passenger's side," she said without looking back.

Dumas watched as she carefully swabbed up some of the blood, placed the swab in a tube, and sealed it. "Nothing on the driver's side?"

"Some on the steering wheel and the door handle," she said. "But not on the seat." Still intent on her work, she stretched her arm out behind her to grip an invisible wheel. "Like it was on the driver's hands."

Carefully moving around the blood-infused mud by the water, he pondered the ground. Dumas could imagine an injured person dragging himself down to the water, or a dead body being dragged. But once there, then what? He gazed up a slight incline at the nearest house. Not likely, he thought. He walked partway up the hill and search the ground, but no blood had been shed there, not even a drop. Trudging back to the road, Dumas leaned against Graham's squad car. "You're right," he said.

"Ya, mon."

"We'll need to search the lake. Can you call it in?"

Graham nodded, but didn't immediately get on it. Instead, he gazed at Dumas for a moment. Dumas ignored him and kept his eyes on the activity around the truck.

"You wish your buddy Rick was here," Graham said. "Don't you?"

"Nah. He deserves his vacation."

"But he'd see the bent blades of grass and follow the killer to his lair."

Dumas laughed. "He's good, but even he's not that good." His cell phone rang.

"I'll put in that call," Graham said.

Dumas nodded and moved aside to take the call from Captain Morris. "Tell me about the truck," she said.

He wondered why she was asking, but related the details: "Late model Chevy, bright green, extended cab, four by four. Blood all over the passenger door and, the techs tell me, on the passenger side of the cab, plus the steering wheel and driver's door handle." He gave her the license number then added, "Why do you ask?"

"It matches," she said. "We've placed a bright green Chevy truck at the scene of a jewelry store robbery Corina is investigating. Not much detail, but the thief shot someone, stuffed him into the truck, and drove off. Any sign of the occupants?"

Dumas, who had started to pace, stopped and gazed at the water.

"Eric?"

"No," he answered. "I think the driver walked off into the sunset. But I don't see how he could have taken an injured man with him, especially one that had lost the amount of blood we're seeing here. I'm guessing the other person is dead and underwater. We've called for a team to try to fish him out."

Morris was silent for a moment then replied, "All right. Sounds like you have it under control. I'll let Corina know."

As he pocketed his phone, Dumas wandered toward the truck again, moving close by the tracks it had cut into the earth. *If only*, he thought, *we* could *follow the bent blades of grass*. Dumas didn't think the thief-turned-killer had hauled away a dead body merely from panic. Panic, certainly, but panic motivated by some reason, some need, some specific fear. What that motivation might be wasn't clear, but he trusted his instincts. Still, he did wish he knew why it felt that way.

He puzzled over this for a time before realizing he had stopped moving and was gazing at a half-formed footprint on the edge of one of the tire tracks. He might not have noticed it in the midst of the tread marks had he not been staring at it for so long.

"Did we photograph this?" he called.

The photographer, Scott Sahin, waved at him. "Every inch from the road down. Why?"

"Did you notice this footprint?"

"Not particularly." Scott walked over and looked, then knelt for a better view. "You want a close-up?"

"Wouldn't hurt. I wonder if there are any others?"

Dumas moved slowly back toward the road, eyes alert for further signs of someone's passing. There were a few. The presumed killer had apparently walked out the way he had driven in.

A few weeks before, Belinda had lost her job. She had worked in the marketing department for a telecom equipment manufacturer, but due to the weakened economy jobs were disappearing all over the country. Jason's job as software developer on a military contract was more stable, so unlike many families they were holding out okay. Monday morning saw him off to work and the children off to school while Belinda stayed home and sifted through online job listings, looking for something up her alley.

"Slim pickings," she had told Peller.

He puttered around the house for a while, looked through the collection of books shelved in their study, tried to read a few pages but got nowhere, shuffled into the kitchen to see if any chores needed doing, and finally wandered to the front window in the living room, where he gazed at the house across the street as though expecting something to happen there. Unable to defeat his restlessness, he told Belinda he might go for a walk.

"Looks like a nice day for it," she said. "There's a park a couple of blocks to the west. There shouldn't be too many people there right now."

He thanked her and set off. It was jacket weather, the sky pouring down sunshine and dotted with a few small, puffy cumulus clouds. He walked by the neatly-kept yards and houses, barely noticing them. It seemed a pleasant enough neighborhood. The park Belinda directed him to was a vast expanse of grass crossed by asphalt walks. Picnic shelters clustered at one end, with a play area populated by swing sets and slides and monkey bars close by. He spotted a couple of joggers and a retiree walking a dog, but otherwise the area was largely empty. He wandered the paths, his mind clearing, and eventually sat on a bench. A short distance away, a young woman was playing with two small children, tossing a bright yellow ball back and forth with them.

He smiled at the simple joy expressed in their movement and chatter. He wondered what had happened to the years. It seemed forever since he and Sandra and Jason had been like that. He thought back to that time, then an earlier moment, and then another, his mind slipping back through time until he came upon a moment he hadn't thought about for a great many years.

Henry Peller, tinkering with the engine of his 1979 Ford Fairmount, looked up, smiling broadly. "No kidding! When do I get to meet her?"

Peller felt half-pleased and half-embarrassed. Sandra was the first woman he'd dated, in part because he'd never had the nerve to ask a girl out. His father had never commented on his lack of a romantic partner, but Peller figured he must have been wondering when the day would come. "I'm thinking I could invite her to dinner with you and Mom this Saturday."

"I'm sure your mom would be pleased to have her. What's her name?"

"Sandra. Sandra Fielding."

"She must be something special, given your general lack of interest in the female of the species."

"Oh, come on. I'm not disinterested. Just..." He leaned over the car and watched his father extract a spark plug.

"Shy. I know. I was, too. The apple doesn't fall far from the tree."

His father examined the plug and set it aside. Taking a new one from a box positioned carefully on the frame of the car, he nodded to a small box of tools situated next to Peller. "Hand me that gap gauge, son."

Peller gave him the requested tool. "Dad, I was wondering."

The elder Peller shot him a quick look. "About what?"

"How did you ask Mom to marry you?"

Straightening, his father regarded him. "Is it that serious already?"

"Well. We've been seeing each other for a couple of months, actually."

With a laugh, his dad made to clap him on the shoulder, then realized that his hand was covered with grease and pulled back. "And this is the first you've mentioned it to your parents. Yeah, that sounds like me." He returned to work. "Well, I'll tell you. It took me a whole month to work up the nerve, but once I decided it had to be done, I just asked her one night over dinner. I didn't have a ring. Couldn't afford both an engagement ring and a wedding ring. So I just told her I loved her and wanted her to be my wife."

"That's it?"

"Sure. What else do you need?"

Peller considered that. Most of the guys he knew who had gotten married had made big productions out of their proposals and even bigger productions out of their weddings. Social convention seemed to call for such extravagance.

"I'm a practical man, son," his father continued. "Flash isn't what counts. Substance is what counts."

"How long were you and Mom together before you asked her?"

"Ah, well." He leaned into the engine compartment to install the new plug. "In our case, a bit over a year, as I recall. But you're asking if it's too soon for you and your lady."

"I guess so."

"All depends. How well do you know each other?"

"Pretty well, I think."

With a grunt of exertion, his dad pulled himself upright. "See, I can't answer the question for you. You two have to answer it for yourselves. Do you see in her a woman of character? Does she see in you a man of character? That's what matters. Get me one of those wires over there, will you?"

Peller went to the shelving unit behind him, where he found a package of new spark plug wires on an upper shelf at about eye level. He opened the package and handed one to his father. "That sounds so—I don't know—dry?"

His dad cracked a smile. "Hard to get weak-kneed over trustworthiness, eh? I suppose. But it's far more important than looks."

"Sandra is definitely that."

"Trustworthy or good-looking?"

"Well, both. But I meant trustworthy. And honest. And straightforward. And compassionate. Yes, I'd say she's a woman of character."

His father was intent on installing the spark plug wire, but he nodded. "Then it's not too soon. Not that it's any of my business, but if I were you, I wouldn't put it off too long."

Peller returned the box to the shelf. "Thanks, Dad."

"Any time. Oh, and one other thing you shouldn't put off too long. Best tell your mother to expect company. You know how she hates to be blindsided."

# Chapter 6

Fog rose up from the river, shrouding the surrounding mountain slopes with an eerie beauty. Standing in the cabin's open front door, the blue-eyed man could see little more than vague shapes melting into the cloud, menacing figures surrounding him like an army of giants waiting for a signal to attack. That they didn't attack disappointed him. He wished they would. He wished someone would put an end to this.

He moved without conviction to a wardrobe huddling against the wall at the rear of the cabin and opened the door. A meager collection of clothing hung within, which he pushed aside to reveal the gun. Gingerly, he picked it up and carried it to the front room, not looking at it. If he didn't look at it, he thought, he might be able to go through with it this time.

The firearm was a Remington Model 870 folding stock pump action shotgun, a twenty gauge, a weapon he had never actually used. He had bought it five years earlier, thinking he might do some hunting, but he'd never gotten around to it. He loaded it, carried it out to the front porch, and sat in the rocker.

He rocked for a while, gazing blankly into the fog.

The gun felt cold in his hands.

He turned it around backwards, slipped the end of the barrel into his mouth, and slid his hands down toward the trigger.

Somewhere out there, a woodpecker hammered a few new holes into a dead tree.

The blue-eyed man did nothing.

For a long time, he did nothing.

Sometime later, he slipped the gun out of his mouth and set it gently on the porch.

Tears filled his eyes while he rocked back and forth, back and forth, somehow seeing *her* moving ghostlike through the fog.

Tomio Kaneko looked up from his computer when the writer knocked lightly on his open door. At age sixty-six Kaneko still had a full head of mostly black hair, although a few streaks of gray were finally showing up. He stood and came to the door to welcome his visitor, shook hands, and introduced himself. Dressed simply but neatly in dark gray trousers and a pale blue shirt, his shoes polished to a soft shine, his office in perfect order, he struck Walters as a meticulous fellow, someone who paid close attention to detail. Maybe Penny had been right. Maybe this was going to work.

"I presume," Kaneko said after offering him a seat and resuming his position behind his desk, "that you are writing a book about the Fibonacci killings and want information."

"Exactly," Walters replied. "Unfortunately, none of the detectives involved in the case will talk to me."

The mathematician folded his hands and gazed evenly at Walters. It made him feel unnervingly like he was back in school being asked a question to which he didn't know the answer. "Did they give a reason for not wishing to talk?"

"No, just a run-around. Mostly they referred me to their captain, who referred me to them."

Indulging in a faint smile, Kaneko said, "I would have expected no less."

"Why?"

The mathematician thought for a moment before answering, his eyes never wavering. "If you were to consider what was written about the case in the press, I believe you could infer the answer. You would not prove it, but yes, you could infer it."

"Or you could just tell me."

"I could, but I will not."

Walters rubbed his forehead. He was getting really sick of this game. Why did everyone feel compelled to play it? "Why not?"

"Because, Mr. Walters, I respect those detectives. They did a fine job under difficult circumstances and should be commended for it. There are those, however, who would try to use certain aspects of the investigation for political gain, to the detriment of those involved."

"That sounds like someone has something to hide."

Kaneko's mouth twisted in disgust. "Not at all, Mr. Walters. But truth is easily turned to falsehood. I do not wish to inadvertently harm friends."

Walters found that tidbit more interesting than anything he'd heard so far. "You consider Lieutenant Peller and the others your friends? I thought you were just a consultant."

Kaneko leaned back, but his gaze remained fixed on the writer. "I do not claim to know them well, but yes, I count them as friends. They all visited me in the hospital while I was recovering and offered assistance to my wife Sarah if she needed it."

In that case, Walters decided, it was time to change tactics. "Do you know Peller lost his wife a few years back?"

Tensing up, Kaneko responded with a barely perceptible shake of his head.

"It was an accident. A hit-and-run, actually." Walters folded his hands in his lap and looked down, feigning sadness. "They never found the driver that hit her."

"He did not mention that," Kaneko said. "But then, he had no reason to mention it."

"No. Still, I think it's eating at him." The writer fell silent and made a point of not looking up, although he was very interested to hear what Kaneko might say next.

When he spoke, his words seemed carefully calculated: "I am sorry for his loss, of course, but I fail to see what it has to do with your reason for visiting me."

"If I were to bring you the available information on the incident..."

The mathematician held up a hand to stop him. "I am not a policeman. I learned that lesson the hard way."

"But you do seem to have a knack for picking out details others miss."

Kaneko stood. "I'm sorry, Mr. Walters, but I think you should go now."

Walters hauled himself wearily to his feet. "All right. I'm sorry to have bothered you."

"It was no bother. I just cannot help you. Goodbye, Mr. Walters."

Walters waved a quick farewell and trudged out of the office, down the corridor, and out of the building. He didn't have much hope for it, but a seed had been planted. With any luck, by the time he returned it might germinate and begin to grow.

⌇

In a room overstuffed with plush purple furnishings, lined with shelves overflowing with books, and draped with English heraldic devices, a scrawny old fellow clad in purple boxers and a purple t-shirt sprawled on a sofa, a book in one hand and a smart phone in the other. From the topmost shelves a number of stuffed purple ravens, mascots of the Baltimore football team, surveyed him.

"You're not supposed to call," he said into the phone as his eyes scanned the lines in the book, an economic doomsday tome by a former World Bank economist.

"It's okay," the growly voice on the other end of the line told him, although its tone was anything but reassuring. The caller sounded just shy of panicked.

"It's not okay. I don't know why I work with you. Are you using your own cell?" He moved the phone away from his ear to flip the page, then put it back again. "What was that?"

"I said it came with the truck. So look, I'm not bringing it after all."

"Why not? No, don't tell me. I should know better than to ask."

"Everything's okay, Duke. I promise."

The old man sat up, put a bookmark in the book, and set it on a nearby table. "Oh God, what did you do now?"

"Nothing. An accident. I can't bring the truck, that's all."

Duke Calvert let the caller listen to dead air for a minute before saying, "Fine. Destroy that phone and lose the parts. And after that..."

"What? What do you want me to do?"

"Don't ever call me again." He cut the connection and threw the phone down on the sofa. He liked to think of himself as an unflappable fellow, if only because in his business he couldn't afford to get ruffled. Panic invited trouble; calm kept things running smoothly. But he had to admit unease now. The caller, one Morgan Parsons, had a knack for car theft but otherwise had very little brains. If he said nothing had happened, something had happened. Something serious.

Rising, Calvert left his purple den, shuffled down the hall to the light-filled kitchen, passed by the brushed chrome appliances and massive cherrywood table, and opened the big French doors. He gazed past the redwood deck to take in the rolling acres of farmland he owned, the collection of houses and outbuildings huddled on the side of the next hill over from his house, the dark clouds rolling across the sky towards him, heavy with rain.

It had taken him a long time to build up this place, to make it secure, unpretentious. Had a crack opened up in his world? If so, it would have to be filled.

He felt a gentle touch on his shoulder, then a feather-light kiss on his earlobe. He turned and put his arms around the lithe blonde who had come up behind him wearing tight jeans and a loose green sweater. Calvert gave her a thin-lipped smile. "Ah, Caroline. Young, beautiful, seductive, and madly in love."

She kissed him on the lips.

"With my money."

Caroline pulled back, her mouth twisted into a half-grimace. "What's eating you?"

Ignoring her, Calvert looked outside again. "Where's Jeff?"

She shrugged. "How should I know? Probably working on that Camry that came in this morning."

"That's not his job."

"Yeah, but you know how he likes to work on the cars."

"Go find him. I have a real job for him."

"What, I'm your runner now?"

"You know you want to see him." She started to protest, but he cut her off. "I understand. I'm not exactly spry anymore."

Caroline was still shaking her head, slightly, but seemed unable to find any words. Calvert waved her on and she left, casting a worried glance over her shoulder. He really should have known better than to take up with her, he thought, but she was at least amusing. Besides, she was ruled by money-lust, so she wouldn't intentionally displease him. It was rather fun having her on his arm, if only to see the astonishment in the eyes of onlookers on those rare occasions when they went out in public together.

Raindrops pattered on the deck outside and a rumble of thunder sounded.

Duke Calvert, composure restored, returned to his purple den and his weighty book.

〜

Rain pelted the windows of Northern District Headquarters as the afternoon wore on. At his desk, Dumas turned his monitor so Montufar could see better, and said, "Looks pretty open-and-shut. Our guy obviously wasn't thinking too clearly. The truck matches one stolen just yesterday at a restaurant in Elkridge. There are prints all over it, but it looks like they belong to only two people. One would likely be the rightful owner, which we'll have to check up on, and the other is this fellow here." He tapped a few keys and pulled up a criminal file.

"Morgan Parsons," Montufar read from her perch on the edge of Dumas' desk. "African-American, six foot two, two hundred thirty pounds. Based on date of birth, he'd be thirty-one now. A number of arrests on minor charges starting with shoplifting when he was sixteen, a minor possession charge, served a couple of months for this, a year for that. Nothing for the past six years, though." She drummed her fingers on the desktop. "And now a stolen truck and a probable manslaughter."

"It's a good bet he's been in the auto theft business for most of those six years."

"If so, he must have a knack for it."

Dumas leaned back and studied the old mug shot. It showed a moderately dark-skinned man with a week's worth of scraggly beard. "I'll say. He nabbed that truck in broad daylight. Most pros prefer to work at night."

"I'll show Ruth Hudson his photo. With luck, he hasn't changed too much since it was taken."

"Right, and I'll track down his current domicile."

Montufar raised an eyebrow. "You learning new words?"

"Incessantly," he replied with a grin.

She shook her head and stood. "Email me that file."

"Will do. By the by, you doing anything tonight?"

"Not particularly."

"Care to join me for dinner at our Chinese place?"

"*Our* Chinese place?" She rolled her eyes, but allowed a hint of a smile.

"Sure, why not?" He smiled hopefully.

Montufar shook her head and started to go, but suddenly stopped and spun around. "Yes." And then she hurried off to her desk.

Dumas leaned back and locked his hands behind his head, intrigued by her response. Only Corina, he thought, could make an acceptance sound like a rebuke.

⌇

"He knows about us."

Jeff Levinson spit the remains of a cigarette from his mouth and crushed it underfoot. The air in the Big Shed, as everyone here called it, was filled with the smell of oil and gasoline and sweat. He was standing beside a current-model Toyota Camry that had been partially disassembled. Tools were scattered about, and a heap of cannibalized parts was piled on the floor nearby.

This was the real business of Duke Calvert's farm: stolen vehicles drove into the Big Shed and came out piece by piece to be re-packaged in the next building over. From there, they were shipped to middlemen around the country for resale to unsuspecting consumers and retailers. Most of the vehicles Calvert's operation took in passed through here. A few choice models, popular mint-condition vehicles, would be sold intact for shipment overseas, but that business had grown risky. Heightened port security in the U.S. and increased vigilance at the Canadian border increased the chances of detection. Worse, Canada had begun beefing up its own port security. Exporters still wanted vehicles, but Calvert always erred on the side of caution. He'd reduced exports and turned instead to local buyers seeking vehicles for use in crimes.

Priority one for Calvert was ensuring that neither parts nor vehicles could be traced back to him. That was where Jeff Levinson came in. Although Levinson enjoyed working on the cars, his primary responsibility was security. Together they'd worked out a double-blind system for sales. They had no idea who bought their products, and their buyers had no idea where they came from. It was a bit complicated, but it worked. They hadn't had a single police inquiry in the ten years they'd been in business together.

Levinson drew another cigarette from the pack in his shirt pocket, lit it, blew a puff of smoke, and smiled at Caroline Fisher. "So what?"

"So *what?*"

He stood only an inch taller than Fisher, but otherwise they were a study in contrasts. She was pale and blonde and beautiful and frequently on edge when she wasn't playing coy. He was a rather plain-looking black man, not particularly strong, but with a smile that put people at ease and that she found irresistible. He flashed her that smile now, and she practically melted into his arms.

"But Jeff…" she started to object.

"Come on, babe, he knows everything that happens around here. He probably has videos of us making out up there in the loft."

She looked up toward the loft, horrified.

Levinson laughed. "I'm kidding. I just mean it's nothing to worry about. So don't."

Resting her head on his shoulder, she said, "He's in a mood, anyway. He wants to see you."

"About what?"

"How should I know? He never tells me anything."

He grasped her shoulders and pushed her back so he could look her in the eyes. His grip was on the rough side, but she had never complained. He suspected she liked a bit of rough handling. "Don't pout. It's not becoming."

"I'm not pouting."

"Good." He kissed her quickly. "I'd better go. Never keep the man waiting."

He marched out of the Big Shed and into the rain, unconcerned that he had neither coat nor umbrella. The lane had nearly become a mudflow as he splashed his way up the hill to the house. The house was large, three stories sided in pale blue with white trim and a dark roof and a porch wrapping around the front and half of the left side. Calvert had built it three years ago and lived there mostly alone, with only his books and Caroline Fisher's on-again, off-again company. Solitude seemed to suit him.

Levinson stomped up the wooden stairs and onto the porch. The noise of his approach alerted Calvert, who opened the front door and looked him over. "You're a mess," he said. "Don't come in."

"It sounded urgent," Levinson said with a grin. "Didn't stop to put on my galoshes."

"Morgan Parsons." Calvert nearly snarled the name.

"He's delivering a truck today."

"Not anymore."

Levinson studied his boss's face and realized from the narrowed eyes and set jaw that something had gone very wrong. "What's the story?"

"I don't know, but he apparently did something stupid and can't deliver. The idiot called my cell to tell me."

"*What?* How did he get your number?"

Calvert arched his eyebrows.

"Right, I'll find out. What about the man himself?"

"Find out what he did and take appropriate action. I don't want the police following him here, and I don't want to hear another word about the matter."

His expression grim, Levinson asked, "What matter?" and turned to go.

"And tell Caroline I'd like her to spend the afternoon with me. I'm in the mood for some poetry, and she has such a nice reading voice. Unless she has other plans."

He looked over his shoulder and found Calvert smiling a disconcerting smile. It irritated Levinson, but he wasn't about to give his boss the pleasure of a reaction. "I'm not her secretary," he replied with a noncommittal shrug. "But I'll tell her."

# Chapter 7

After school, Susie and Andrew vied for their grandfather's attention. He fixed them some peanut butter and jelly sandwiches, listened to them talk about what they'd done that day, and helped them with homework. The afternoon was bright and warm, and he accompanied them out back to play on their swingset and toss a large ball back and forth. When they had worn him out, they went inside and settled in front of the television.

At the dining room table, Belinda was chewing on a pen and frowning at her laptop computer. "You okay?" Peller asked her.

"Just frustrated. I spend most of my day searching job listings and sending in applications, but I hardly hear from anyone. I've only had one interview in the past two weeks."

"Tough times," Peller agreed, "but keep at it. Something will turn up."

She nodded absently. "Did you ever go through anything like this?"

He pulled out the chair next to her and sat. "No. I guess I was fortunate. I got a job on the force in Lockport right after high school, and after a few years as a patrol officer had a chance to move into investigations. About a year after that, I applied for and got a position in Howard County. I've been there ever since."

She scrolled through the information on the screen. "I don't suppose layoffs are a big problem in your business."

"Not generally, but if the budget turns sour, even police positions can be on the chopping block. It's a lot more political, though. People don't like to sacrifice police and fire, but they don't much like paying taxes to support them, either."

Belinda laughed. "I'm as guilty as the next in that! What about Sandra? Did she ever find herself out of work?"

Peller didn't answer at first. There had been one time, but it was long ago and it took him a minute to dredge up the memory.

Belinda didn't seem to mind his silence; she went on working as before, without comment.

"When we moved to Maryland," Peller finally said. "She'd been working at Greenway, the agricultural co-op in Lockport, since before we met. There weren't many openings in her field at the time we moved, so she was out of work for almost two years."

"What did she do?"

"It worried her at first, but at some point I remember her saying we should trust God. After that, I don't remember her ever being worried." He thought back, trying to recapture the feeling of that moment. "I think I was skeptical for a long time. It was only later that I realized that she didn't mean she expected God to find her a job. She simply meant that whatever happened, things would work out."

Belinda lifted her hands from the keyboard and looked at him. Although she didn't speak, he knew what she was asking.

"In hindsight, they actually did. For one thing, she got pregnant."

Belinda smiled. "Jason. So she had time to give him a start in life before going back to work?"

Peller nodded. "It wasn't until he was born that I realized what a blessing her being out of work was. I've never been incredibly religious, but I have to admit she was right. It's something I've tried to remember since then, although it can be hard."

Belinda pushed her chair back and stood. "Yes, I think she was right. On that note, I have to start dinner. I guess I just have to trust that things will work out, too. Thank you."

Peller nodded. She moved into the kitchen and he looked out the window, thinking back, not seeing the houses and trees and sky beyond the glass. He wondered if there was a God, if there was some grand plan for his life, if there had been some purpose in Sandra's death. It had been such a random thing, a freak accident. Although it hadn't been his job to investigate it, he'd obtained all the files and memorized every detail. He had even, on several occasions in the weeks after her death, visited the scene, trying to replay it in his mind, to see what had happened, to envision what the witnesses had seen, to read the signs left on the pavement and in the grass by the side of the road.

But even he couldn't see what wasn't there.

He could see Sandra driving westbound on Frederick Road, passing farm fields and small stands of trees. He could see the dark blue pickup truck charge into the road from the farm lane, perhaps trailing a cloud of dust. He could feel the impact and knew that Sandra had died in the instant, never knowing what had hit her. He could see the truck push her mangled car off the road, just missing a telephone pole. He could see the truck back up suddenly, then turn and race westward, vanishing into the distance.

But all to no avail. Peller had replayed events time and again, how many times he no longer knew. It always played out the same way. He had studied the photos until every detail was burned into his memory: every contorted bit of metal, every drop of blood, every fragment of bone. Shattered pieces of the truck's headlamps and grille had been intermixed with the debris from Sandra's car and scattered all over the road. He revisited each image, each detail, knowing that he'd seen it all before and that nothing would be different.

But now, with the shock of a thunderclap, he realized something he hadn't before.

Scattered across three of the photographs he could clearly see pieces of a license plate holder. The letters on it, although fractured, were visible. He couldn't be certain, but Peller wondered if it might be the name of a dealership.

He buried his face in his hands. Why hadn't someone seen that before? Why hadn't *he* seen that before?

He thought he felt a gentle touch on his shoulder, thought he heard Sandra's voice—soft, forgiving.

*It's okay. You were in pain.*

⟅⟆

Obtaining accident reports in the digital age proved as easy as typing: Walters entered a few details on the police website, printed out what came up, and added it to his growing file on Sandra Peller's death. Undoubtedly more existed in police files than could be found on the website, but it was a good start.

His working hypothesis remained that the pickup involved had been stolen, and he saw confirmation in the police reports, the statements of the witnesses, and news reports. The truck had clearly been driven recklessly. Warping out of nowhere, it had t-boned Sandra's car, backed up, and raced off without hesitation, according to one of the witnesses. The driver didn't appear intoxicated: the vehicle sped away down the middle of the proper lane, never wavering despite its flight.

The farm from which the truck had come belonged to an elderly couple, Arne and Lucy Folsom. The police had interviewed them, but they claimed no knowledge of the truck's presence or its driver. No vehicle matching its description had ever been registered in their names or at their address, so the cops had accepted their statements. But clearly there had been suspicions. A question lay like a shadow in the background, raised in passing but not answered in the report: if the vehicle wasn't theirs, what had it been doing on their property?

Shuffling through the papers, Walters used a yellow high-lighter to mark key information. An image emerged as he did so. The driver of the truck must have been on the Folsom property without permission. Something had happened, and the driver had panicked. He—or she—jumped into the truck and raced away, not realizing until too late that they had burst onto the road at exactly the wrong moment. They could see Sandra Peller, knew what they had done before the cars stopped moving. Terror added to panic, they fled.

But what had the driver been running from?

Monday afternoon's storms were followed by a night that began clear and starry, but before dawn more clouds rolled in, the temperature dipped, and a cold drizzle spattered central Maryland for most of Tuesday. Dumas hated this kind of weather, but he had to go out in it. He'd located Morgan Parsons and was ready to arrest him on the first of what probably would spin up into a long list of charges.

As he drove through Columbia, windshield wipers running on intermittent, he thought about the previous evening. Dinner with Montufar had been pleasant enough. Initially they had talked about the case while waiting for their food to arrive. Montufar told him that Ruth Hudson had identified Parsons as the robber outside the jewelry store. He filled her in on the body that had been pulled from the water near the abandoned truck, dead from a gunshot wound to the abdomen and the attendant loss of blood. A tool box, probably one that had been in the truck, had been duct-taped to the body in an attempt to weigh it down. Given how long it had taken to locate the corpse, it was submerged surprisingly close to the shore near the truck.

Shop talk soon gave way to other subjects: weekend plans, the annoyances of apartment life, and how their boss was enjoying his vacation. All in all a comfortable evening, Dumas thought as he turned from Tamar Drive into the Columbia Landing apartment complex. Comfortable, yes, but it had brought no clarity to their relationship.

There would be time for that later, though. Right now, he had work to do.

Shrouded in trees, the complex consisted of about twenty buildings arranged in a square with the parking lot and more trees in the middle. He parked near the building where Morgan Parsons lived and waited for the squad car that was not far behind. Shortly it arrived, and a pair of officers, one a burly Hispanic fellow and the other a lanky black man with an unassuming air about him, emerged. Dumas beckoned to them. The three entered the building and mounted the stairs to the second floor. Locating Parsons' unit, Dumas knocked and waited.

No answer. He listened carefully but heard no sounds from within. Knocking again, he called, "Mr. Parsons! Howard County police. We need to talk to you."

Still nothing.

"After the day he had yesterday, I'd have thought he'd be sleeping in," Dumas said.

"Maybe he is," the Hispanic officer said.

"We'll find out. Run down to the rental office and have them send up a key."

"You got it."

Dumas and the other officer waited, staring at the walls.

"Is it supposed to rain all week?" the officer asked abruptly.

Dumas shrugged.

"I hope not. I mean to get out the ol' golf clubs this weekend."

"You a golfer?" Dumas asked before he realized what a dumb question it was.

"I swing the club, and usually the ball flies somewhere out in front of me," the officer said, waving a hand to illustrate. "Does that count?"

The detective laughed. "Why not?"

"You into any sports?"

"Not really. I watch baseball sometimes. Lately I've been jumping emotional hurdles."

Shaking his head, the officer grumbled, "Women."

Dumas heard footsteps coming up the stairs. Happy to drop the subject, he looked down and saw the other officer leading a young woman up the stairs. From the top he could mostly see her hair: lots of strawberry blonde hair interlaced with swirls of green and pink. Once she reached the top, he noted that her skin had the darkened, slightly fried look of someone who'd spent too much time on tanning beds.

"I hope this is okay," she was saying. "You have a warrant, right?"

"Yes, ma'am," the officer assured her wearily. She must have asked the question already, Dumas thought, possibly several times.

Arriving at the apartment door, she suddenly gave Dumas an unfriendly scowl. "Who are you?"

"Detective Sergeant Dumas," he replied, and extended his hand. She shook it tentatively. "I need to talk to Mr. Parsons, but either he's not home or he's asleep. Or just not answering the door." He avoided mentioning the fourth possibility—that he was dead. "If you could let me borrow the key, we'll go in and have a look."

She twirled the key but didn't hand it over.

"I'd let you do the honors," Dumas told her, "but frankly, ma'am, this guy might be dangerous. I'd rather you weren't in the way if any unpleasantness started."

Her eyes widened and she took a step back. "You'll give it right back?"

"As soon as I can, yes." He held out his hand, palm up, and waited.

After some internal debate, she set the key in his hand and hurried down the stairs as though chased by demons.

Dumas held up the key. "Shall we?"

"Ready when you are," the Hispanic officer said. They drew their guns and waited.

The detective unlocked the door and slowly pushed it, standing off to the side. Nothing happened. He looked into the darkened apartment. "Foyer's clear. Go ahead."

The officers moved in ahead of him and began a careful search, announcing that each room in turn was clear. Every curtain was drawn, every light out. A faint smell of grease hung in the air. The place was well-furnished. A huge TV, the centerpiece of a home theater, hung on the wall. The styles and colors clashed, but Dumas thought that in full light it probably was a flashy place. Aside from the TV, the walls held posters of bikini-clad women.

Dumas pulled out a dining room chair, sat, and studied the kitchen, where piles of dirty dishes occupied every available surface, including sink, stove, countertops, and the top of the refrigerator.

The officers returned from the back of the apartment. "He's not here," one of them said.

"Figures," Dumas groused. "I wonder where he's gone?"

⟿

At that moment, Morgan Parons might have preferred to be in the hands of the police. A big man with strength to spare, he wasn't much afraid of anyone. The lunatic now confronting him was one of the few exceptions.

Standing almost seven feet tall, Orion Speros looked like the Greek hunter whose image had been immortalized in the stars. All he needed was the club and shield to complete the picture. But it wasn't his physical size or strength that frightened Parsons. It was the manner in which Speros had arranged their little "talk."

Parsons had been jarred from sleep at six that morning by pounding on the door and someone outside bellowing, "Morgan! Come out, Morgan! Hurry, hurry! Morgan!"

Barely awake, he leaped out of bed and rushed to the door, clad only in his boxers, and opened it. "What? What's going on?"

Speros shoved him aside and strode into the living room. "Get dressed, Morgan. We've got to hurry!"

"Wait a minute," Parsons stammered. "Who the hell are you? What's going on?"

Spreading his arms so wide it looked as though he could gather up all the furniture with them, the intruder said, "Everyone knows me, Morgan. I'm Orion!" And then he slugged Parsons in the stomach so hard it knocked the wind out of him. By the time Parsons had recovered enough to speak, Speros had snagged a blanket from the bedroom and wrapped him in it. "Come on," he said cheerfully. "We need to go someplace we can talk."

"We can talk here," Parsons objected, his voice quavering.

Speros hit him again, doubling him over. "No, it's not safe here."

After that, things were a bit of a blur. Hurting and terrified, Parsons was dragged from the apartment out into the cold rain, stuffed into a car, and driven for what seemed hours although it probably hadn't been nearly that long. He thought about jumping out of the car, but Speros saw what he was thinking and said, "I'll run you over if you do." Parsons believed it.

Eventually they arrived at a barn out in the middle of nowhere. Speros pulled inside, closed the barn doors behind him, and dragged Parsons from the car. Throwing him to the ground, he gazed down at him, smiling as if they were best friends.

"What do you want?" Parsons asked. He tried to make it sound like a demand, but it came out pathetic.

"Oh, Morgan, you've been a bad boy. Jeff is upset."

"Jeff Levinson? I got nothin' to do with him."

"You called the man's cell phone. Jeff didn't like that."

Parsons shook his head, but he knew lying was pointless.

"How did you get that number, Morgan?"

"Du, I mean, the man gave it to me."

Speros' boot connected with Parsons' face, knocking him over backwards. Overwhelmed by pain and pinioned by the blanket, Parsons writhed about. By the time he'd freed himself, blood was all over the blanket and the ground.

"I found it!" he whimpered. "I found it, okay?" He gingerly felt his nose. Agony erupted at the slightest touch.

"Found it where?"

Nausea roiled in Parsons' gut. He gasped out, "In the Big Shed, last time I made a delivery. There were some papers lying on a desk, and a planner with a pink cover. I think it belonged to that slut Jeff hangs with. I looked through it while I was waiting. There was a list of numbers in the back. It was there."

"You shouldn't read other people's stuff, Morgan. That's not polite."

Still probing his face with his fingers, Parsons whined, "Polite? I think you broke my nose!"

Speros grinned. "You want me to fix it up?"

"Stay away from me!"

"You think I like this, Morgan?"

"You sure as hell do! You're insane!"

Squatting down in front of Parsons, Speros looked him in the eye. "You're not very nice, are you? Now tell me. What happened to the truck?"

"An accident. I ran off the road and into a pond."

Hanging his head in disappointment, Speros clicked his tongue a few times. "You still haven't learned not to lie." He smacked the top of Parsons' head, eliciting a yelp. "Never lie to a lunatic, Morgan. You might get hurt. What happened to the truck?"

Parsons was too terrified to speak further. If he told the truth, he was dead. If he didn't tell the truth, he was likely dead anyway. He wanted to escape, to hide, to never let anyone touch him again. He didn't remember doing it, but he found himself curled up into a ball. He glanced up.

Speros had a gun in his hand and was examining it lovingly, as though it were made of solid gold. "I heard some upsetting things about what you did yesterday. Jeff told me to make sure you weren't going to lead the police to the farm. You wouldn't do that, would you, Morgan?"

He tried to shake his head.

"Would you?"

The gun was pointed at his forehead. "No," he whispered.

The gun pressed into his forehead, cold, harsh, digging into his flesh.

"No!" he screamed.

Speros stood and tucked the gun away. "Now Morgan, I want you to pay attention. It's a good bet the cops will find you. Given the things I heard, you're probably going to jail for a long time. Probably the only way to avoid it is to give them something more interesting than your own pathetic self."

Nudging Parsons with his foot, he said, "But if you do that, I'll have to kill you."

Parsons blinked up at him but couldn't find his voice.

"You know how little pleasure that would give me," Speros said. Returning to the car, he opened the driver's door. "I hate unpleasant work. So if it came to that, I'd have to make it fun."

With a playful wink, Speros slipped into the car, started the engine, and threw the vehicle into reverse. Flooring the accelerator, he smashed through the barn doors and drove off.

The sound of the engine receded, leaving in its wake the patter of soft rain. Parsons stared at the splintered doors. Beyond them, cloaked in gray rain, he thought he saw Death raising his scythe.

# Chapter 8

The search of Parsons' apartment was still in progress when Dumas' cell phone rang. Checking it, he was surprised to find Peller calling.

"Hey Rick, how's Denver?" He was seated at the dining table shuffling through some old mail that had been found jammed in the bottom of a drawer. There wasn't much of interest, mostly old bills and credit card offers.

"Not bad. The Rockies are even better than the pictures. You should come up here sometime. Any excitement back home?"

"The odd mugging, a voluntary manslaughter, a truck and a body dumped in a lake. You know the drill. Nothing we can't handle. Anyway, you're supposed to be relaxing, not checking up on us."

"I am relaxing," Peller said, although his voice didn't sound relaxed. "I just wanted to ask a favor. When you have a spare minute, could you have a look at the photos from Sandra's accident? There are fragments of a license plate holder in several of them. I think it may have had the name of a dealership on it."

Dumas dropped the papers and leaned back. Peller had pored obsessively over those photos for a long time after the accident, to the point that many of his colleagues worried over his mental state. Then one day he gave up on them, and hadn't mentioned them since.

"Eric?"

"I can. But, Rick..."

"I don't need a lecture, Eric. I need to know if I'm right."

"What if you are? What difference does it make now?"

"Probably none at all, and I may be wrong anyway. But I need to know."

Feeling like an enabler, Dumas said, "All right. But don't you go nuts on us."

Peller laughed. "I promise."

"Why couldn't you have asked Corina?"

"She would have given me a lecture."

Dumas couldn't help but smile at the observation. "That she would have," he said lightly. "That she would have."

At that moment, Montufar's thoughts were far from lectures. A stack of paperwork needed reducing, most of it sufficiently routine for her to do with both eyes closed. Her mind was only half on her work anyway.

Eduardo. She was worried about her brother, whose frequent inability to find words nagged her. She wanted him to ask his doctor about it, but she knew he would shrug the matter off as simply part of his recovery process, convinced that he'd be back to normal in no time.

She silently offered a brief prayer on his behalf.

Maybe that was it, she thought. Maybe she could talk to the pastor at St. John's. If anyone could make Eduardo see reason, a priest could. But she didn't know any of the local priests, not having set foot in a church for nearly eight years.

She felt guiltily as though she were making excuses for her reluctance. Speaking to a priest shouldn't be a problem. After all, her job entailed talking with strangers all the time. But this was different, somehow. It seemed a bit like asking a bank for a new loan after having defaulted on the last one.

Her desk phone rang, and she answered it absently.

"Sergeant Montufar, this is Phil Walters. I'm sorry to bother you again, but I was wondering if I could ask a small favor?"

"Who?"

"Phil Walters. The writer. I visited you at…"

"Oh. I'm sorry, Mr. Walters, but you already have my answer."

"It's not about that," the writer said quickly, perhaps afraid she was already hanging up. "This is about an entirely different matter."

"Like what?"

"I was wondering if I might be able to get copies of any photos the department has related to the accident that killed Sandra Peller."

Montufar felt a sudden rush of heat and nearly did hang up. "Why do you want that?"

"To help."

"I doubt that."

"Freedom of Information Act?"

"Fill out the paperwork and pay the fees." She rattled a handful of documents. "I'm doing mine right now and don't have time to do you favors."

"I could, but I was hoping..." His voice trailed off in discouragement.

"Why would you call me about this?" Montufar demanded.

"To be honest, Sergeant, I really was hoping you wouldn't mind doing me the favor. I want to help Lieutenant Peller. The case isn't under investigation any longer due to the statute of limitations. But there is no statute of limitations on auto theft."

Montufar closed her eyes and took a few breaths to steady herself. "You're sleuthing without a license," she said. "What does auto theft have to do with it?"

"It's just a hypothesis based on what I know of the facts. The photos might help." She was about to tell him to forget his hypothesis when he added, "I'm hoping Tom Kaneko might look at them with me."

"Oh God," she muttered, then said sternly, "Please leave that poor man alone. He's suffered enough for his involvement in police work."

"It's up to him. I think he's interested."

"No favors, Mr. Walters. If you want the photos, I'm sure you know how to get them. Please don't call me again."

She slammed down the phone. A couple of detectives at nearby desks jumped and cast her looks both surprised and irritated.

She pulled her papers into order and glared at them.

The phone rang again.

"I'm going to kill him," she said, but knowing it might not be Walters again, she answered with as much calm as she could muster.

"Hey Corina," Dumas' deep, gravelly voice replied.

"Oh, Eric. Thank God."

"Now what?" He sounded alarmed.

"Nothing. Just that writer, Walters. He called and asked me… well, never mind. It's not important."

"His dogged pursuit of the almighty dollar is impressive," Dumas laughed. "Listen, I need a favor."

Montufar sighed. "Theme of the day. What is it?"

"Rick called me a few minutes ago. He wanted me to look for something in the photos of…"

She waited, but it seemed he couldn't finish the sentence. And then she realized what it had to be. "The world is going mad around me," she muttered.

"Sorry? I didn't catch that."

"What does he think he remembers?"

"A license plate holder," Dumas said. "Possibly with the name of a dealership. He said fragments of it appeared in several photos."

"Walters thinks the pickup was stolen."

Dumas didn't answer at once. Montufar jammed the receiver between her ear and shoulder and pulled a sheet of paper to her, studying it.

"Why is Walters looking into that?"

She told him what the writer had told her.

"I'll be back shortly. We didn't find much here except some tools of the auto theft trade. And it sure looks like Parsons had more disposable income than he had any right to, so he must have done a good business. Let's get those photos and go over them together. I'm starting to get a funny feeling about all this."

"You get funny feelings about everything," she said, feigning boredom. She had actually been looking forward to a bit of boring paperwork, but obviously fate had other ideas.

Dumas laughed. "That's why I need your analytic mind, to keep me grounded."

"Great. We're an ideal couple."

Oddly, he didn't laugh at that, but after a beat said, "I'll see you shortly," and hung up.

She returned the receiver to its cradle, gently this time, and shook her head. Her life had become too complicated, and although she didn't care to admit it, Eric Dumas was among the complications.

∽

The photos had slumbered quietly in a folder in a box for years. Spreading them gingerly on the desk, Montufar felt like she was slashing open an old wound, and she sensed that Dumas, standing at her side, felt something similar. Neither spoke for a long time, nor did they really look. The images lay before them, harsh, cold, and evil, daring the detectives to set eyes upon them once again. They had both studied scores of similar photos in the course of their careers, but these were different. In painfully exquisite detail they depicted the death of one who had been the whole world to their mentor, their friend, and whose friendship with themselves had been an unexpected gift.

Eventually they had no choice but to look.

"Oh," Dumas said miserably.

Montufar put her hand over her mouth.

Sandra had been driving a silver Dodge Neon. The side of the vehicle had been ripped open by the collision and its insides pushed every which way. In some of the photos, it was barely recognizable as a car. Sandra's body had been similarly ravaged.

Other photos showed the debris field, both in overview and in detail. The majority of the scattered wreckage appeared to have come from Sandra's car, but here and there a bit of different-colored material testified to the truck's role in the accident. Picking through the images was exhausting, heart-wrenching work.

Finally, Montufar said, "Here," and pointed to one of the photos.

Dumas looked, nodded, and examined another from a nearby area. "And here," he said.

"And this one." Montufar picked up a third photo and studied it.

They looked at everything again, but only those three showed what they were looking for: the shattered, twisted remains of a license plate holder.

Montufar showed Dumas the photo she was holding. "These two pieces. Ford." The break occurred down the middle of the "r," but there was no question about it.

They studied the rest in silence for a few minutes. Finally, Dumas said, "Got it. Andy Abramson Ford."

"Hunt Valley," Montufar added.

Dumas set the three photos aside, then quickly gathered up the rest and returned them to their envelope to get them out of sight. "I'll check with Rick, see if he wants copies of these three."

Lining them up in front of her, Montufar looked from one to the other. "What good are they? We have a dealership and maybe a make on the truck, but we don't have a model year. It's not much to go on."

Captain Morris came up behind them. "What's not much to go on?" Montufar silently offered the photos. The captain's eyes closed for a moment, and she leaned on the desk as if for support. "Christ, not this again."

"Don't ask me how, but Rick pulled a rabbit out of his hat," Dumas said. "Look here." He pointed to the bits of license plate holder.

"I thought magic was your department," Morris said, but she took the photos and studied them carefully. "He figured this out while wrestling with his grandkids?"

"Apparently."

The captain straightened. "We can't reopen the case. You both know that."

Montufar and Dumas exchanged a glance. "We know," Montufar replied. "Rick just asked us to see if he was right."

"Okay," Morris said, but the line between her brows proclaimed her apprehension. "Then again, if you happened to be car shopping up in Hunt Valley and felt like asking a question or two, I don't see how I could stop you." She walked off, shaking her head.

"Not really any point," Montufar said quietly. She stacked up the three photos and handed them to Dumas.

"No," he said, taking them. "It's not likely anything would come of it."

"When should we go?"

"I'm free tonight. You?"

"I could manage it."

Dumas nodded at the photos. "I'll make some copies and call Rick back."

Montufar watched him go, ideas chasing each other through her mind. She wondered if the writer, Walters, had hit upon something with his stolen vehicle idea. She wondered if the pickup was one of the dark blue trucks sold by Andy Abramson over the year prior to the accident. If so, where was that truck now? Had it been repaired, repainted, resold, stripped, shipped out of the country, or dropped into a deep, dark hole? Almost anything was possible. She wondered what Rick would do if by some miracle these questions and the dozens more swirling around this one unsolved case could be answered.

She wondered if faux car shopping with Dumas constituted a date.

"Now I need a vacation," she muttered, and without the least enthusiasm resumed her paperwork.

Irritated but not deterred, Walters visited Northern District Headquarters, paid for expedited processing of his Freedom of Information request, and in due course obtained everything available on the case.

Eventually, Parsons dragged his pain-wracked body to the barn door and peered into the rain, hoping for some sign of where he was. Tree-studded hills surrounded him. Off to the left, a furrowed field stretched across rolling land, while to the right tall grass bent under the assault of wind and water. He couldn't see any other buildings from this vantage point, but somewhere there must be some.

On the opposite wall of the barn a second door stood slightly ajar. He inched his way across to it and pushed it open only to find more of the same: hills, fields, grass, trees. Leaning out into the rain, he looked about. A few hundred yards away, atop a rise, stood an old farm house. Light shone from several of the windows.

Parsons pulled himself out of the rain and slid down against the wall to sit on the dirt floor. Pain made it difficult to concentrate, but he had to come up with a plan. He might steal a car, except he didn't have his tools. He could ask for help at the house, but anyone finding a nearly-naked man wrapped in a bloody blanket on their doorstep would instantly call the police. Worse, what if the man who called himself Orion lived here or used this place because he had friends here?

A wave of nausea overtook Parsons. He turned onto his hands and knees, retching, but nothing came up. Trembling, forcing himself to breathe deeply, he waited for it to pass. He didn't think he could make it to the house, much less to one further away, yet he knew he needed help. God only knew how much damage that maniac had inflicted. He might die out here.

Making the only decision he could, he slowly gathered himself up, wrapped the blanket around his body and over his head, and, drawing a deep breath, set out into the icy rain.

⟿

Among the farm's many buildings was a modest house set well downhill from Duke Calvert's. Grayish and oldish, it was almost invisible in the rain. The blinds were nearly always shut, so little light escaped to betray the presence of inhabitants. Its purpose was twofold: on the one hand, the few outsiders who came to the farm conducted their business here; on the other, this was where Jeff Levinson lived.

Levinson's tastes were as plain as Calvert's were opulent; his surroundings spartan. Furnishings were stripped to bare essentials—a few blonde wood pieces upholstered in bleached canvas scattered the rooms—and beige walls bore little in the way of art. No knickknacks spoiled the simplicity of line. Levinson didn't want the place to stand out in any way, although some who passed through it found its minimalism memorable if not desirable.

On this rainy Tuesday afternoon, he was playing host to Orion Speros. The man gave him the creeps and could have easily split him in two, but he was useful. Levinson was always careful to avoid antagonizing him, though.

Speros was saying, "I think he'll be a good boy." They were seated at a round table in the kitchen. To gratify his unpredictable employee Levinson had supplied him with a bowl of pistachios. Speros was crunching through them as though they were the most desired delicacies on the planet.

Levinson regarded Speros. He thought of him as his dog: huge, ugly, and ill-tempered. Speros probably wouldn't bite his master, but it was best not to take chances. He put a casual hand over the loaded .38 tucked into his belt. His t-shirt covered it but left a noticeable bulge. "I hope you didn't have to rough him up too much. Strange as it may seem, he's one of our better suppliers."

"Nah. I just reminded him how important security was to you."

Which, Levinson figured, meant Speros had beat the hell out of Parsons but left him alive. "You should play for the Ravens," he remarked, forcing a smile so as not to appear too sarcastic.

"Amateurs," Speros replied. "Anybody wants to have fun off the field, send 'em to me. I'm a great teacher." He laughed heartily.

Levinson didn't. "Just don't get sloppy. You know what the man thinks about sloppiness."

Speros had continued opening pistachios, and now had a small pile of them. He gathered them up in his hand, asked, "You afraid he'll take your whore away from you?" and popped them all into his mouth, grinning while he chewed. The effect was unnerving.

Levinson bristled at Speros' mention of Caroline Fisher, and was sure that Speros was well aware of his disgust. But he kept his temper in check. "I can always find another girl. You're not so easily replaced. The man could arrange your disposal if he wanted. You're not invincible."

Speros leaned back, spread his arms wide, and roared, "Of course I am! I'm Orion!"

Whenever he did that, Levinson thought, Speros seemed to expand to fill up the whole room. With a shake of his head he asked, "How in the name of God did you ever get to be like this?"

"I was born this way," Speros laughed. "I didn't always know how great it was, but once I learned that, everything else fell into place."

"And how did you learn it?"

"Now that's a tale, Jeff. That's a tale. Let's just say I had three teachers: one who never taught again, one who never walked again, and one who will never stop looking over his shoulder."

A shiver chased its tail up and down Levinson's spine.

"Don't worry about Morgan," Speros said, grabbing another handful of pistachios. "Even he isn't that stupid." He tossed the nuts into his mouth, shells and all, crunched them up with his teeth, and spat the whole mess out onto the floor.

"Yick," he said. "Take my advice, Jeff. Don't ever try that!"

The woman who opened the door must have been about eighty. Tall and large-boned, she was clothed in an ankle-length blue dress patterned in little white and yellow flowers. Her eyes widened as she took in the bloodied, blanket-wrapped man standing before her.

"My goodness!" she gasped. "What happened to you? Has there been an accident?"

Parsons could barely think, but the word felt like a good one to use. "Accident," he stammered.

"Gene!" she called over her shoulder. "Gene, get in here! There's a man in a terrible state!" She took Parsons by the shoulder and gently guided him into the house, through the living room to the kitchen, and settled him in a chair.

A rail-thin man with a mop of white hair came up behind her. "What's wrong?" he asked. "Who is this?"

"Don't know." The woman began to unwrap Parsons, then quickly folded the blanket back into place. "Good heavens, what became of your clothes?"

Parsons shrugged.

"He's a mess, Gene. Says he was in an accident. You'd better call an ambulance."

"Don't worry, son," Gene said. "We'll get you some help." He shuffled to the telephone hanging on the wall at the back of the kitchen, dialed 911, and reported a traffic accident with injuries.

# Chapter 9

The after-school ceremonies on Tuesday went much as on Monday: Peller made peanut butter and jelly sandwiches, listened as the children recounted their day, helped them with homework, and took them outside for a round of swinging on swings and sliding on the slide. Part of him thought he could do this forever and be happy, but part of him was anxious for Dumas to call back.

The call came just after he had settled Susie and Andrew in the family room with their TV show. Belinda was filling out an online job application at the dining room table. He walked out the front door to take the call so he wouldn't be overheard.

"You were right," Dumas said.

Peller closed his eyes for a moment. "And?"

"Andy Abramson Ford in Hunt Valley."

"So now we have a dark blue Ford pickup bought at that dealership."

"Could've been purchased used, though, in which case the make might be different."

"Maybe, but I have a feeling not. So now I have to figure out what comes next."

"No need," Dumas said. "Corina and I are going car shopping tonight."

"You don't have to do that. Captain Morris..."

"Has already let us know that she'll look the other way, so long as we're not on duty."

Peller gazed at without seeing the house across the street, a pale yellow place similar in style to Jason and Belinda's. "I don't want to drag all of you through this again."

Dumas didn't respond for a moment. Peller could usually read him pretty well, but now he didn't know what was going through his colleague's mind.

"It's not again," Dumas finally said. "It's still. Like it or not, we're in it with you."

"Thank you, Eric. Thank you both. You tell Corina I said that."

"I will."

Peller pocketed his phone and breathed in the cool air. He couldn't count the times he'd felt himself blessed to have known and worked with Montufar and Dumas. Their support in the aftermath of the accident might have been the only thing that got him through his grief, a grief they had shared because they both had known Sandra. Sandra had connected with them from the very start. She'd had a way of doing that.

It had been nine years since that day, the day Detective Lieutenant Jim Cowden met Peller and his team in the parking lot of Northern District Headquarters. Although Cowden didn't have all the details, he'd heard enough from the radio chatter to know that things had gone badly, that the team would need his moral support. He wanted them to know, just as soon as possible, that they had it.

Peller, recently promoted to Detective Sergeant, had been dropped into a nasty case, a series of brutal attacks on teenagers near Oakland Mills High School in Columbia. The perpetrators had to be found and stopped immediately. Peller had the best of help, in Cowden's view: Detectives Corina Montufar and Eric Dumas, both young, energetic, and very sharp. Against all odds, the trio had resolved the case in a single day.

But not without cost.

Cowden watched them climb wearily out of Montufar's car, a dark red Dodge Shadow. He and Peller resembled each other to the extent that colleagues made jokes about their having been cloned: just under six feet tall, broad-shouldered, lean-faced, square-jawed.

But Cowden's sandy hair and blue eyes came from northern stock, while Peller's dark hair and hazel eyes proclaimed a different lineage. They couldn't be truly confused, yet sometimes people looked at them oddly, as though trying to figure out whether they might be brothers.

As the three detectives approached, he said, "Good work, people. Very good work."

Peller nodded, but said nothing. Montufar's eyes were downcast. Dumas drew a breath and let it out slowly, looking skyward.

"They ambushed us," Dumas said. "Two officers down, two of the perps dead and the other nearly dead. It sure doesn't feel good."

"Our guys will pull through," Cowden assured him. "I just got off the phone with the hospital five minutes ago. The paperwork can wait. You want to go someplace to unwind? My treat." To anyone else he would have explicitly offered drinks, but oddly none of these three were drinkers. Peller had grown up in a Methodist family that didn't drink, Dumas had sworn off alcohol for reasons Cowden didn't know, and he had no clue as to Montufar's story.

"Might not be a bad idea," Peller said. He looked at Montufar and Dumas for approval, but they didn't get a chance to speak.

"Well, hello, stranger!"

Peller's face lit up as he turned to the woman who had spoken behind them. "Sandra! What are you doing here?"

A woman dressed casually in jeans and a t-shirt printed with a bevy of flowering plants approached them. A good five inches shorter than her husband, Sandra Peller stood on tiptoes to peck a quick kiss on his lips, as if she were shy of their audience. "What am I doing here? Don't tell me you forgot that your car was in the garage. I'm here to take you home." She brushed a lock of wind-tossed brown hair back from her heart-shaped face. "Assuming you want to go."

Peller looked embarrassed. "I did forget, totally. God yes, get me out of here."

"Bad day?"

"The worst."

A look of concern stole the light from her face. "What happened?"

He glanced at the others. "Oh, Sandra, this is Lieutenant Cowden, and Detectives Montufar and Dumas. This is my wife Sandra."

Sandra released her husband and shook hands with the others amid a murmur of pleasure-to-meet-you's. Then she fixed Peller with a motherly look. "So what happened?"

"A trio of thugs knifing kids to get their expensive sneakers. The cut up their victims pretty bad." He shook his head. "For shoes."

"That's sick," she said with a grimace. "Was anyone killed?"

"Only the bad guys. Well, two of them. The other might pull through. We thought we had them cornered, but..." Peller rubbed his eyes. "Two of our officers are in the hospital, in addition to eight victims."

"You all look like hell." She regarded each of them individually. "Would you like to come to our place for dinner? It won't be anything fancy, but I can throw something together."

"Oh, I don't want to be any trouble," Dumas said quickly, and Montufar began, "No, that's all right—", but Sandra cut them off.

"You have family?" she asked.

Dumas shrugged.

Montufar nodded, but something in her nod suggested reluctance.

"Then come on over to our place. You shouldn't have to go home to an empty house." Her tone made it sound like an order from a superior officer. Then, more softly and with a hopeful smile, she added, "Friends are always welcome in our home. Say yes?"

"Well," Montufar said.

Dumas hesitated, then said, "If you insist."

Sandra turned her smile on Cowden. "You'll join us?"

For a moment he couldn't find his voice. He felt as though an angel were addressing him.

"Please?"

He shook his head. "Thank you, but it was their bad day, not mine. And anyway, I have a meeting on the schedule."

She cocked her head and kept smiling.

"But, ah, I could take a rain check."

Relenting, Sandra said, "Okay. But I'll hold you to that."

Cowden couldn't help but crack a smile. "Yes, ma'am. Get some rest, guys. Don't second-guess yourselves. You did good. I'll see you tomorrow." With a wave, he returned to the building. Once indoors, he looked back. The Pellers and the others were getting into their cars, after which Sandra led the procession off the lot.

Cowden watched them go, wishing he could join them but knowing it was better this way.

"There's no accident," Kevin Graham told the lady of the house, who had identified herself as Clara Sudworth. Clara was seated on a comfortable couch in their sensibly-furnished living room while her husband Gene hovered nearby, seemingly unable to either sit still or stand in one place. An open door in the back of the room led into a bedroom, where the accident victim had been settled in bed with a pile of clean blankets and a cup of hot tea. Now the paramedics were bent over him.

"He said he was in an accident," Clara said firmly. "Not that I heard or saw anything. We're well back from the road here. But he was soaked to the bone, so he must have been walking for a time."

"You said he wasn't wearing much."

"That's right, just a pair of boxers and that blanket."

Whatever had happened, Graham thought, it wasn't any usual sort of accident. "And he'd been bleeding?"

"Yes, a lot by the look of him and the blanket. I think he must have smashed his face on something. That happens if you're not wearing your seatbelt, doesn't it?"

"It can," Graham agreed. "But where is his car?" He thought for a moment. "You mind if I look around outside? I wonder if he somehow got off the road, came up your drive, and ran into something." *While on drugs*, he didn't add.

Clara started to speak, but before she could, Gene asserted his authority over his realm. Waving a hand towards the front door, he said, "Be my guest." Clara rolled her eyes.

"I'll be back in a bit," Graham told them. He poked his head into the bedroom, directing the EMTs not to leave without him, then went outside. The rain had tapered off, but the ground was saturated. Little in the way of clear footprints would be preserved, although he thought he saw a few signs of the injured man's passing. They pointed towards a barn over a hundred yards off. Careful not to disturb the vague marks, he moved toward it.

A door on the side of the barn facing the house gaped open. Graham approached carefully. He found no one in the barn, but neither did he find any sign that animals had recently been kept there. No trace of feed, straw, or hoofprint was apparent. There wasn't even any old harness or other equipment that might remain from an earlier time. Whatever had been happening here, it hadn't involved sheep or cattle.

What he did see was blood. A trail led into the shadowy depths of the structure, and he followed it, only too aware that whoever was responsible for the beaten man in the Sudworths' back bedroom might still be within. When he saw the splintered double doors through which livestock had once been driven, he stopped and gaped.

Tire tracks gouged into the dirt floor seemed to indicate that a vehicle had been rammed through the great doors. What was left of them hung drunkenly from their track, exploded outward by the force of the blow that had shattered them. Graham crossed the open space to the doors and looked out.

No vehicle.

"Somebody," he said to nobody, "isn't being straight with somebody."

By the time Graham got back to the house, the paramedics were loading the victim into the ambulance. "Can he talk?" he asked.

"He's in shock," one of them replied. "I don't think he'll be saying much for a little while."

"All right. We'll pay him a visit a little later." He watched the ambulance leave, its flashing lights igniting red sparkles in the water droplets clinging to the vegetation, then returned to the house.

"Did you find anything?" Clara asked.

"For one thing, I hope you have good insurance." Graham watched their reactions, but saw only confusion. Probably, he thought, the guy really did tell them he'd been in an accident. "Your barn door is all smashed up."

Gene's face reddened in anger. "What? He ran into my barn?"

"I don't think it was him."

"Who else would it be?" Gene demanded. He thumped his fist on the wall surprisingly hard for a man his age.

"If it was him, he's a magician. There's no car out there, Mr. Sudworth. Someone else drove through it, and drove off."

Clara stood and put a hand on Gene's shoulder. Her touch seemed to calm him. "Officer, are you saying..." She scowled, working it out, then put her hand to her mouth.

"Yes, ma'am," Graham replied. "I am indeed."

∽

Hunt Valley, about thirteen miles north of downtown Baltimore, is the northernmost of the city's suburbs, sandwiched between Interstate 83, which takes the traveler north to York, Pennsylvania, and York Road, which predated the Eisenhower administration by one hundred and thirty years. A hub of commerce and light industry surrounded by uncrowded housing, some of it on the luxury end of the spectrum, it had been carved out of wooded hills and felt much farther from the city than it actually was.

That, at least, was Montufar's sense of the place as they drove through on their way to Andy Abramson Ford, a dealership located on York Road just sound of the Hunt Valley Village Centre. They pulled into the lot of a flashy glass-and-chrome building and parked near a showroom filled with bright, new cars and bright, eager sales-people. This evening, the place had attracted a good number of potential buyers.

The detectives entered and took a quick look around at the sales floor. "Here's one for you," Dumas said. "A shiny red Mustang, fully loaded." He ran a finger down the sticker. "Just on the high side of thirty thousand. Good thing you have a lucrative government job."

Montufar opened the driver's door and considered the interior. "Nice. You could buy it for me for my birthday."

"I'll start saving."

"Good evening, folks," a cheery voice said behind them. "I'm Bruce. Bruce Waggoner."

They turned to find a short, rotund fellow reaching out for a handshake. Dumas obliged first, saying, "Hi, I'm Eric, this is Corina."

The salesman shook Montufar's hand a bit less vigorously than he had Dumas'. He put her in mind of a hobbit that had gone into the automotive business. She wouldn't have been surprised if he'd said his name was Bilbo Waggoner. The image made her smile.

"Let me guess. You're into sports cars, but your husband wants a family car." He winked, as though sharing a joke with her.

"Actually," she replied, deadpan, "I want a helicopter and he wants a motorcycle." She looked around. "But I don't see either."

Waggoner blinked. "No, I'm afraid not. Is there something else I can help you with, maybe?"

Before she could say anything else foolish, Dumas told him, "Actually, we're interested in trucks."

That put the dealer on terra firma again. "Of course! We have a good selection on the lot. Do you have any preferences?"

"Something in a dark blue."

"And possibly stolen," Montufar added.

Waggoner frowned at her. "Look, I'm sorry if I said something wrong. Maybe we should start again."

Montufar instantly repented her words. The man didn't deserve the sharp edge of her tongue; he was just trying to make a living. "I'm sorry. But we're with the Howard County police. We're hoping you can help us with a small matter."

He looked from her to Dumas, nonplussed. Dumas nodded. "Do you have ID?" he asked finally.

Montufar produced her badge. "About four years ago there was a hit-and-run accident in our jurisdiction. We never had much to go on. Witnesses described a dark blue pickup leaving the scene. But we realized today that photos of the debris from the accident show a license plate holder from this dealership. It could only be from the truck."

Dumas took out the photos and showed them to Waggoner, pointing out the relevant fragments. The salesman studied them closely and nodded. "Takes a bit of doing to see them, but I do believe you're right."

"It's possible," Dumas told him, "that the vehicle was sold here, but it's also possible it was stolen from you."

"And you want to know if we could search our records for a match."

"Exactly."

The salesman pondered. "I've been here five years," he said, "and I can't recall us losing any trucks to theft in that time. I can ask. As for sales, we sell about thirty trucks per year, so even going back a couple of years prior to your accident wouldn't produce too many vehicles. Yes, I think we could do that."

"We really appreciate it," Montufar said. "Motorcycles and helicopters notwithstanding."

This time he laughed. "You must think me over-sensitive."

Montufar shrugged. "My mouth gets ahead of my brain sometimes."

"I suppose we all have that problem. Come with me. I'll introduce you to our manager. He can probably pull up the information you need."

⟞

An hour later they were in a nearby diner, eating crabcakes and coleslaw and looking at a sheet of paper on the table between them, a paper bearing the name and address of a customer who had purchased a dark blue F250 a mere month before Sandra was killed. As luck would have it, the buyer lived just to the south in Cockeysville, or at least had at the time, although it was too late to pay a visit tonight.

"Think they're still there?" Dumas asked.

"God only knows. But we have to find out."

"Yeah."

They ate in silence for a few minutes, not looking up from their plates.

"Eric?"

"Hmm?"

"Do we look like a married couple?"

Dumas set his fork down and considered his dining partner. "I don't know. What does a married couple look like?"

"Dumb question, I guess."

"But if I ever got married..." he began, but paused before finishing the sentence.

Montufar waited. Eventually Dumas looked away, apparently embarrassed. "Oh." She picked up her napkin and patted her mouth. "Oh. Thank you."

Dumas kept looking away.

"Seriously. Thank you," she repeated.

"You're welcome." He shook his head and said with a half-hearted laugh, "I think it's time to change the subject."

"But if we're going to go around pretending to be married, we need to think about it," she pointed out.

"It's awkward."

"Well, yes. It's going to be. But I think that's because we both have family issues."

Dumas finally looked at her. "I have issues," he said. "You have a good family."

"My mother is dead, my father doesn't recognize me anymore, my brother may have brain damage, and my sister falls apart at the slightest touch." She laid down her fork and sighed, leaning her head up on her hands. "Yes, a good family, but not without its problems."

Dumas copied her pose. "Plus that Fibonacci business. Too much stress lately. And now this." He nodded at the paper. "You know this is just going to make it worse. The statute of limitations means no chance for justice. Even if we find out who killed Sandra, there's nothing we can do, unless the vehicle was stolen. What do you think Rick will do if we do find the driver?"

"You don't think he'd go vigilante?" she asked in horror.

"I doubt even he knows what he'd do. I think that's part of what's kept him away from his family until now. If he didn't see them, he didn't have to see it, either." That didn't make sense to her, but Dumas continued, "Think about it. He wasn't with them three days before he realized that license plate holder was hiding in those photos."

Montufar thought about it. Maybe Dumas was right. "But we have to follow through," she protested. "We can't just let it go."

He nodded agreement.

Reaching across the table, she took his hands in hers. "We're in this together. All three of us. That helps, doesn't it?"

He folded his hands around hers. "That's what I told Rick." Unconsciously, he had begun gently caressing Montufar's fingers. She found it soothing and said nothing, allowing him to continue for a moment, before pulling her hands away. "We should get back to work," she said with a halfhearted laugh, "and stop acting like a married couple."

He arched a flirtatious eyebrow. "Should we resume acting like it later?"

She smiled at the table, a quiet private smile. "I guess we'll see."

# Chapter 10

Late Tuesday afternoon on the campus of Johns Hopkins University in the city, a student was peppering Professor Tomio Kaneko with questions.

Mathematical questions.

Questions Walters could hear but didn't understand except for an occasional mention of a number or a mathematical operation. From his carefully-chosen position near the mathematician's office door, he listened, hoping for a speedy end to the conversation. The few passersby paid him no mind. He could have been just another grad student waiting his turn with the professor.

Checking the time on his cell phone, he grumbled to himself. He'd been waiting here for over fifteen minutes, with no letup in the rapid-fire questions. Kaneko handled the barrage with practiced calm, directing, guiding. Walters had the sense that the professor wanted the student to find the answers himself and was merely acting as a catalyst.

Ten more minutes passed.

Finally, the student thanked Kaneko and left, barely noticing Walters as he passed by.

"Come in, Mr. Walters," Kaneko called.

Startled, Walters wondered how the mathematician had known he was there, but he wasted no time entering the office. He took a seat opposite Kaneko and slid the folder of information toward him.

"You know what this is," he said. "I'd very much appreciate it if you'd look at it and give me your impressions."

Kaneko sighed but pulled the folder to himself, squared it, and opened it. He sorted quickly through the papers, making neat piles: official reports in one, photos in another, news articles in a third. Sitting perfectly erect, he started on the reports without saying a word.

Walters leaned back and waited.

He waited forty minutes.

Kaneko restacked the materials in the folder and pushed it back to the writer.

"Well?"

"It is curious," Kaneko mused, "that the truck was on that property. The owners denied any knowledge of its presence. Moreover, it is curious that it should have exited the property at such high speed. And finally, it is very strange that it should have done so just as Mrs. Peller was driving by."

"I agree with you on the first two points. The last, though, is just coincidence."

"Perhaps. But given the volume of traffic at that hour, statistically the truck would have been far more likely not to strike another vehicle, or for another driver to have enough time to avoid a collision. Mrs. Peller apparently had no time to react."

Walters frowned at the papers. "Meaning what?"

The mathematician stated precisely, "It may not have been an accident."

Stunned, Walters leaned forward and folded his arms on the desk. "But that makes no sense. If you want to kill someone..." Kaneko waited patiently for him to continue. He felt unnervingly like a student being challenged to work out an answer. "It's just too risky, Professor. Why would anyone commit a murder that way?"

With a shrug, the mathematician said, "I don't know. But you asked my opinion, and in my opinion the circumstances suggest it wasn't merely a careless accident. If it was not an intentional act, the driver of the truck was at least running away from something."

This, Walters thought, changed everything. Due to the statute of limitations, the police would no longer investigate the case as an accident. He had hoped to be able to show that the vehicle had been stolen, which would allow the investigation to be reopened. He still considered it worth pursuing. But if the accident hadn't been an accident? There definitely was no statute of limitations on murder.

He would need more than Kaneko's hunch before he could talk to Peller, but it was a lead worth following.

Kaneko interrupted his thoughts. "There is one other thing."

The writer leaned back. "What's that?"

"Something is missing from the files."

"Missing?"

Kaneko nodded. "There is no mention in the official reports of any interviews with employees of Andy Abramson Ford in Hunt Valley."

That evening, Peller sat down to dinner with his family and waited in silence through prayers. He found it interesting that Jason had apparently preserved this tradition. When Sandra was alive, they had started each meal with silent prayers—her way of living her beliefs without imposing them on anyone—and although she had taught Jason a few children's prayers, as he grew it became his choice whether to say them before meals.

After the serving dishes had been passed and plates were full, Belinda asked, "Whatever happened to the dog?"

"The dog?"

"The one you ran into the day you met Sandra."

Peller glanced at Jason. His son was unconcernedly taking a bite of salad. "Well. The dog. He lived, but we never found his owner. I asked around the department, and Mom put the word out, but nobody was interested in adopting a Dalmatian. Mom visited him every day while he was recovering, and eventually named him. She called him Talisman." He smiled, remembering how she had talked to the animal, petting it as if it had been hers forever.

"There were rescue outfits that would have taken him in, but she couldn't bear to see him go. She kept pestering me to find him a home nearby so she could visit him. Finally, one of my friends on the force took pity on me said he'd keep Talisman, just until Mom had a place for him. Later, he gave Talisman back to us as a wedding present."

Jason looked up. "I remember Zorro." Catching Belinda's raised eyebrows, he added, "Our black Labrador. But I don't remember a Dalmatian."

"He died about a month before your second birthday. We found out he had a tumor, and it was too late to save him. We had to put him down. Mom was heartbroken." Peller remembered that, too, the way the days stretched into weeks and months while Sandra mourned, and how even years later a sad look would sometimes suddenly fill her eyes and she'd tell him how much she missed Talisman.

"How big was Talisman?" Susie asked.

Peller laughed and tousled her hair. "As tall and as heavy as you, young lady, but a lot longer, and he had as much energy as you and your brother combined."

Susie's eyes widened with delight.

"Can we get a Tall Man dog?" Andrew asked excitedly.

Jason feigned horror. "It would pull you around like a motorboat towing a skier!"

"That would be fun!" Andrew told him.

Belinda narrowed her eyes at Peller. "Now look what you've done, Grandpa."

"That's my job," Peller said, grinning. "Fortunately, I don't have to deal with the consequences."

⤳

Later, after the kids were asleep and Peller had retired for the night, Jason and Belinda turned out the lights and settled in bed. Belinda rested her head on Jason's shoulder. "What do you remember about your mother?" she asked him.

He wrapped his arms around her but lay silent in the darkness, his chest rising and falling slowly with each breath. She waited, wondering how he would answer, or even if he would answer.

Finally he said, "So much it sometimes hurts."

"I dreamed about her last night."

"I'm not surprised. She's been the main topic since dad arrived." He didn't quite sound bitter, but she sensed he was still trying to hide from the subject.

Belinda propped herself up on her elbow and looked at him in the darkness. "It wasn't like that, though. It was like…"

He waited, silent.

"It was more like she visited me. It's hard to explain."

"What, the two of you had tea and crumpets?" He nudged her to show he was kidding.

"Not quite. We talked. No, she talked, I listened."

Another silence, then he prompted, "And?"

"She told me not to be afraid. She told me your father wasn't alone, that God had given him helpers. I thought that was a strange thing to say, but I couldn't tell her so. I couldn't speak at all. Then she kissed my cheek and told me that He had given us all helpers. 'Even you,' she said. I didn't understand but still couldn't speak."

Jason said nothing, and Belinda settled her head on his shoulder again. He held her in silence for a time, their breathing the only sound in the room. Eventually, he answered her original question: "Strange, but that's one of the things I remember best about her. She was always helping people. I think that's why everyone thought so highly of her."

"Yes," Belinda said. "It's odd, but I always thought of her as a second mother. Usually that's the kind of thing a woman doesn't want her mother-in-law to be. But Sandra made it feel—oh, natural I guess is the word."

"She was kind to everyone. Unassuming, but always there when you needed her to be. Although she didn't mince words when it was time to be direct. She gave me a good talking-to once, when I was in high school."

Belinda felt him trying not to laugh. "Really? What did you do?"

Jason turned to face her. "Maybe I shouldn't tell you this."

"Oh, it involves a girl!"

"Yeah," he answered sheepishly. "Her name was Amanda. She was the most...well, the most beautiful girl I'd seen up to that point."

"Nice recovery. So she had a great body." She poked him in the ribs. "Go on."

"I'm not sure Dad noticed anything, but Mom sure did. I must've been talking nonstop about her, or not paying enough attention to my schoolwork or chores or something. Anyway, she sat me down one day after school for a talk."

"Must have been awkward."

"I'll say. But it sank in."

"What did she say?"

Jason pulled Belinda close and rested his forehead against hers. "After I told her how gorgeous Amanda was, she said, and I quote, 'Physical attraction is normal, but even the vegetables in the garden have a sex life. You're not a vegetable, so don't act like one. Never mind what Amanda *looks* like. What *is* she like?'"

"Then what did you say?"

"I couldn't say anything. I had no idea what Amanda was like."

"Did you ever find out?"

He rolled onto his back.

Belinda tugged his ear. "Nothing under the makeup and short skirts, was she? Bit of a letdown, huh?"

"It was, but that just proved how smart Mom was." He rolled toward her and took her in his arms again. "And next time, I knew what I was really looking for."

"So I guess we're both in her debt," Belinda said, and kissed him. But after she drew back, he seemed unusually still, and she sensed something unsaid was bothering him. "What?"

"There was something else, too. Just before we moved out here, I stopped by my parents' house to collect some of my old things. I'd been up in my room, packing, when the doorbell rang. I didn't think anything of it. One of Mom's friends, I thought, or maybe Aunt Karen. Then I heard a man's voice that I didn't recognize. I couldn't make out any words, but from the sound of the conversation it must have been someone Mom knew. I couldn't think of who it might be. Somebody I didn't know, anyway. Then it got quiet, and I assumed he must have left. I finished getting my stuff together and headed back downstairs. But as I was coming around the landing I saw Mom standing in the living room with someone. At first I thought it was Dad, but this guy had light hair, not dark like Dad's. And he was standing very close to her, holding her hands."

Jason fell silent, but his rapid breath betrayed the alarm of that moment and its clutch on him even after so many years. "Holding her hands? Your *mom's*? What did you do then?"

"I slipped back upstairs. Ten minutes later, when I got up the courage to come down again, he was gone and Mom was sitting at the dining room table, looking shaken. I asked her what was wrong, but she said she was fine."

"What did you think?"

"I hate to admit what my first thought was."

"Well," Belinda interrupted, "it would be a logical thing to occur to you."

"I didn't want to believe it, of course. Mom couldn't be like that. And then seeing her so upset, well, I just didn't know."

"Did you tell your father?"

Jason shook his head. "How could I? If I was wrong, he'd be mad at me for accusing her, and if I was right, it would have destroyed him. Mom was his whole world."

"Don't doubt her," Belinda said soothingly. "You know her. You said it yourself. She was always helping people. And as far as we know, nothing bad came of it. Whoever this guy was, he wasn't important enough to her to replace your dad. Maybe he was an old friend from school or work who needed help, or brought some bad news about someone they both knew."

"I suppose you're right," Jason said, weariness filling his voice. "Then again, we moved out here a couple of weeks later. We weren't around to see. So how can we know?"

Corina Montufar, scrubbed and nightgowned, laid her hairbrush down and paused to regard the photo on her dresser. Tonight it seemed to her that the light-faded picture was a metaphor for time. Frozen in an ornate gold metal frame chosen by her mother, a fourteen-year-old Corina, her parents, and Eduardo and Ella smiled out at an unforgiving world. How, and when, had life become so complicated? It never used to be that way, or at least not as she remembered it.

A close-knit clan, the family had migrated to the U.S. when her father, an engineer, landed a job with a company willing to sponsor him for permanent resident status. The move had been an upheaval—it meant leaving behind grandparents and cousins and friends—but had been filled with excitement, too. Corina quickly took to her new surroundings, made friends, and excelled in school. Eduardo married. Corina graduated from high school. Her interest in law enforcement led her to apply to the Howard County Police Department, where she was promptly accepted as a recruit. Ella, vivacious and popular, had a string of boyfriends. Everything had seemed to work out. Sure, there had been some rough spots—her academy experience among them—but her parents and Eduardo had always been there to keep her focused and on track.

Now her mother was gone and her father was slipping away in the haze of Alzheimer's. Only Eduardo was left, and since the accident he hadn't been entirely right. She wondered if he was nudging her towards Dumas because he, too, feared she might soon be left alone. Yet she didn't trust her feelings enough to let Dumas that close, to allow herself to become that dependent upon him. Maybe, she thought, in time, but not so soon.

She needed someone she could trust implicitly.

Opening the top drawer, she took out her rosary, then sat on the edge of the bed and ran it through her fingers. Its crystal beads caught the glow of the ceiling light and filled with a soft fire.

Grandma Alessandra had given the rosary to her for her First Holy Communion. She could still see the carefully-wrapped package in her grandmother's hands; she remembered the crystal sparkles in the warm spring sunlight. It was the most beautiful rosary she had ever seen.

"Remember always," Grandma said, "Our Lady will lead you to Jesus. Even when the road is lost, or seems impossible. Ask her to help you, and she always will. She will never say no." And she swept

Corina into a hug that seemed as warm and loving as the Blessed Mother's.

Fleetingly the adult Corina wished she could be embraced again by her grandmother. Swept into the excitement of her new country, bewildered by the choices and distracted by all the enticements hurled her way, Montufar hadn't prayed the rosary very often after they came to the United States. Once she was on the force, she had ignored it completely.

Until recently. Over the past few weeks she had begun making a habit of bedtime prayers again. In part, she knew, it was a reaction to stress, a grasping for something familiar and solid in a world increasingly making little sense, a desire for something so simple it could shield her from chaos. Yet it was more, too: a sense that she had fallen asleep and needed to wake before it was too late. Dumas had said it one evening not long ago, sitting at Peller's table, when she had wondered aloud if God were listening: "He is. Usually we're the ones who aren't."

She knew now that she needed to listen. She hoped she would hear, and understand.

# Chapter 11

"Good morning. Do you know where you are?"

Morgan Parsons frowned at the nurse. She was an older woman, probably nearing retirement, he thought, with gray hair peeking out from under her cap and blue-framed glasses. She peered at him as though he were a specimen in a petri dish. "Why wouldn't I?"

Her lips turned up in a smile. Her eyes did not. "That's not an answer."

The head of the bed had been raised about halfway. He slowly tugged the sheets up higher and adjusted the pillow, making her wait. It didn't seem to perturb her in the least. "I'm in the hospital. Duh. When can I get out?"

"That depends on the doctor." She came to his side, checked his IV connections, and put a blood pressure cuff on him. "You're banged up pretty good, but nothing's broken other than your nose. No internal injuries. You'll probably be out by tomorrow." The cuff inflated and squeezed his arm uncomfortably.

"I'd rather go now."

"I daresay."

"Can't I release myself?"

The nurse looked at him over the top of her glasses. "You can sign a waiver and walk out whenever you want. But it would be a stupid thing to do."

"Get it for me."

She ran a thermometer over his forehead and looked at the reading. "Don't you want to talk to the doctor first?"

"No. I want to get the hell out of here."

"I see. Give me an hour, then." She started packing up her equipment.

"How hard can it be to get a piece of paper?"

"You're not the only patient in the hospital. Or the worst off." She headed for the door. "Besides," she said, looking over her shoulder, "you have visitors."

No sooner had she left than a pair of men entered the room, one white and wearing a tie, the other black and in a police uniform. "Oh no," Parsons muttered.

"Good morning, Morgan," the white man said, thrusting out his hand. "I'm Detective Sergeant Eric Dumas, and this is my good friend Officer Kevin Graham. Officer Graham investigated your accident last night."

Parsons didn't accept the proffered hand. He knew he should have, to look friendly and cooperative, but he was shaking too much. They could probably see how scared he was. No need to let this detective feel it, too.

Dumas dropped his hand. "Oddly, I was at your apartment yesterday morning, but you weren't there. I guess you were busy."

Graham pulled a couple of chairs over and the two of them sat. "Busy at a farm out in the west end of the county. Strangest thing I've ever seen, mon. How'd you get way out there and get into an accident without a car?"

Parsons shrugged. He needed a story, and he needed it quick, but he was too scared to think. He was too scared to even talk.

"Look, Morgan," Dumas told him. "You're in trouble. I can see you know you're in trouble. The doctor tells me you were beat up, not enough to do any permanent damage, but it must've hurt and you sure are scared. You're a big guy. I can't imagine what could scare you that much. Why don't you tell us what happened?"

"It..." He closed his eyes and tried to get his nerves under control. He couldn't. "It don't matter," he said. "I'm fine."

Graham shook his head. "You're not fine, mon. You're going to jail. We got you for the robbery at Giulio's. A witness ID'd you. And we got you for auto theft. She also ID'd the truck, which you stole and dumped in that lake. And we found the body of the man you shot. You're in big trouble."

The world falling apart around him, Parsons wondered why he'd been so stupid. He should have stuck to stealing cars. He was good at that. It was the only thing he was good at. The jewelry store had been a spur-of-the-moment job, a temptation he should have resisted. But it had seemed so perfect. All he'd had to do was watch and wait. Someone was bound to come out with some nice stuff, and then all he had to do was take it from them. Why had that fool tried to stop him? As soon as that had happened, he was done for. He couldn't take the truck to the farm after that, and no matter what he did, the cops would eventually have found him.

"Morgan," Dumas said, leaning close and lowering his voice. "The only way out is to help us. We can put two and two together. That robbery wasn't your style. You didn't steal that truck for a joy-ride, and you didn't steal it as a get-away car. You were going to sell it, weren't you?"

Parsons wanted to say no. All he could do was shrug.

"Auto theft is big business. You're just the supplier. Who's your customer? Help us on that, and we may be able to get you a reduced sentence."

All he could see was that lunatic's smile. All he could hear was Orion's promise to kill him and "make it fun."

"Auto theft and manslaughter," Graham said ominously. "I'll bet we can pin more than one stolen vehicle on you. You could spend the rest of your life in prison."

"I was beat up," Parsons whispered. He wanted it to be an explanation, a statement of innocence. He knew as soon as he'd said it that it was neither.

"By someone hired by your customer," Dumas replied. "Because you did something foolish. But we can protect you if you help us."

He tried again. "I mean I was beat up and robbed and dumped in that barn." He looked from Dumas to Graham and back again. They seemed to be waiting for more. "It had nothing to do with any-thing else."

"Who beat you up?"

"I don't know. Some guy I never saw before."

"Did he tell you his name?"

Parsons shook his head. "He just beat me up."

Dumas nodded. Maybe, Parsons thought, this would work. He needed *something* to work out right.

"In the barn." Dumas made it a statement, as though relating a fact.

"Yeah."

"Is that where you met him?"

"Well..."

"How did you get there, then?"

"He took me there."

"From where?"

Realizing his mistake, Parsons pressed himself back into the pillow and closed his eyes.

"Come on," Dumas prompted. "We can't help you if you don't cooperate."

He figured it out. A story. A good story, he hoped. "I had a flat tire. He stopped, like he was going to help, then he knocked me senseless and took me to that barn."

Graham laughed. "Come on, Morgan, we know that's a lie! Your car is still in the parking lot at your apartment complex!"

Feeling like he was going to throw up, Parsons forced himself to sit. "He came to my apartment, all right?" he snapped. He glared at Graham, hoping he looked defiant, but he knew it wouldn't work with these two. "He beat me up, pulled me into the rain, threw me into his car, and drove me to that barn. Then he beat me up some more and left me. That's all I know!"

"Oh," Dumas said as though suddenly understanding. "So it wasn't really a robbery?"

"Well..." Parsons blinked at him. Why did everything seem to go from bad to worse? "Well, yeah, it was."

Dumas' eyebrows lifted in surprise. "But Morgan, robbers don't drag their victims halfway across the county to rob them."

Parsons couldn't think of a reply, so he just shrugged again.

"Okay, you're scared to talk. Tell you what. Let me make a guess and you just nod if I'm right. After you botched the robbery at the jewelry store, your customer got mad. They knew we'd find you and didn't want you leading us to them. They sent one of their thugs to put the fear of God into you. He gave you a sample of his wares, then told you he'd kill you if you talked to us. Am I warm?"

It was as though Dumas had watched everything happen. How could he know so much? Was it just a guess, or had there been a witness? Maybe the old couple at the farm had seen something?

Graham nodded sagely. "You're red hot, mon," he told Dumas. "Look at that look on his face." He leaned closer to Parsons. "So what's it gonna be? You want to go to jail forever, or do you help us so we can get you out of this mess?"

"You can't get me out of it," Parsons moaned. He hated sounding so weak, but he felt as though he was no longer in control of himself. Animal instinct possessed him. He was trapped, no place to run, his drive for self-preservation forcing him to flee into doom.

"Give me a name," Dumas said. "Just a name. I'll do the rest."

Parsons looked away. "I can't."

"Can't?" Graham asked, "Or won't?"

Maybe, he thought, they hadn't heard the name before. Was that possible? Probably not. But his only hope now was that they couldn't do anything with it even if he gave it to them.

"Just a name," Dumas insisted. "That's all we need."

"Orion," Parsons whispered.

"What?"

"Orion."

Dumas and Graham both sat back and exchanged a glance.

"Orion?" Graham asked. "Like the constellation?"

"I don't know. He just said it was his name. That's all he said."

"Okay," Dumas said. "What does he look like?"

"Big. Strong. Crazy."

"What else?"

"I don't know!" Parsons snapped. "After the first punch, I was in no shape to think!"

"Okay." Dumas rose and Graham followed suit, although looking reluctant to go. "We'll see what we can find on this Orion. You rest up and get better."

They started to leave, but at the door Graham paused and looked back. "Oh, and Morgan, you might want to think twice about discharging yourself. They'll know we were here. You'd be safer staying in bed." He winked. "Rest easy, mon. Catch you later."

Parsons watched them leave. His life was over. He could feel it. It might have been better if Orion had killed him. He thought that Dumas fellow was probably on the level and would try to protect him, but he didn't think it would be possible.

As for Graham, Parsons hated him.

Montufar placed a bowl of instant oatmeal and water in her microwave, punched the "start" button, and picked up the telephone. While the oven hummed, she dialed the number Bruce Waggoner, the salesman at Andy Abramson Ford, had given them. Not knowing whether the number was still good, she was relieved when it rang and a voice mail greeting played:

"You've reached the Palmer family," an austere female voice pronounced. "Leave a message and we'll either call back or ignore you, as appropriate."

Montufar couldn't help but laugh and barely managed to stop before the tone sounded. "Hello, this is Detective Sergeant Corina Montufar from the Howard County police. I'm calling about an F250 you purchased from Andy Abramson Ford about four years ago. I was wondering if we could..."

Before she could finish, a male voice came on the line, "Hello! This is Douglas Palmer. Did you find my truck?"

"Hello, Mr. Palmer," Montufar answered. Everything, she thought, had just changed. Stolen vehicle. No more statute of limitations. "We didn't exactly find it, but we have reason to believe it was involved in an accident about a month after you bought it."

"That figures," he said. "Not that it matters after all this time, I guess. Insurance covered the loss. But I did really like that truck, for all of about twelve days."

"So it was stolen, then?"

"Right out of my driveway. I thought you knew."

"The Baltimore County police would have investigated the theft," she told him. "We have a hit-and-run on the books with a vehicle that matches the description of yours, but until just recently we didn't have any idea where to look for it."

Palmer was silent for a moment, then he asked in a subdued voice, "Someone was killed?"

"Yes, I'm afraid there was a fatality. But don't blame yourself. If it hadn't been your truck, it probably would have been someone else's."

"I suppose so."

"If you don't mind, I'd like to have one of our detectives visit you and take a statement. It won't take long, I promise."

"Anything I can do to help," he said. "I'm getting ready for work now, but I'll be home by six this evening. Any time after that will be fine."

After thanking him and hanging up, Montufar poured herself a cup of coffee and sat down at her kitchen table with her breakfast. A few things fell into place. Stolen vehicles often ended up in saleable pieces, but they were increasingly used in the commission of crimes. The fact that the truck had been where it had no business being and had been driven so recklessly suggested crime rather than the alternative. From what she recalled of the reports, the investigators hadn't looked around the farm from which the truck had come. They had asked the owners, but they had denied any knowledge of its presence. Maybe it was time for another look, although it wasn't likely there would be anything to find after the passage of so much time.

She ate most of her meal while pondering their next move, then sent a brief text to Dumas to let him know what she'd learned. Then, with the brisk efficiency she was known for, she gathered her dishes into the sink, traded her slippers for heels, snatched up her purse and jacket, and hurried on her way to work.

⟿

At first, Penny Lowell was puzzled when early Wednesday morning Phil Walters told her they were going car shopping. Over a breakfast of toast, strawberry preserves, and coffee, he related to her Kaneko's observations.

"Too bad he won't open up about the Fibonacci case," she said, "but I called it right, didn't I? He knows more than the police do."

"He's definitely smart," Walters agreed. He took a sip of coffee. "And it does seem the police overlooked those license holder fragments."

"Doesn't give a person much faith in law enforcement." She said it gravely, but she couldn't help smiling. A woman with confidence in her own intelligence, she liked being right and she especially liked the occasional opportunity to help Walters in his work. He was just as bright as she, but in her view sometimes got too tangled up in details to see the big picture.

"To be fair, I didn't catch them, either. Look." He took the three relevant photos from his folder and shoved them towards her.

She studied them. It was like searching the jumbled pieces of a jigsaw puzzle, but she kept at it until she found the important fragments. Pointing them out, she said, "If I can get it, the cops should have been able to get it, too."

"You already knew what you were looking for."

In her opinion, that didn't matter, but she decided not to argue the point. "Either way, we're ahead of them."

Packing the photos back into the folder, Walters nodded. "I doubt the case can be solved, but for now I just need to give Lieutenant Peller a reason to hope."

"I'm sure he'll be grateful."

He gave her a peculiar look, as though he wasn't at all sure.

"It's worth a shot, at least," she added.

"Except that I'm starting to think I'm wasting my time. I should probably find a more likely project. This might never pay off."

She reached over and patted his hands. "I believe in you."

Taking her hands in his, he studied her face. "That's what keeps me going," he said. "Whatever you see in me, I hope it's real."

"Me, too." She winked at him. "I expect we'll find out soon enough."

⸺

Captain Morris didn't hesitate when Montufar and Dumas told her the news. "I'll reopen the case. But bear in mind that it's low priority for now. I don't want you two going nuts over it." She looked sharply at Dumas. "What did you learn from Parsons?"

"He didn't confess to anything, but he didn't deny it, either. I think we have enough on him for auto theft, plus armed robbery and manslaughter. He says he was beat up by a guy named Orion."

"Orion?" Morris searched her memory. It sounded familiar.

"It's from Greek mythology," Montufar supplied. "A prominent winter constellation, too--Orion the hunter. It's also probably an alias."

"You into astronomy?"

"She's into internet," Dumas said, grinning. Montufar gave him a long-suffering look.

There was something about that name, Morris thought, a strange case some time ago in Baltimore that had ended in an acquittal. She turned to her computer. Dumas and Montufar waited patiently, curiosity painted on their faces, while she searched.

After a good five minutes, Morris read from the screen. "Here it is. Orion Speros. He was tried on homicide and assault charges, but pleaded self-defense and was acquitted. The guy looks like he should be playing for the Ravens. Come look at this."

Rising, Montufar and Dumas went around the desk to look. Speros stood six foot nine, weighed over two hundred eighty pounds, and sported a mountain-man beard. In the mug shot, his eyes appeared to be sparkling, although his mouth was set in a firm line.

Morris skimmed through the text. "The details are kind of confused, but apparently Speros thought he was owed some money for some 'demolition work' he'd done for one Keylon Wynne. Wynne was a local drug lord, so the phrase demolition work seems suggestive, but details of the alleged job were never uncovered. Speros killed

Wynne and left one of his bodyguards, a Roscoe Hammond, with a broken back that paralyzed him from the waist down. There was allegedly a third party involved, possibly another bodyguard, but he was never located."

After a bit more scrolling, Morris continued, "The incident took place on a sidewalk in front of some derelict row homes. Well this is weird. Speros himself called the police. When they got there, they found Wynne dead on the ground, his skull bashed in. Hammond was next to him unconscious, and Speros was sitting in a chair at a table he'd hauled out from one of the row homes, drinking wine straight from a bottle. He told them the men on the ground had attacked him, and he wanted Hammond arrested."

"That must have taken some nerve," Dumas commented.

Morris nodded. "Hammond later described a different encounter. He said Speros had gone berserk when Wynne refused to pay. According to him, Speros never did any work for Wynne."

"Why the acquittal?" Montufar asked. "It's presumably clear that Speros did the damage."

"Guns were fired, but not by Speros. He actually took a few bullets, one in his left arm and two in his right leg. He got off on reasonable doubt. The jury found him more believable than Hammond, who apparently was a first-class jerk, insulting the judge, all the lawyers, and the jury itself."

Dumas returned to his chair, while Montufar continued to look through the information on the screen. "What kind of weapon did he use?"

"His bare hands," Morris replied, "assisted by a nearby brick wall and the sidewalk."

"Christ," Dumas said. "No wonder Parsons is terrified of him. Bullets won't stop him."

Finished reading, Montufar sat down. "They will if they hit him in the right place. That jury must have been deluded. He obviously started it."

Morris agreed with her assessment, but there wasn't any point in second-guessing the outcome. What was done was done.

"Speros has been off the radar since then?" Dumas asked.

"Seems so. Either he's been a good boy, or he's very careful."

Dumas shook his head. "He's somebody's enforcer now, and in our jurisdiction. That's not a happy feeling."

A sickly look crossed Montufar's face, but she didn't say anything. At first, Morris thought she was reacting to Dumas' comment, but as she watched, she realized something else was behind that look. Wheels were turning, rapidly, and their destination wasn't a pretty place.

"What?" she asked.

Montufar shook her head.

"You've connected Speros to something, haven't you?"

"Not really."

Now Dumas was studying his colleague's face. "Corina, we know that look."

"It's just..." She waved her hands vaguely. "Speros sounds like a lunatic, like a guy who'd do any insane thing just for the fun of it."

Morris frowned and consulted her computer again. "Fair assessment, I guess."

"It also looks like he's involved with a stolen vehicle racket."

Dumas nodded. "Seems so, from what Parsons told us."

"A lunatic in a stolen vehicle," Montufar said quietly. "Does that remind you of anything?"

# Chapter 12

Food was running low in the cabin. He'd have to go to town.

The blue-eyed man avoided Centerville as much as possible. It wasn't that he didn't like the town or even its people. He'd had too little interaction with anyone there to either like or dislike them. But he didn't wish to be drawn into interactions, not with anyone. When he first arrived his priority had been safety, and safety meant keeping his distance. Dangers lay in questions. Better to be thought aloof, a loner, even peculiar, than to risk discovery.

As time passed, discovery no longer frightened him. Often he'd pondered what relief it might bring, but only if it meant death. That, he knew, was the problem. Maryland's death penalty had been suspended years earlier. He could only meet death through violence, and that he would not risk. He did not wish to take anyone with him, and he much preferred to be imprisoned here in the mountains than in a corrections facility. At least here he could be alone.

He shuffled about the small kitchen, taking stock of his supplies. He'd lost considerable weight over the past few years, a thought which sometimes made him consider starvation. If he simply stopped eating, in time he would die. But no. Starvation would be too unpleasant, and in any case his instinct for self-preservation would take over. He wouldn't be able to see it through. He lacked the self-control required for that means of escape.

Self-control. That had always been his problem. Not in all areas of life—in certain matters, he was the master. In others, he had failed miserably. Money. Women.

One woman in particular.

*Damn. Why must her specter always rise?*

If only he could have been with her, he might have truly lived. In separation from her, he had only died.

And his greatest anguish: that he himself had sent her away, never to return.

⟿

Bruce Waggoner spotted the couple looking over the red Mustang and walked briskly to their side. The glossy exterior drew customers to its side like an aphrodisiac. They clung to the car, admiring the interior and caressing the upholstery, but after a nod toward the price tag they shook their heads and departed, murmuring, for less expensive models. Still, Waggoner held out hope that he'd be the one to sell it, and he never missed a chance to talk up any customers who lingered over it.

A twinkle in his eye, he opened with a variant of the line he liked to use with women: "Now you look like a woman who's into sports cars."

The couple turned and smiled. Waggoner stuck out his hand, introducing himself. The woman shook first. "Penny Lowell," she told him with a warm smile. "And this is my gentleman friend, Phil Walters."

"Very pleased to meet you both," Waggoner replied. "You're obviously a couple with refined tastes."

Walters returned the salesman's smile, but it looked forced. "Actually, we're interested in trucks."

Waggoner's smile froze on his face. He could feel it freeze but found himself unable to change his expression.

"Possibly a stolen truck," Lowell added with a giggle.

"You're joking."

"Nope. We're looking into an accident that occurred about four years ago. It involved a dark blue truck that we think was sold here."

"But someone was here just last night. We gave them the information."

The couple glanced at each other, clearly caught off-guard.

"You are with the police, aren't you?" Waggoner persisted.

Walters shook his head slowly.

"The police were here last night?" Lowell asked. "Baltimore County police?"

"Howard County." Waggoner suddenly thought he may have said too much. "Who are you? Why do you want to know?"

Walters seemed to regain his composure. "I'm a writer. I'm investigating a case that the police have closed."

"It sure sounded like an open case last night. Why are you investigating it?"

"I told you, I'm a writer. I'm writing about it," Walters said testily. "I don't know why the police were here last night, but it's probably because I was asking questions to which they didn't have answers. Was the truck stolen from you?"

Waggoner wasn't sure what to say. The safest course, he decided, was to send them up the chain of command. He didn't get paid to deal with this kind of thing, so he wasn't about to risk getting fired over it.

"I think you should talk to the manager," he told the couple.

Half an hour later, Walters strode furiously across the lot, Lowell teetering after him in her high heels, and barely waited for her to get in before gunning the motor and pulling recklessly into the flow of traffic.

*I shouldn't let him drive*, Lowell thought, wincing as they avoided sideswiping a bus by the merest hairsbreadth. But a moment later, she found herself laughing.

"What's so damned funny?" he snapped.

"I love you Phil, you know I do. But sometimes you're just so clueless."

He shot her a glare.

"You didn't notice, did you? You were so busy arguing that you just didn't notice."

"Notice what?"

"The papers on the desk. The sales manager had pulled the files on the truck so he could give the cops the information they wanted. They were still there."

"You're kidding."

"While you were trying to argue him into giving you the information, I just read it off the papers. It's in my phone's notepad."

"You said your boss had texted you."

She smiled. "How about that?"

"Good lord, Penny." Walters burst out laughing. The car immediately veered toward a passing Silverado. She put a hand on the wheel to steady it while he added, "It's a good thing you're on my side!"

Making himself useful, Peller was in the kitchen frying up a pound of bacon for Belinda, who was busily chopping vegetables for dinner. The bacon sizzled and popped, and a spatter of hot grease stung his hand. The meat's savory aroma filled the air.

"Turn the heat down a tad," Belinda told him.

He did so. "It's been awhile since I did this. I used to fry bacon all the time for Sandra. Usually on Sunday mornings. We'd always have something special for breakfast on Sundays."

"We try to do that, too, although it doesn't always work out."

His cell phone, tucked in his left pants pocket, rang. "Things are more hectic these days, I guess." He retrieved the phone and checked the sender. Dumas. "What's up, Eric?"

"We have news," Dumas said, his voice less than clear over the network. "You might want to sit down."

"Can't. I'm at the stove, frying bacon."

"Then try not to set yourself on fire. We visited that Ford dealership. They were able to identify the truck and gave us the buyer's name and contact info."

Peller turned a slice of bacon, then set the fork down on a plate next to the stove. "And?"

"The truck was sold about a month prior to the accident and stolen twelve days later. Everything fits. We at least have an auto theft case now. Captain Morris authorized reopening the investigation."

Peller placed a hand on the counter and leaned on it. He wasn't sure whether he felt relief or anxiety.

Dumas' anxious voice asked, "You okay?"

"Yes, Eric. Thank you. It's still a long shot, but it's the best news I've had since..." He glanced over his shoulder at Belinda who, rinsing a huge mass of greens in the sink, apparently had her whole mind on her unruly subject.

"By the by," Dumas continued, "do you recognize the name Orion Speros?"

Peller started to say no, but then something registered, something about a trial that had gone wrong and a killer who had walked free. But nothing concrete materialized. "Sounds familiar. Why?"

"Speros came up in connection with another case involving a stolen truck. Looks like he's somebody's enforcer now."

Peller heard Dumas draw a breath. He flipped the bacon slices. "What's that have to do with us?"

"Maybe nothing. Probably nothing. But after Corina reviewed the information on Speros, she had a thought."

Peller waited, but Dumas seemed unwilling to continue. He didn't have to. It was easy to anticipate Montufar's thought. Something had connected for her, something that placed this Speros guy in the truck that had killed Sandra.

The identification, tentative as it was, struck him like a blow to the stomach. He turned off the fire, walked to the dining room table, and sank into a chair. Belinda looked up from her work but said nothing. "Why would she think that?"

"Let's just say Speros is a larger-than-life character. A risk taker, almost to the point of insanity. Corina put it this way: a lunatic in a stolen vehicle. She thinks it fits too neatly to be coincidence. But then again, it's just a hunch."

A wave of anger overwhelmed Peller. In his mind's eye he saw himself throw his phone through the window, heard the glass shatter, watched the sunlight glint from the smooth faces of a swarm of keen shards.

Belinda lifted the leaves from the sink with a final shake, carried them to the worktable, and turned to face him. He forced a few slow breaths until some measure of calm returned. Speros might not be the right man, probably wasn't the right man. He needed to keep his emotions in check until they were sure.

*But Corina suggested it. I trust her hunches.*

"You'll be paying Speros a visit, I assume?"

"It's on my list," Dumas assured him. "He's likely to be a tough customer, though: confident, audacious, and undoubtedly as dangerous as Beelzebub."

Anger-crazed, Peller's mind swiftly constructed conclusions: Speros charged, Speros convicted, Speros imprisoned. Or Speros confronted, Speros attempting escape, Speros dead.

Justice for Sandra. Justice for all those who had known and loved her. Justice for himself and Jason.

"Rick?" Dumas sounded concerned.

Belinda's eyes remained on him, but a calmness clothed her. Her hands lay relaxed on the block table, reaching neither for the pile of greens awaiting her attention nor the waiting knife.

*Do I want justice, or revenge?* He pushed the question aside. Someday he would have to confront his motivations, but not today. Possibly he would never need confront it: Speros might prove a dead end. Peller might face the dissolution of hope.

Again.

Dumas was still waiting silently on the other end of the line, but the tension had gone from the room. "Uh, yeah, Eric," Peller said.

Relieved, Dumas said, "I'll give you an update when I can."

"Thanks again, Eric. Both of you."

"Our pleasure, boss."

Peller pocketed his phone and took a deep breath. It seemed to him as though he stood in a room containing everything and nothing, as though the universe itself had been fitted carelessly into a point devoid of space.

"Everything okay?" Belinda asked.

"Yes. No. I'm not sure."

"Should I finish the bacon?"

Dinner. That was it. They were making dinner. "No, I'll finish it."

Belinda started in on her pile of spinach. Peller returned to the stove and relit the burner. The simple task focused him. Grease sizzled once more, and before long he had a pile of fried bacon draining on a plate layered with paper towels. "What's next?" he asked.

"You can crumble it for me." She finished her chopping and placed the vegetables in a stock pot, then turned to watch him. "Anything you want to talk about?"

Peller shook his head.

"Maybe later?"

"Maybe." In fact, later was a certainty. He couldn't keep this from her long, nor from Jason.

⤳

With such an unusual name, Orion Speros wasn't difficult to find. He owned a house on a rural road off of state route 94 southwest of Lisbon, in the northwestern part of Howard County. Dumas arranged for a pair of male officers—strapping young men—to accompany him. If Speros turned out to be homicidal, he wanted solid backup. "You just need someone who can shoot straight," Montufar had told him in a bland voice, but they both knew how easy it was for things to go south.

Initially Montufar had wanted to accompany him, but he didn't want her anywhere near Speros. Instead, he had reminded her that she had planned to check out the farm at the accident scene, and she had conceded the point.

Now Dumas stood before a fair-sized ranch-style house of the sort constructed in the late 1950's or early 1960's, painted tan with dark brown shutters. A detached garage sat to the right, at the end of a long driveway that ran past the house. A dark gray Toyota Tundra pickup was parked halfway up the drive. The vehicle looked reasonably new, or at least well cared for.

He rang the bell and looked around the yard while he waited for an answer. There was little landscaping, but the lawn was neatly mowed and several large trees flanked the house on either side. It was a warm, partly cloudy day. Birds chattered in the trees.

The door opened to reveal Orion Speros: huge, bearded, smiling warmly. He was a few years older than in the photos Dumas had seen, but his face had scarcely changed, and in real life he appeared exactly as the detective expected.

"This is a pleasant surprise," he said. "I don't often play host to Howard County's finest."

"Orion Speros?" Dumas asked, although there was no need.

"At your service."

"I'm Detective Sergeant Eric Dumas. I was wondering if I could have a word with you."

"My pleasure, Eric. Please, come on in." Speros held the door open as though inviting them in to a party.

The room they entered surprised Dumas. Filled with neo-classical furniture and artwork inspired by ancient Greece, it felt like a curious sort of pagan temple. Speros must have spent a fortune on this stuff, Dumas thought as they crossed an elaborately tiled floor. Just as notably, there were no electronics in evidence: no television, no DVD player, no video games.

"Sit anywhere," Speros told them, and settled himself in an enormous chair big enough for two average-sized people. "What's the topic of discussion?"

Dumas sat on a sofa opposite him, while the officers remained standing and alert. "What can you tell me about a fellow named Morgan Parsons?"

"Morgan Parsons. Can't say I know anyone by that name."

"That's odd, because he knows you."

Speros made a "Who, me?" gesture.

"Okay, I'm exaggerating. He only knows your first name, and that you gave him a good talking-to the other day."

"Really? That's interesting. What did I say?"

Dumas leaned back and studied the ceiling. A border wrapped around the top of the walls looked like a Greek temple frieze. "He's a bit vague on that point, but given his injuries that's not too surprising."

"Oh, did he get hurt?"

"You know he did."

Speros shook his head. "I don't see how I could know any such thing, Eric. This fellow, what did you say his name was?"

"Morgan Parsons."

"Yes. He must have me confused with someone else."

Dumas directed a bland look at Speros. "Orion, how could anyone possibly confuse you with someone else?"

Speros doubled over, laughing so hard and so long that Dumas wanted to clap his hands over his ears to shut out the noise. When the big man finally caught his breath, he said, "Oh, Eric, that's the best line I've heard from anyone other than myself in a long time!"

"Glad you enjoyed it," Dumas replied dryly. "But let's stop with the games. You grabbed Parsons from his apartment, took him halfway across the county to a barn, and beat him up. Presumably it was a warning. Against what?"

Still amused, Speros shook his head. "If I actually had done all that, do you think I'd admit it, much less tell you why I'd done it?"

"Not really, but it doesn't much matter. We already have Parsons on auto theft, armed robbery, and manslaughter. You're looking at an aggravated assault charge."

"Then arrest me." Speros grinned. "I've beaten worse charges than that."

"Yeah, I know all about that."

"I can see." He nodded to the officers. "Not taking any chances, are you?"

"None."

"Don't worry. I admit to being a thrill-seeker, but I'm not so stupid as to assault a police officer. You guys don't know how to take a joke."

Dumas studied Speros for a few minutes in silence. He had to give him credit for coolness and intelligence, but there was more to him than that. He was playing chicken with Dumas. Dumas wasn't about to step out of the way. It was time to up the stakes.

"Okay, Orion, let's talk about something else for a minute."

"Shoot. Metaphorically, that is."

"Does the name Peller ring a bell?"

The humor left the big man's eyes. "Should it?"

"Four years ago, a stolen dark blue F250 charged off a farm lane and smashed into a car. The driver, Sandra Peller, was killed. The truck left the scene. Sound familiar now?"

Frowning at the floor tiles, Speros shook his head. "Sounds like a nasty business. Maybe I heard about it on the news. But no, I don't know anything about that."

"You're lying about Morgan Parsons. Why not lie about Sandra Peller? It's certainly your style."

Speros' hands tightened on the arms of his chair, his expression suddenly violent. Dumas glanced quickly at the officers, who had taken note of the change in mood and had tensed, hands on their holstered guns, ready to react as needed. "My *style*? What do you know about my *style*, Eric?"

"You enjoy hurting people. That much is obvious. You smashed a guy's brains out on a brick wall, broke another man's back, and gave Morgan Parsons enough terror to last him a lifetime. Crashing a truck into an innocent woman's car, watching her die up close and personal—does that excite you?"

Speros locked eyes with Dumas. In a moment Dumas understood Parsons' terror. "Are you going to arrest me, Eric?"

"Eventually."

"Not now?"

Dumas shook his head.

"Then get the hell out of my house."

The detective didn't move. Speros' eyes drilled into him. What, Dumas wondered, had triggered this rage?

He stood. "All right, Orion, we'll go. But I suggest you think about cooperating with us. We know you're working for someone who deals in stolen vehicles. They're the ones we really want." He took his time walking to the door, aware of Speros' hot gaze following him the whole way. The officers followed, but kept an eye on their host.

Before he closed the door, Dumas turned. Speros was still in his chair, gripping the arms as though to crush them. "God help you if you are the one who killed Sandra Peller. She was a cop's wife. Killing her was worse than killing one of us. A lot worse."

He closed the door, and the five of them walked slowly back to their vehicles. Just before he closed his car door, Dumas thought he heard the roar of a grizzly.

Set amidst rolling hills, its house and barns and other structures set well back from the road, its fields woods-edged, the Folsom farm had a tranquil air, as though upon crossing into its space one entered a different world—an older, calmer world where life moved at a gentle pace and nothing ever went wrong. Montufar, having driven halfway up the lane from the main road, got out of her car and breathed in the serenity. She had trouble believing that such a place could have played a role in a tragedy.

She'd stopped at the crest of a small hill. Looking back towards the road, she could see a good third of a mile in either direction, although trees dotting the roadside hid the road at a few points. An old stone building about the size of a large shed stood near the end of the lane. She wondered when it had been built and what purpose it had served.

What would the driver of the F250 have seen cresting this hill and starting down to the road? Traffic had been light that day, according to the reports. Montufar noted a few cars moving in each direction. If she were in a hurry to leave the farm, she could race down the hill, hit the brakes just before the road, and insert her car into the flow of traffic without losing more than a few seconds. Even if she were fleeing in blind terror, she thought it unlikely she would hit someone square in the side. At the very least, she'd certainly have to slow to make the left turn.

Returning to her car, Montufar puzzled over that. It made no sense. Judging from the lay of the land, the truck had intentionally hit Sandra's car. Would even Orion Speros do such a thing? Ram a pickup truck into a random car passing by? It occurred to her that maybe the driver had been suicidal, that they'd hoped to die in the accident. But that seemed an incredibly stupid thing to try in a truck. One of the golf ball-sized cars so popular these days, maybe, but not a truck.

She drove further up the lane, passing recently sown fields, until she arrived at a huge walnut tree that seemed to mark the boundary between the lane and the dooryard. The other buildings lay farther back along the lane. She parked beneath the tree and got out for another look around. It looked like any other farm. The lane stretched into the distance beyond the house and over another rise. She could see no reason why a stranger would come up here, unless the reason lay farther back. But really, what could be so interesting back there?

Montufar went to the door and knocked. A moment later, a young woman opened it and looked her over. She was short, barely five and a half feet tall, with long brown hair pulled back in a pony-tail. She was wearing a lace-collared white blouse and dark jeans. Her expression was wary as she asked, "Yes?"

Montufar smiled in what she hoped was a nonthreatening manner. "I'm sorry for the intrusion. I'm Detective Sergeant Corina Montufar, Howard County police." Montufar held up her shield. "I know it's been rather a long time, but I need to ask a few questions about the accident that occurred out on the road four years ago."

"That's ancient history by now," the woman said. "What's left to know?"

"Would it be possible to come in?" Montufar persisted.

The other considered it for a moment, then opened the door wide. "I guess. But I'm afraid I can't be much help. I wasn't living here then. I just know about it."

"Ah, I see," Montufar said. "I was wondering. I didn't recall anyone of your age being mentioned in the reports."

The woman led Montufar through an austere kitchen into an equally austere living room where a few ladder-back chairs and a small colonial sofa had been arranged around the periphery. Framed family photos hung alongside a cheap reproduction of a painting of

Jesus. To her practiced detective's eye, the Savior appeared to be approximately forty-seven years of age.

They sat in two of the chairs.

"I'm Arne and Lucy's granddaughter, Hannah Worth. I was just a teenager at the time, but of course I heard about the accident from them. From what they said, it was quite awful, and they talked about it for months afterward."

"Are your grandparents here today?"

Worth shook her head. "Grandpa died about a year ago, and Grandma is in a nursing home. She's ninety-three now and her mind comes and goes."

So much for that, Montufar thought, but she held out hope that somehow the grandparents' handed-down recollections hid some useful fragments of information. "Do you remember them talking about the truck that was involved?"

"Yes, they talked a lot about that. It was a real mystery to them. It had been here on the farm just before the accident, right?"

Montufar nodded.

"They couldn't understand why. They hadn't known it was here. My dad thought that the driver probably got lost and pulled into the lane to turn around."

"Could be," Montufar said. "But he was in a terrible hurry to get back onto the road, or at least it looks that way."

Worth glanced towards the window as though trying to catch a glimpse of that long-ago day. "Yes. At the time, I remember thinking whoever it was had to have been up to something. But what? I took a look around the barns and garages, but didn't see anything wrong. I don't think he even got as far up the lane as the house."

"Would anyone have known if the truck had driven by the house?"

"That's hard to say. My grandparents might not have noticed. They were both hard of hearing. But they weren't the only ones here that day."

"Who else was here?"

"My Uncle Jimmy and Aunt Christine, and my cousins Jean and Abby and Randall. But none of them ever said they noticed the truck up this way. Randall was the only one who actually saw it."

Montufar sat forward. The reports hadn't mentioned any witnesses from the farm. "What did Randall see?"

"Not much. He'd gone out to water the garden that morning. On the way, he had to walk up a hill just to the west. That's where he was when the accident happened. He heard the noise, but by the time he looked it was all over. He just saw the truck leaving the scene like a bat out of you-know-where."

"Could he see the driver?"

"Not in any detail. Just a big man with a beard."

"A big man with a beard," Montufar repeated.

Worth nodded. "Lots of those around here, though."

Montufar had a particular one in mind. "I need to talk to Randall," she said. "Do you have his phone number?"

"It might take me a couple of minutes to round it up," Worth said, getting up and heading for the kitchen. "Would you like some coffee?"

# Chapter 13

Behind his house, a swimming pool slumbered under its winter cover, waiting for summer. Behind the pool sat a shed, and behind the shed a woodpile, and well back of the woodpile a downed tree. The tree had died a year ago. Rain water had washed down into cracks and crevices, rotting out the interior about five feet above ground level until, during a fierce autumn storm, the weakened trunk had splintered under the canopy's weight and the tree had crashed to the ground. Over the months since, he had cut parts of it up for firewood, using chainsaw or axe as suited his mood.

Today he attacked it with his axe.

He wielded the axe to vent the rage burning white hot in his head.

He had held his fury in check through an entire afternoon and evening and a mostly sleepless night, but in the red of Thursday's dawn, he could no longer contain it. The tree became his victim, a surrogate for the people he wanted to kill.

He wanted to kill that cop, that Eric Dumas.

He wanted to kill Morgan Parsons.

He *really* wanted to kill Jeff Levinson.

Each blow of the axe dispatched one of them. It murdered them over and over and over again. Wood chips flew, becoming to his eyes splatters of blood signaling the death of his victims, time after time. Dumas, who had taunted him. *Whack!* Parsons, who had betrayed him. *Whack!* Levinson, who had lied to him. *Whack!*

Especially Levinson. A cop's wife! Was he insane?

With all his might, Orion Speros slammed the axe down on the foot-thick trunk, imagining it to be Levinson's chest, and drove the blade deep into the heartwood.

"I could station an officer outside Parsons' room," Captain Morris said. "But if Speros wants him, I don't think we can protect him. Dropping his name probably wasn't the smartest thing to do."

Dumas looked around the captain's office, a place almost as familiar to him as his own apartment. Located in the corner of the building, it featured windows on two sides. The available wall space was covered by bookcases packed with professional tomes. She kept a photo of her husband, physician Daniel Morris, and their three children on her desk along with her computer and a notepad, but nothing else. A sense of order and control always pervaded this office.

"Speros needed some prompting," he told her. "He may be a lunatic, but he's the master of himself. He isn't about to do anything stupid. I think he'll wait until Parsons is out of the hospital. That's why I plan to arrest the poor fellow as soon as he's discharged, before he gets out the door. We won't give Speros the chance to get to him."

Montufar, who was seated next to Dumas, tapped the arm of her chair as though considering options. "From what you described, it sounds like he nearly lost control."

"That's right. I don't get that part," Dumas admitted.

"Obviously," Morris said, "he knows about Sandra. Either he was the one who killed her, or he was somehow involved with whoever did."

"Agreed, but why would he nearly explode when I mentioned it? He beat up Parsons, too, but being accused of it didn't rattle him in the least."

"You accused him of enjoying it," Montufar pointed out.

"So what? He does enjoy it, I'm pretty sure. Why should being called out on it make him mad?"

Montufar sprang to her feet and went to the window. Looking out on the nearby trees, she said, "Maybe he didn't enjoy it. Maybe something about it bothered him."

"Not Orion," Dumas said flatly.

"Maybe it was an accident. Maybe it wasn't what was supposed to happen."

Morris leaned back and studied the ceiling. "Speculation, Corina."

Montufar glanced back at her, then resumed looking out the window.

"I want to nail whoever killed Sandra as badly as you do," Morris said. "But we need to be certain. We can't be a lynch mob, especially not on this."

"I'm aware of that, Captain. And we might have the evidence we need." Montufar turned and leaned against the windowsill, arms crossed. "I've got a call in to a Randall Sommers, who was present on the farm the day of the accident and who saw the truck leaving the scene. According to Hannah Worth, he says the driver was a big man with a beard. He might be able to identify Speros."

Morris frowned. "Wait a minute. We missed a witness?"

"He was out doing chores when the incident occurred. I gather he didn't get back until much later."

The Captain relaxed. "That would explain it. I'll be interested to hear what he says." She turned to Dumas. "Meanwhile, what's next for Parsons?"

"I'll look in on him shortly, let him know that Speros probably wants to see him again. That might loosen his tongue."

"Or give him a heart attack."

Smiling impishly, Dumas stood to go. "I'll break it to him gently," he said.

Douglas Palmer seemed a pleasant enough fellow, Walters thought as he put his cell phone down on the kitchen table next to his laptop. He almost felt guilty about the deception, but honesty hadn't helped him much thus far in this venture. People, it seemed, were more likely to talk to the police than a writer, so Walters decided to feign cophood.

Unsuspecting, Palmer had been happy to tell Walters that a detective had already come around yesterday evening to take his statement. He assured Walters that he'd given the detective as full an accounting as possible, given the lapse of four years. He didn't recall the detective's name, but it had been a woman. No, her last name wasn't Montufar. It was the name of some bird, but he couldn't remember which one. Stork? No, that wasn't right.

Walters had told him it wasn't important, thanked him and said goodbye. But now he was at a loss for a next step. If Dumas and Montufar had stumbled across the fact that a stolen truck had killed Sandra Peller, the case would certainly be reopened and he had lost his potential leverage with Lieutenant Peller.

Unless he could identify the driver.

How could he do that?

Walters poured himself some cornflakes, sliced a banana into the bowl, and poured in milk. He made a cup of coffee and added two sugar cubes, then sat and ate while pondering the problem.

Kaneko thought the driver had intentionally killed Sandra Peller. Would the killer have stolen the truck for that purpose? Probably not. Auto theft was a business staffed by experts. Unless the killer was also an auto thief, it would have been far easier to buy a stolen vehicle. And if that had happened, then maybe somebody would have put two and two together. If so, Walters simply needed to find that person. He needed to talk to someone who knew the business.

Who would that be?

He pulled his laptop over and did a search on auto theft in Baltimore, hoping to find a few names of convicted thieves. He could visit one or two of them in prison, maybe get some leads from them.

He hit paydirt immediately. The first result was a news item from the *Baltimore Sun* detailing a recent armed robbery and homicide. A stolen truck had been used in the crimes, and the suspected perpetrator, one Morgan Parsons, was now in the hospital being treated for injuries. A police spokesman speculated that he'd stolen the truck to sell it; the robbery, most likely had been an impulsive act that went wrong. Charges had not been filed, but appeared to be not long in coming.

Walters put down his spoon and reread the article with great interest. Twice.

Although he'd given a couple of speeches in his life, Peller didn't fancy himself a speaker and didn't much care to stand up in front of an audience. This, though, was a special case. The audience consisted of a class of grade-school students, including his beaming granddaughter, and rather than standing he was sitting in a small chair that, he thought, made him look like a giant.

Susie had told her teacher that her grandfather the detective was visiting, and the teacher, a pretty young woman named Clara Nuñez, had sent a note home asking if granddad would be willing to visit the class and tell them about his work. He could have resisted Ms. Nuñez's invitation, but not Susie's pleading.

Hoping not to say anything too scary, he told the class that detectives look for clues at crime scenes to figure out what happened and who the criminal was. He talked about fingerprints and pieces of cloth and interviewing witnesses. When it was time to field questions, he quickly learned that not too much scared these kids.

"Have you ever seen blood all over the walls?" one boy asked with a ghoulish grin.

Peller took a deep breath. "Well. Yes, I'm afraid I have."

Behind the boy, a redheaded girl shouted out, "What about cut-off heads?"

"No, that doesn't happen too often, thank goodness."

"If they steal the head," another boy said sagely, "he has to get DNA to figure out who it was."

"Actually," Peller began, but he didn't have a chance to finish.

"Or teeth," a second girl chimed in. "They can use teeth, too. I saw that on TV last night."

"There's no teeth if the head's gone," the boy objected. "There's only DNA."

Hoping to change the subject and still appeal to his forensics-show fans, Peller asked, "Okay, now that's an interesting subject. Do you know what DNA is?"

"That's what you get from the blood that's all over the walls!" the first boy crowed.

"It comes from cells," Susie interjected. "It's what tells cells how to make a person. Everyone's is different." She smiled at her grandfather.

"Yes, very good, Susie. We use DNA to identify people."

"Headless people," the boy who had brought it up added.

"Well, usually not. Usually it helps us find the criminal, because they leave bits of it behind. Sometimes it tells us who the criminal is not rather than who it is. That keeps us from arresting the wrong person."

"Spit," a girl in the front row said.

"I'm sorry?" Out of the corner of his eye, he caught a glimpse of Ms. Nuñez putting her hand over her mouth to stifle a laugh.

"That's where you get the criminal's DNA. Criminals are always spitting."

Peller tried not to laugh, too. He almost succeeded. "Yes," he said. "Some of them are."

When Walters knocked on the open door, Parsons jumped. He looked scared, the writer thought, almost terrified. Given his predicament, he had good reason. But why hadn't the police stationed an officer nearby? Surely the man was a flight risk.

Still, the absence of police was a gift he wasn't about to question. He smiled warmly in an effort to put Parsons at ease and introduced himself.

Parsons blinked, seemingly unable to process the information. "Mind if I sit down?"

"A writer?"

"That's right."

The other mulled that over. "You don't work for the man?"

"Who?"

"Nobody."

Walters didn't care to press the point. Whatever this man's troubles, the only value he had for the writer lay in what he might know about one particular pickup truck. "I was wondering if you could help me. I'm researching something, nothing to do with what put you here, but it does have to do with auto theft, and I gather you're something of an expert in that area."

Parsons shook his head. "I don't know nothin' about that."

"I'm not with the police. The police don't know I'm here, and I don't want them to know I'm here. I'm not going to tell them anything you tell me."

Tugging the sheet up to his neck, Parsons looked away. "Suits me. I still don't know nothin'."

Ignoring the denial, Walters pressed on. "Four years ago, a dark blue F250 was stolen in the Hunt Valley area. Not long after, it was involved in an accident near West Friendship. A woman was killed. The driver of the truck fled and was never caught." He watched carefully but Parsons didn't react in the slightest. "Did you hear about that?"

"Nope."

"I'm not suggesting you stole the truck. I'm just wondering if you heard about it."

Parsons shook his head without making eye contact.

"The woman who was killed was a cop's wife."

"I don't know about it."

"Who would?"

Parsons shrugged.

"It's really important that I find out."

That got a reaction. Parsons' head swiveled slowly around, and he looked Walters over very carefully. "How important?"

"Very."

"Get me the hell out of here important?"

Walters hadn't expected that, but he was willing to play along. "Maybe. Do you know something?"

"Get me the hell out of Maryland important?"

"I can't promise that."

"Then I don't know nothin'."

Walters frowned. Given that the police were likely going to arrest Parsons, it might be a criminal act to help him flee the state. It might even be a criminal act to help him flee the hospital. Then again, he could plead ignorance. After all, they hadn't charged Parsons yet. "What if I can?"

"Then I might know somethin'."

"Like what?"

"I'll tell you when we cross the state line."

"How do I know it'll be worth it?"

"You don't trust me?"

Walters grinned. "As far as you trust me, Morgan."

Parsons didn't look amused. In fact, he looked even more disturbed than before. "Okay," he said. "I'll tell you this much. I stole that truck. I wish to God I never had." Without warning, he sat and swung his legs over the edge of the bed. "Now get me out of here."

Walters put a hand up. "Whoa, I don't know how to undo an IV."

"I'll take care of that. See if there are any bandages in those cabinets." He stood and unplugged the IV unit from the wall.

Walters, suddenly fearful of the new direction his goal had taken him, went to find the bandages.

Although he knew next to nothing about his friend's background, Kevin Graham had always regarded Eric Dumas as a stable, level-headed guy. He took his job seriously but liked to joke around. He dabbled in sleight of hand, and although he lived alone and seemed fairly uninterested in women, he probably would have made a good father. But sometimes, Graham thought, he could get weird. Like now.

Riding the elevator up to the third floor of the hospital, Graham mentioned in passing that his anniversary was this weekend and he still hadn't figured out what to get his wife.

"How long have you been married?" Dumas asked.

"Seventeen years."

"Seventeen good years?"

Graham raised an eyebrow. "If they hadn't been, it wouldn't be our seventeenth."

"But they can't all be good, can they?"

"What kind of question is that?"

"Just…" Dumas shrugged. "Life isn't a fairy tale, is it?"

"No." Graham waited, presuming that Dumas had a point and would come to it sooner or later, although in his case later sometimes took its time arriving.

"It's a risk, then, getting married."

"It's a risk being born, mon."

Dumas gave him a funny look.

The elevator dinged and the doors slid open. The two of them exited and turned toward Morgan Parsons' room. "Being born isn't a choice," Dumas finally replied.

"You telling me you're thinking about getting hitched?"

"Did I say that?"

"Who's the lucky girl?"

"I didn't say that."

Graham gave Dumas a gentle nudge in the ribs. "Does she even know you're interested?"

"Come on."

"Okay, okay." They made a right at the nurse's station. "Yeah, there are ups and downs. But you enjoy the ups and weather the downs. That's life, you know?"

Dumas stopped short at Parsons' door so quickly Graham almost ran into him. He half-turned as if to speak, but said nothing. Graham looked over his shoulder into an empty room.

Graham caught at a passing nurse. "Where's Morgan?"

The nurse glanced into the room and scanned the hallway. "I don't know," she said with a frown. "Let me check." They followed her to the nurse's station, waiting while she tapped at the computer and puzzled over the screen. "He's not scheduled for anything that would take him out of the room."

"Where's the security video?" Dumas asked. "Maybe he walked out."

Now the nurse looked alarmed. "I'll see what I can do," she said, picking up the phone. Within a few minutes, a guard arrived to escort the police down to the security offices on the first floor.

The security personnel were housed in a surprisingly up-to-date facility. Efficient to a man, they quickly located the images Dumas and Graham requested. The policemen watched as Parsons, dressed in his street clothes, his head turning nervously every which way, slipped away in the company of a sandy-haired man. He'd made his exit a mere five minutes before they had arrived.

"I'll be damned," Dumas said. "Back that up and play it again."

"What is it?" Graham asked as the guard complied.

"Stop it there," Dumas said. "I don't believe it."

"You know that guy, Eric?"

"It's that damn writer. Phil Walters!"

Checking an online map, Montufar noticed that Randall Sommers lived only a quarter mile east of St. John the Evangelist Catholic Church in Columbia's Oakland Mills Interfaith Center. A resident of the Forest Ridge Apartments, Sommers had agreed to meet with her at one o'clock that afternoon. That would give her plenty of time to meet with a priest if one was available, so she called the church, where she was put through to Father Owen, who told her he would be glad to see her at twelve-thirty.

When she arrived at the Interfaith Center, she stood beside her car, staring at the building. It didn't feel like a church to her. She remembered attending Mass as a child in her hometown of Amatitlán. The church where she had been baptized, San Juan Bautista, was a beautiful old church, white land gold on the outside, gold lines spiraling up gleaming pillars to the heavens; while inside great arcs of bright fabric in the colors of the liturgical season hung suspended overhead and ornate statuary graced the altars and alcoves. By contrast, the Interfaith Center looked, at least on the outside, like an office building: brownish brick, blocky, corporate.

Columbia's interfaith centers seemed to Montufar's classically-trained mind like the stereotypic good intention paving the way to Hell. In the mid-1960's when the community was being planned, its designers cherished the notion of a place that would erase barriers between people. A shared space for congregations of various religions was among their innovations. But in sacrificing the identifying marks of creed and denomination, Montufar thought, something important had been lost: the beauty and grandeur befitting the transcendent. And through its loss, the unification wrought by a common art had been weakened, for she could mentally fit neither a cathedral nor a Quaker meetinghouse into the building that stood before her.

She went inside and followed the signs to the parish offices. The interior of the building looked a bit less corporate, more inviting. Public spaces seemed open and light. It didn't have the majestic beauty of the church she remembered, but she thought it would be a comfortable place for a conference or convention. She would have to ask Eduardo what he thought of it. Montufar couldn't remember him ever describing the place or expressing an opinion on it.

Reaching the offices, she found a fiftyish woman seated at the reception desk. A tall, lanky man in a clerical shirt and black jeans was consulting a stack of papers he held in his hand. "We'll have to work around that," he was saying, "but no matter. Monsignor can't be in more than three places at once."

The woman chuckled. "Don't tell *him* that!"

Montufar knocked lightly on the door to get their attention.

"Ah, you must be Ms. Montufar," the man said. When she nodded, he added, "I'm Father Owen." He set the papers on the desk. "Very pleased to meet you. Come on back to my office."

He led her through a door in the back into a short hallway leading to a series of small rooms. Montufar thought of a monastery. To the right a door stood ajar, and Father Owen pushed it open, motioning her to go first. The room was barely big enough to hold the miscellanea of items within: a scarred desk, a couple of uphol-stered chairs in an uneasy relationship with a small round table, a wall of bookcases with books and papers shoved in every which way. A purple chasuble hung from an old-fashioned coat rack hiding in the corner. Montufar felt a slight shock—the sight seemed faintly sacrilegious.

"Sorry about that," he said, following her gaze. "I was in a hurry. Don't worry; I'll get it back to the sacristy." He scooped a handful of books from one of the chairs. "Please, have a seat."

Montufar parked herself uncomfortably on the edge of the chair. The priest seated himself across from her and smiled apolo-getically. "And sorry about the general chaos. I haven't had time to get organized for the past fifteen years." He smiled warmly.

Montufar collected herself. For the first time she took a good look at the priest. He must have been in his sixties, his hair half-white and his face creased as though he had seen more joy and grief in his lifetime than others might in ten. His eyes were startlingly blue. In that moment she decided that, whatever the condition of the church he pastored, she liked him. More than that, she trusted him. "That's all right. In my line of work, I see far worse sometimes."

"And what line of work is that?"

"I'm a detective with the Howard County police." Seeing his smile start to fade, she added quickly, "But I'm not here on business. I'm here because of my brother."

"Ah! I thought I recognized the last name. Eduardo, isn't it?"

"That's right."

"A very fortunate young man. I saw him in the hospital shortly afterward."

Montufar thought it would have been more fortunate had he not been in the accident at all, but she pushed that aside. "He's recov-ering well. Physically, that is. But I'm worried he may not be doing as well as he thinks. He's been having trouble finding words when he talks, words he shouldn't have trouble finding."

"I see. Has he talked to his doctor about this?"

Montufar shook her head and looked down at her hands, clasped in her lap. "I've encouraged him to do so, but he's convinced he's doing fine."

Father Owen leaned back and studied Montufar, a thoughtful look on his face, but he said nothing. Still looking down, she felt his gaze and sensed he was waiting for more. She had nothing else to say but to state her request: "I thought maybe a priest could talk to him, convince him that he needs to take it seriously."

"Yours is a close family, isn't it?"

"Yes."

"I see a lot of people and hear a lot of names, so sometimes it takes me awhile. But now that I think about it, I'm sure he's mentioned you more than once. I don't recall his actual words, but I have a sense that he's very proud of you."

Montufar didn't see what that had to do with anything, but she couldn't help smiling as she finally looked up at the priest. "I suppose he is. He was always one of my champions, especially when things looked impossible."

"And it's obvious that you care deeply about him, because you wouldn't be here otherwise. But I think you should know that it will be hard for me to broach the subject with him. He'll want to know why I think he has a problem. If I tell him that you brought it up, he may resent that you've involved me."

She hadn't thought about that and wondered how it could have escaped her. But she didn't know where else to turn, so she pressed on. "Maybe, but I think he would listen to you anyway."

"Are you a parishioner elsewhere?"

This wasn't an avenue she wanted to pursue right now, but she felt compelled to respond. "N-no," she stumbled. "Not for a long time now."

"Just curious," Father Owen said, smiling to signal he wasn't accusing her of lapsing. "You're always welcome here. But I just thought that maybe you could come to Mass with his family on Sunday. That way he could introduce you to me and we could all have a friendly talk. If I notice anything amiss in his speech, then I'd be in a position to talk to him about it."

A reasonable suggestion, she thought, yet she hesitated. She wasn't sure she was ready to return to the rituals and practices of her youth. Even if she did, she wasn't sure she wanted it to happen in a place like this. Yet Father Owen hadn't asked her to do anything other than accompany her brother. Why should that be so hard?

She wished Dumas were here, even if only for moral support. But that, she scolded herself, was stupid. He was even less of a Catholic than she was and couldn't possibly be of much help.

"Or," the priest continued, possibly sensing her discomfort, "I might have time to pay him a visit this weekend. I visited him in the hospital, but haven't been able to see him since. I really should."

"Yes," Montufar said, a bit too quickly. "That would be good."

"All right then. Why don't you give me your phone number? I'll check my schedule and give you a call. You can drop by his place at the same time."

"Thank you, Father. I really appreciate it." She rose and shook his hand. "I'm afraid I have to run."

"Back to police business?"

"Back to police business," she affirmed.

Father Owen showed her out of the office, and when she emerged from the building into the bright sunlight, she paused and drew in a breath. A crew of landscapers was piling mulch around the trees at the edge of the parking lot, and its earthy smell filled the cool spring air. She felt suddenly at ease, as though she'd passed some critical test. The sensation puzzled her. There was no reason she could find for feeling that way.

Dumas called in for data on Phil Walters and soon had his address and phone and license plate numbers. He issued an APB on the car, then called the phone number. Nobody answered. After contacting the Baltimore County police, he and Graham drove to

Walters' place in Catonsville, where they were met by a pair of officers from that jurisdiction. Nobody was home.

"He lives with his girlfriend," Graham said, fiddling with his smart phone. "Penny Lowell, a nurse at Spring Grove Hospital Center."

"That's close by," one of the Baltimore officers said. "It's a nut house. Excuse me. A psychiatric hospital." He grinned.

Dumas didn't. "How did you find that?" he asked Graham.

Graham held up his phone. "Social media. Nobody keeps anything private anymore, mon."

Dumas shook his head. "I should've known. All right. Let's pay Ms. Penny a visit."

When the apartment door opened, Montufar found herself looking at a man totally unlike the one she'd expected. Randall Sommers, hardy farm boy, ought to have been tall and fit, a moving advertisement for a health club. Instead he was on the short side, a bit overweight, bespectacled, and starting to lose a bit of hair on the top. Dressed in jeans and a plain green t-shirt, he seemed more of a couch potato than a hiker.

He greeted her warmly, though, and invited her into his living room, where he fussed over getting her coffee or tea or water or juice or whatever she'd like, plus a plate of almond cookies. She tried to dissuade him but eventually accepted his offer of a glass of water and picked up a cookie, just to make him feel more at ease.

"I'm doing some follow-up work on the accident that took place in front of your grandparents' farm four years ago. Your cousin Hannah tells me you saw the truck leaving the scene."

"That's right. I didn't see much, but it was a dark blue Ford."

"What about the driver?"

"He looked to me like a big guy. He had a beard. But I'm not sure I could really describe him."

Montufar opened a folder she'd brought with her and took out four photos, all of big, bearded men. One was Orion Speros, two others were mug shots of convicts, and one was a photo of a police officer out of uniform. She handed them to Sommers. "Was he one of these men?"

He looked carefully at each one. "Hard to say. Not this one, I don't think. His face is too narrow." He set aside one of the convicts. "Not this one, either." He put down the police officer. After studying the remaining two, he leaned back and closed his eyes. "I can still see the truck, and the mangled car. The truck flew like the wind, straight west. The driver, he looked, I don't know. Not like someone who'd just been in an accident. More like he was mad about something."

"You could see him that clearly?"

"He wasn't more than a hundred feet away, I don't think, when he passed me." Randall opened his eyes and looked at the photos again. "I think it was this guy. If not, it was someone who looked a lot like him." He handed a photo to Montufar.

She took it and looked at it.

Orion Speros.

# Chapter 14

"We need another car!" Parsons wailed. "Once the cops find out I'm missing, they'll come looking for us!"

Walters was about ready to push him out of the vehicle, story or no story. Driving west on Interstate 70, he had planned to pick up U.S. 15 going north from Frederick. Once near the state line, he figured he'd kick Parsons out, leaving him to make his own way into Pennsylvania. If questions arose later, Walters had a story ready: he had gone to interview Parsons, who said he had discharged himself and asked for a ride home. Walters had only realized later that Parsons was trying to flee the state. He was pretty sure a jury would believe him over a convicted criminal accused of killing a man.

Unfortunately, part of the plan had been to get Parsons to talk before giving him the boot, and that hadn't happened. The thief—big man though he was—had done nothing but whine and complain since they left the hospital.

"You're stuck with my car," Walters snapped. "Just take it easy, will you?"

"You think they won't know it was you? The hospital has security cameras. They'll be looking for you!"

"I suppose you want to stop and steal a shiny new BMW? I'm not making myself an accessory to auto theft."

"No time for that. We need to see the man. He'll sell us a car."

"What man?"

"The guy who buys cars from me. He's got some to sell. He's always got some to sell."

Walters shook his head. "I doubt you have few thousand in cash on you."

Parsons put his hands on his head and squeezed his eyes shut. "Don't be stupid, man!"

"Forget it, Morgan! I'm not buying a stolen vehicle!"

Parsons slammed his fist on the dashboard, hard, then rubbed his hand in pain. "Wait. We can rent it. You can return it after you drop me off in Pennsylvania. A day's rent, that's not much. He knows I'm good for it."

"If I were him, I'd have bumped you off a long time ago. Are you always this hyper?"

Parsons glared at him, but at least he shut up for a few minutes.

They drove in blissful silence.

"Take the next exit," Parsons eventually said.

"Why?"

"The man's place. We see him or I tell you nothin'."

"I don't want to see anybody you know. I don't want to be any more mixed up in your insanity than I already am. God, I wish I'd never talked to you!"

Walters took the next exit anyway.

⟿

The day's agenda, at the outset, looked pretty boring: inspect the security systems, double-check arrangements for a few outbound shipments, meet with Duke about some potential new customers.

Boring was good; it gave one time to relax and enjoy life. Jeff Levinson liked such days. He liked them even more when Caroline Fisher showed up, craving his attention. She'd been extra feisty this morning, perhaps having finally worked out that Duke Calvert didn't care that she was fooling around with his underling.

Afterward, she'd fallen asleep. Leaving her in bed, he had set about his business, armed with a cup of coffee and his laptop. He accessed each of the farm's security cameras in turn, verifying their operability, their image quality, their coverage. It took time, but the scenery was pleasant: the hills, the spring greenery, the stands of wood. Absorbed in the view, he jumped when something slammed against the front door, once, twice, three times.

"Jeff! We have to talk, my man!"

Levinson cringed. He made sure his gun was loaded and ready for action. "In the kitchen!" he called.

The door banged open, thudded shut. Orion Speros appeared in the kitchen doorway, seeming to fill it so completely that not even air could squeeze past him. He didn't look happy. In fact, Levinson thought, he looked ready to kill.

He forced a calmness he didn't feel into his voice. "What's wrong?"

Speros only glared.

Levinson pushed himself back from the table but didn't rise. His right hand near the gun, he motioned with his left. "Have a seat. You want some coffee?"

"Guess who came to my house yesterday?"

Levinson waited.

"The police."

*Not good*, he thought. "What did they want?"

"Morgan squealed. He led them right to me. They know I worked him over, but that's not the problem."

*Very bad*. "Damn. If he told them about you, he probably told them about the farm, too."

"The farm can go to hell," Speros snapped. "Somehow they've fingered me for that wreck four years ago. The one *you* hired me to do, Jeff. The one *you* said was to get rid of some annoying competition for somebody. The one *you* lied about."

Keeping his expression bland, Levinson slipped the gun out of its holster and set it on the table, his hand resting atop it. Speros didn't look at it, possibly didn't even care.

"Do you know who was in that car, Jeff?"

Levinson shrugged. "You know I don't. All either of us had was the guy's name and the description of the car."

"Except it wasn't him, was it? It was his wife."

"We've been over this a million times, Orion. It wasn't our fault. The client gave us bad information. He knew it was his fault, too. He never came back, never demanded we return the payment.

Okay, I know you don't like taking out innocent bystanders, but it just wasn't our fault. Yours or mine."

Speros took a few slow steps toward Levinson but didn't make any threatening moves. He knew the gun was there, knew Levinson was skilled in its use, and kept his anger under control.

"Shall I tell you who was in that car, Jeff?"

Frowning, Levinson wondered where this was going. "The guy's wife. You already said that. We've known that for years."

"He's a cop! She was a cop's wife!"

Levinson could feel the color drain from his face. He put both hands on the gun, just in case. "How…"

"How do you think, you moron? They told me! When the cops questioned me about Morgan, they told me!" Speros pointed a meaty finger at Levinson. "If they pin this on me, I swear I'll kill you. And that little toy gun of yours won't stop me." Before Levinson could respond, Speros spun around and surged from the house. The front door crashed behind him.

But before Levinson had time to catch his breath, Speros suddenly reappeared in the doorway. He held a living room chair before him like a shield. Without warning, he heaved it at Levinson, who barely had time to raise his gun before the chair slammed into him, knocking him to the floor. The gun flew harmlessly from his hand into a remote corner of the room. His head hit the floor, hard. Pushing the chair away, he tried to scramble up, feeling like dog on roller skates, his uncoordinated limbs working at cross-purposes.

He finally got his feet under him and stood.

Speros, now impossibly close, slammed a fist into his jaw and knocked him down again.

His head ringing, fire roaring up his face, Levinson heard screaming. His eyes registered light, but his brain couldn't assemble it into anything meaningful.

The screaming went on and on, filling his head, filling the whole world.

Until it stopped.

Something landed on him. Something heavy, something warm. Too yielding to be furniture, too heavy to be anything else. He pushed feebly at it and realized in horror that it wasn't something.

It was someone.

Caroline Fisher.

Still naked.

Very dead.

Sited on a two hundred acre campus, Spring Grove Hospital Center appeared peaceful. The rolling land, bordered by thick stands of trees, was pleasantly landscaped and populated with buildings of varying styles from old to modern. An unpretentious wooden sign almost small enough to overlook marked the entrance, giving the impression that the hospital would rather that passersby didn't know it was there. Drinking up the view, Dumas felt himself relax as Graham eased the car around the winding road leading to the main hospital building.

Once there, they entered and presented themselves at the information desk. Dumas showed his badge and asked for Penny Lowell, and the smartly-dressed African-American man asked them to wait while he called for her.

Five minutes later she came down the corridor, moving quickly, her face covered in concern. When she saw the police officers she stopped short.

Stepping forward, Dumas introduced himself and Graham. "I don't want to alarm you, but we need your help. We're trying to locate Phil Walters. Do you have any idea where he might be?"

She looked from Dumas to Graham and back again, puzzled. "Phil? If he's not at home, he's probably off somewhere doing research. He's a writer."

"Yes, I know. He approached me a few days ago about one of his projects."

"Oh, I'm sorry. You must be one of the Fibonacci detectives."

"You could say that. It's really important we find him, Ms. Lowell."

Now her brow furrowed. "He's not in trouble, is he?"

Dumas hesitated, unsure how much Lowell knew about Walters' involvement with Parsons, or indeed if there was much to know in the first place.

"Do you think he is?" Graham asked.

She stared at him then turned to Dumas, anger welling up. "Whatever concerns Phil concerns me. What's going on?"

"He was seen this morning in the company of a suspected criminal," Dumas told her.

She shook her head. "That doesn't make any sense."

"As you said, he might have been doing some research. Unfortunately, we were about to arrest this guy, but it appears he may have gotten Mr. Walters to give him a ride somewhere. So we need to find them, both to make sure Mr. Walters is safe and to see what he knows about this other man."

Lowell shook her head, denying that Walters could have done any such thing.

Out of the corner of his eye, Dumas noticed Graham nod towards the exit. "All right," he told her. "Let me give you my cell phone number. If he contacts you, please find out where he is and let me know. Tell him it's important that I talk to him." He handed her a business card.

She took it and stared at it as though not knowing what it was for.

"Okay?" he asked.

She nodded.

Once outside, Graham said, "She's on the level."

"Thank God somebody is," Dumas replied.

Walters, turning each time Parsons told him, eventually pulled off the road, followed a paved drive up one side of a hill and down the other, and drove around a bend, arriving at a 1930s sort of farm house, square and sturdy, that might have been deserted for all he knew.

"Pull off here," Parsons instructed. "I'll see if Jeff is in."

"Who's Jeff?" Walters put the car in park.

"The guy I talk to."

"Another code name for 'the man?'"

"Nobody talks to the man except Jeff."

"Why not?"

Parsons gave him a scolded puppy look. "Don't do this. Nobody talks to the man, that's all. We go through Jeff."

Walters threw up his hands. He had long since regretted this course of action, but he was in too deep to back out now. He just hoped that it would prove worth the trouble. Given that Parsons had stolen the pickup truck that later killed Sandra Peller, it stood to reason he knew considerably more about the matter, but more and more it looked like only an act of God would get Parsons to talk.

Parsons quietly closed the car door and started for the house, but abruptly halted. A moment later, he crept forward. Now what? Walters wondered. Then he noticed that the front door was ajar.

*Great*, he thought. *Another complication.* He considered leaving but decided he might as well wait this out, too. It hardly seemed that matters could deteriorate any further. As Parsons cautiously pushed the door open and stepped into the house, Walters turned on the radio, absently scanning through the stations.

Just as he reached a song almost worth listening to, Parsons erupted from the house. Skidding on damp turf and loose gravel, he scrambled into the passenger seat and slammed the door, screaming, "Go! Go!"

"What's wrong?"

"Just go! We gotta get Duke!"

"Who?"

Parsons grabbed for the gearshift. "Go!"

Shaking his head, Walters put the car in gear and continued up the road, which changed from gravel to erosion-rutted dirt. The car jounced along, finally arriving at a second, more modern dwelling. Parsons jabbed a finger at Walters. "Stop. Stay here. Don't get out of the car." He jumped out and ran up to the house. Walters watched him pound on the front door as though trying to break it down.

The door opened a moment later, but all Walters could see was a shadow within, to which Parsons babbled and gestured wildly. The shadow shifted and leaned forward as though to look down the road, then ducked back inside.

The door closed. Parsons raced back to the car and threw himself inside.

Walters asked, "Well?"

Breathless, Parsons pointed. "Up the road to the Big Shed. Duke'll have someone take care of..." He shook his head. "Never mind. I'll tell you when we get there."

"I gather Duke is 'the man.'"

"Come on!"

Walters did as instructed.

The Big Shed appeared to be a maintenance garage with five large bay doors. Two of them stood open, revealing a small collection of vehicles—all no doubt stolen, Walters thought—in various stages of disassembly. He pulled through the nearest door and turned off the car. "Now what?"

Parsons indicated a man approaching from the driver's side. "He'll get us a rental."

The man, a young Mexican about six feet tall and wearing grease-spattered overalls, waved to them, a smile beneath his thick mustache. Parsons got out of the car and called, "Hey, Esteban! Long time no see."

"Six months, no?" Esteban replied in a heavy accent as he and Parsons shook hands.

Whatever had panicked Parsons seemed to be over. Walters climbed out of his vehicle and leaned against it.

Esteban ran an appraising eye over Walters' car. "Not much use for that one," he said. Walters wasn't sure whether he should feel insulted or be happy that the crooks didn't want to rob him.

"We're just storing that for a day or so," Parsons told him. "The man said you'd fix us up with a loaner."

"That's not the word I got."

Parsons looked confused. Walters cynically thought confusion was his natural state.

Esteban pulled a gun from inside his overalls and trained it on Parsons. "Sorry, man. He wants you to wait in the office." He nodded to Walters. "Both of you."

Walters seemed to see himself from a distance. He felt no fear; he was beyond fear. Anger was a different matter. Enraged, he wanted nothing more than to crush them under the wheels of his car. At the same time, he wasn't about to argue with a loaded gun. Hands balled into tight fists at his side, he did as he was told.

Those who worked for Duke Calvert seldom dealt with anything more violent than vehicle disassembly, but they were all involved in a criminal enterprise and knew how to keep secrets. Nor did he need to give instructions. When he told an underling to take care of a matter, it was taken care of, and he never heard about it again.

Thus, a pair of them transported Caroline Fisher's body, wrapped in several layers of sheets, deep into the farm's acreage for burial. After a few seasons, no one would ever guess its presence. Another removed Jeff Levinson, reduced to incoherent mumbling, from the scene and took him to another building where he was cleaned up and his injuries treated. The crime scene was thoroughly scrubbed several times, eradicating all traces of violence. Their chores completed, the accomplices melted away to their regular duties.

While his flunkies carried out their orders, Calvert read a book for a full hour, then pulled on a pair of boots and walked to the house where Levinson had been taken. He came quietly into the mudroom, stripped off the boots, and donned a pair of polished loafers waiting on a shelf. He was dressed in a conservative navy blue suit with a blue and red striped tie. He hadn't come to visit the sick but to conduct business, crucial business, something he never did without dressing the part.

In the living room, Levinson slumped on a plush burgundy sofa, staring at the floor. Behind him stood another hired muscle, his expression bored. With a slight wave of his hand, Calvert dismissed the man.

Calvert examined Levinson as though he were an insect pinned to a display board. Given Levinson's state, he doubted he could get much useful information out of him, but Levinson alone knew what had happened, who was responsible, and how great was the danger to their operation.

Actually, Calvert reflected, why was probably more important than who. Fisher hardly seemed a likely target for assassination, unless the killer had been a jealous lover. He doubted he and Levinson were the only men she'd had. One of them might have followed her to the farm. In that case, there was no danger to his operation. What bothered him was that Levinson hadn't been killed, too. If a jealous lover had found Fisher with another man, how likely was it he would have killed her and left the man alive? It was possible, of course, but seemed unlikely. So was the murderer targeting Calvert—or his business—from a distance?

"Can you talk?" Calvert finally asked.

Levinson didn't give any sign of hearing.

"Did you hear me? I need information."

No response.

Calvert pulled a ladder-back chair from the corner, positioned it across from Levinson, and sat. "Who attacked you?"

Slowly, Levinson's gaze rose to meet his.

Calvert scowled. "Snap out of it. Tell me who it was."

Levinson shrugged.

"Oh God, Jeff, I thought I could trust you. What have you done?"

Under the prodding of his voice, Levinson seemed to awaken. He scanned the room, frowning. "What am I doing here?"

"You're telling me what happened."

"What happened when?"

*Why*, Calvert asked himself, *must everyone I employ turn out to be a moron?* Aloud, he said, "You were attacked. You and Caroline."

"My face hurts." Levinson probed gingerly at his chin.

"I'm not surprised. Who hit you?"

All Levinson could do was shake his head.

"Caroline is dead. You do know that, don't you?"

"Caroline? Who's Caroline?"

Calvert rose and stared at Levinson with contempt. What the hell had happened? Stupidity. What an adversary stupidity was. One moment, he had had an amusing companion and a key team member—the next, they were gone. But even worse than that, whoever was responsible for the carnage knew far more about his operation than he should. And, whoever it was, he was completely beyond Calvert's control.

He returned to the mud room, removed his shoes, and donned his boots. He would pay another visit. It was just possible Morgan Parsons could tell him something. Parsons was in frequent contact with Levinson. He was a fool, but perhaps he would possess some useful piece of information. Although probably, Calvert thought, he wouldn't realize it if he did.

As for Parsons' chauffer, whoever it was, it would be best to eliminate him.

# Chapter 15

The definition of frustration, Dumas thought, might well be needing to get something done but having no way to do it. At the moment he needed to locate Phil Walters and Morgan Parsons, but with no idea where they were going and no information to hand beyond Walters' license plate number, finding them would require a massive amount of dumb luck. He could do little but wait at his desk, where the usual flood of paperwork failed to preoccupy him, and hope that a patrol would spot Walters' car.

Fortunately, Montufar arrived with news capable of distraction: "Speros is our man."

Dumas shoved his chair back and looked up at her. She was wearing that look of intense concentration he knew so well. "Sommers was that certain?"

"I'm that certain."

"Corina..."

"Sommers picked the photo of Speros as the most likely candidate," she insisted. "He was sure it was someone who looked very much like Speros and was pretty sure the driver was angry as he sped away. Think about that."

Dumas did so while she settled herself on the edge of his desk. "Anger doesn't make sense. Fear, yes. Horror, maybe. But anger?"

"Exactly. It wasn't an accident, Eric. Speros intentionally rammed Sandra's car. Only it wasn't supposed to be Sandra. It was supposed to be someone else. When he realized he hadn't hit the target, he was angry. Furious."

The scenario worked, Dumas thought, yet it raised a slew of new questions, and the evidence was still thin. But one more piece fell into place. "Could be. He's mad about something, for sure. Remember what I said about his reaction the other day when I raised the subject? Furious isn't an exaggeration."

"Yes," Montufar said thoughtfully, but ventured nothing more.

As soon as he had mentioned the possibility, though, he wondered if he had read the signs wrong. "But it doesn't sound like him. He's too smooth--doesn't make mistakes. Not when he's in charge, at least." He sat silent for a moment, turning over possibilities in his mind. "Try this on for size. What if he was working on contract and his customer gave him bad intelligence? He wouldn't have been mad at himself. He would have been mad at whoever hired him."

Montufar regarded him archly. "You like to complicate things, don't you?"

"I'm the crazy idea guy, remember?"

"How could I forget?"

"Well, think about it. If Speros wants someone dead, they're going to be dead. If he made a mistake, he'd correct it. We should check, but as I recall the first homicide following the accident was five or six months later and was resolved in about a week. Either Speros missed his intended victim, or he did it so well we never knew about it."

"He may have," Montufar said. "But if he was hired to kill someone and the job went wrong, he may have refused to make a second attempt. Especially if he'd already been paid enough for his trouble."

"Right."

"Okay, hotshot. How do we prove it?"

"Beats me. He sure isn't going to turn himself in anytime soon. Maybe we can find whoever hired him." But as soon as the words left his mouth he knew they were in vain. Who would be stupid enough to admit to having hired Speros? Nobody.

"Well." Montufar slid off the desk. "We'll have to tell Rick about Speros, at least."

"I'll do it," Dumas volunteered. "But this must be turning into a hell of a vacation."

"He started it." She tried to smile, but the result looked more sickly than playful.

Before he could reply, his cell phone rang. He didn't recognize the number, but picked up anyway. "Dumas."

A frantic woman's voice came over the line. "Sergeant Dumas, this is Penny Lowell. I've heard from Walter. He's in trouble. You've got to help him!"

∿

The man named Esteban followed behind Parsons and Walters, his gun trained on their backs. Walters, still fuming, tried to memorize their path, hoping to find a way out but knowing there wouldn't be any. The place was too open despite the maze of stolen cars in various stages of disassembly and the equipment of the trade scattered about. In addition to the large bay doors, there were four human-sized doors, two along the left wall and two along the right. The office towards which they were marching was in the back, its door ajar. If he tried to run, Esteban would gun him down before he could reach cover.

Walters could see only one possibility of escape: the cell phone he carried in his left trouser pocket. Given a few moments unobserved, he might be able to get a message to Penny. He would have to do it soon, though, before Esteban or someone else decided to frisk them. And he didn't dare think what might happen if Esteban caught him in the act. Depending on the man's loyalty, his reaction could be anything from confiscating the phone to putting a bullet in Walters' head.

Ten feet from the office door, Parsons suddenly turned. "Look, man, this has to be a misunderstanding."

"Don't whine." Esteban motioned toward the office with the gun.

"C'mon, we're friends. Right? Friends?"

Walters kept up a steady pace until he entered the office. Outside, Parsons still moaned and complained, but Walters ignored him. A quick look around the small space revealed no other exit, not even a window. A beat-up metal desk holding a computer sat dead center. The space not taken by the computer and its peripherals was covered in newspapers, printouts, and a precarious stack of auto manuals. Two cheap plastic chairs angled away from the desk as though their occupants had only recently left; another held a pile of boxes. Walters perched on the chair closest to the door, snatched his phone from his pocket, and grabbed a section of newspaper. Placing the paper on the chair next to him, he slid the phone into its midst, then sat back and waited.

Presently Parsons entered, still protesting, the barrel of Esteban's gun prodding him in the back. There was nothing friendly about Esteban's expression anymore. "Over there," the Mexican growled. "Put your nose against the back wall." After one terrified backward glance, Parsons obeyed. Esteban turned to Walters. "Up."

Walters rose.

"Empty your pockets. Put everything on the desk."

Walters produced his wallet and car keys, then turned his pockets inside out to show they were empty.

Esteban gestured with his gun toward the opposite wall. "Nose against this wall," he ordered.

Deciding that discretion was the better part of valor, Walters complied. The barrel of the gun now pressed into his back while Esteban's free hand patted him down.

"Keep your nose against the wall."

The pressure from the gun vanished. Walters heard Esteban give Parsons the same order. A moment passed. "All right. Both of you sit down, and don't try anything stupid."

Walters returned to his original seat, while Parsons sat on the far side of the desk. His wallet and keys were gone from the desk, along with whatever Esteban had confiscated from Parsons. Walters briefly wondered if Esteban had put them in one of the desk drawers. But no, that would be too obvious.

"The only way out of here is the door," Esteban said unnecessarily, "and I'll be watching it. The man will be here soon." He left, slamming the door behind him.

"Are all your friends like this?" Walters asked.

"Shut up, man. Just shut up."

"With pleasure. You do the same while I try to get us out of here." With a glance at the door, he retrieved his cell phone from under the newspapers and launched the maps app. GPS wouldn't work without a clear view of the sky but, as he recalled, the phone would use data about nearby cell towers to approximate his position. He just hoped it would be close enough. Keeping an ear open for sounds of approaching footsteps, he surreptitiously texted Penny Lowell that he was being held captive at the coordinates provided by the app, and that she was not to text back but to immediately contact the police. Once the message was away, he deleted it from his phone and powered off the device. Assuming he wouldn't likely be searched again, he returned it to his pocket.

When he looked up, Parsons was grinning at him. "Don't get too excited," Walters whispered. "They might kill us anyway, before the cops get here."

Parsons stopped grinning. "Oh God, you didn't call the cops, did you?"

"Not directly, but they'll be here soon enough."

"You shouldn't have done that!"

"What, you wanted me to call the nearest convent?"

"Oh man, Duke's gonna kill you! He'll kill us both!"

Walters crossed his arms over his chest, leaned back, and closed his eyes. "Maybe. But I'll bet he's in for some lumps, too."

"You're insane! You know that, don't you? What kind of a man are you?"

Eyes still closed, Walters smiled. "I already told you. I'm a writer."

His face still hurt.

Jeff Levinson touched it gingerly. Something had happened, but he didn't know what. Maybe he'd fallen?

No. Someone had told him he'd been attacked. But by whom? It didn't make any sense. He studied his clothing: jeans and a brown button-down shirt. They looked clean, not like he'd been in a fight.

Someone had mentioned a woman, too. Caroline. Who was she? Where was she?

Dead, he imagined. Whoever had attacked him must have killed her. Had he been defending her? But he didn't know any Caroline. At least, he didn't think he did. Had they confused him with someone else?

He tried to recall any attack, any fighting, any death.

Nothing.

But his face still hurt. That much was certain.

He needed to think.

No, he needed to work. Work on some cars. Work was therapeutic. He liked working with his hands, working on cars. Something out in the garage needed fixing, he was sure. He remembered they always had cars, lots of them, needing work.

Leaving the house, Levinson started up the road to the Big Shed.

Immediately after talking with Penny Lowell, and with no idea what they would find at the coordinates she'd given him, Dumas called for four squads to converge on the location. Then he and Montufar raced off in her car to meet them. Montufar's driving always unnerved Dumas, but he held on and kept his mouth shut as the miles disappeared beneath her wheels. Their destination appeared to be a farm in the northwest part of the county, north of Interstate 70. The online maps indicated a couple of houses and other building there, but it wasn't clear in which one Walters was being held.

Why Walters was being held puzzled him, too, although he figured it had something to do with Parsons. Maybe Walters hadn't been helping Parsons after all? Whatever was going on, it gave Dumas a feeling of very bad karma.

Once out of the mud, Calvert again exchanged boots for shoes. As he approached the office near the back of the Big Shed, he saw one of the workers fiddling with something at a workbench. A gun rested nearby amidst tools and a jumble of loose metal and car parts. He didn't know the man's name. He purposely knew the names of only his top people, and they were the only ones who knew his name. But everyone, high or low, recognized "the man".

He asked, "Where are they?"

The worker, a Mexican fellow, looked up. "In the office, like you wanted."

"Any trouble?"

"Morgan was a bit whiny. The other one behaved. They've been quiet as mice since I shut them in there."

Calvert grimaced. "Mice eat holes in your socks," he said, and continued on. He could feel the worker's eyes following him.

"You want me to come in?"

"No. But if anyone other than me comes out, kill him."

He entered the office and closed the door firmly behind him. Parsons jumped at the sound, but it was easy to scare Parsons—his eyes were wide with fear, and Calvert hadn't done anything yet. Calvert didn't like the fact that he and Parsons knew each other by name, but his association with Parsons predated most of the security arrangements he and Levinson had worked out. Someday he'd have to have the fool eliminated. Maybe even today. That was an interesting thought, almost pleasant. He lingered over the prospect for a moment.

Calvert then sized up the second captive. Short, with an air of terminal boredom about him, the guy didn't even bother to look up. Calvert wasn't sure what to think. Was he trying to play cool, or be submissive, or was he simply an idiot?

"Hey, Duke," Parsons ventured.

"Shut up." Calvert spoke to the stranger. "You. What's your name?"

The other man finally looked at him. "Phil."

"Phil what?"

"Just Phil."

"You can't be famous enough to be mononymous."

Phil regarded him steadily. "That's a big word. I'm impressed."

"Phil the chauffeur, you'd be well advised not to annoy me." He turned back to Parsons. "What happened to Jeff?"

Parsons' voice edged up the scale. "You think I know? C'mon, Duke, he was all banged up and Caroline was already dead when I got there. I didn't see nothin' else."

"But you know what happened."

"No, Duke! I swear!"

Calvert reached for a chair loaded with papers. He tipped the papers onto the floor, shoved them out of the way with his foot, and sat. "Engage your brain for a moment, assuming you have one. Whoever did it had a reason. I need to know who and why." Calvert glanced back at Phil. The man was scowling. Probably he didn't know anything about either the beating or the killing. That meant he was useless. "Tell me what you saw."

Parsons shifted in his chair. "Just Jeff lying there with Caroline on top of him, dead."

"Where was Jeff's gun?"

"Gun?"

"Jeff always carried a gun. You know that."

"I didn't see it," Parsons said. "Wait, how could anyone have done that to him if he had a gun?"

*Save me from imbeciles,* Calvert thought. "Just tell me what you saw."

Parsons shifted again, as though moments from bolting. "I was scared, Duke. I didn't stop to look around. Wait a minute." His face screwed up in concentration. "There was a chair, one of the chairs from the living room, lying on its side."

"Like somebody threw a chair at him," Calvert supplied.

"Oh my God." Terror filled Parsons' eyes.

"What?"

"Orion," he nearly whispered. "I'll bet it was Orion."

Orion. Calvert had heard Levinson mention the name, although he didn't recall having met its owner. Maybe the name would snap Levinson out of his mental snake pit. Standing, Calvert gave Parsons a look of disgust. He would rather scrape manure off of his boots than talk to this idiot. As for Phil—Calvert shifted his gaze to the chauffer—he was as useless as a regifted knickknack.

Without a word, he made to leave, but when he had opened the door halfway, he stopped, unnerved by what he saw.

Jeff Levinson, his hands filthy, was hard at work under the hood of a Honda Civic. As he worked, he was smiling.

And talking to a complete stranger.

The detectives rendezvoused with the squad cars on the road a hundred feet from the entrance to the farm. Dumas had received word while they were en route that a search warrant had been issued, but they would need to move fast to locate Phil Walters and ensure his safety. After a quick consultation, they opted to split into teams to hit as many buildings at once as possible. The officers would start with the houses while Montufar and Dumas checked out the other buildings.

Returning to their cars, they drove up the lane. One of the squad cars pulled over at the first house, a rather plain-looking structure that almost had an abandoned feel to it. Farther up the road, a much nicer house sat atop a hill. Another of the squads pulled over there. Montufar and Dumas continued past a third house, where the next squad stopped. Ahead, a collection of outbuildings loomed, and Dumas directed Montufar to make for the largest of these, built like a garage on steroids, several of its bay doors standing open as though to swallow up anything that happened by.

To minimize noise, Montufar had dropped her speed below the tooth-jarring pace she had up till now been setting. When she finally pulled the car to a stop, they quietly exited the vehicle and moved in for a look. Five cars—some clearly in the process of disassembly and none with license plates—were inside. An abundance of tools and shelves lined the walls and occupied cluttered work benches. On the left and the right, doors exited to the outside. A door at the back seemed to lead to another enclosed space. Other than themselves, only two people were present: both male, one black, one Hispanic. The former was working on the engine of a Honda Civic, the other was at a workbench with his back to them. Dumas nodded toward the man working on the Civic. The detectives carefully approached him. He didn't seem to notice until they were right beside him. Then he looked up, surprised, flashed them a winning smile, and said, "Hi there."

"Hello," Dumas replied. "Busy?"

"Nah, just relaxing. I enjoy tinkering." He turned back to his tools.

"Are all these your cars?"

"No, they're not mine. I just get to work on them when I feel like it."

Montufar nudged Dumas and nodded toward the Hispanic man, who had apparently heard them talking and was now staring at them, wide-eyed.

In a friendly fashion, Dumas asked, "What's your name?"

"Jeff. What's yours?"

"Eric. This is Corina."

"Pleased to meet you. I'd shake your hands, but mine are pretty dirty."

"That's okay. Who's your friend over there?"

"Oh, that's Esteban. Hey, Esteban! Come on over. This is Eric and Corina."

Esteban continued to stare as if frozen.

"I guess he's shy," Jeff told them confidentially.

"So who does own the cars?" Dumas asked.

Confusion flickered across Jeff's features. "I'm not quite sure. I'm not feeling quite right today. I got hurt, I think."

"Oh?"

"That's the funny thing. I don't remember. Someone told me I was beat up."

"Beat up?" Montufar asked, surprised.

Jeff shrugged. "Like I said, I don't remember. Maybe I got a concussion. Can't have been too bad, though, 'cause here I am, working on cars like always."

"When did it happen?" she asked.

He touched a bruise shadowing his cheek and winced. "Today, I guess. My face hurt for a while. It's not so bad now." He turned away and resumed working on the engine.

Without warning, Esteban rushed out of the garage and vanished around the side of the building. Montufar started after him.

"Careful," Dumas warned.

"I won't get any closer to him," she assured him. "I'll just see where he's going."

Dumas didn't like it, but he couldn't stop her, so he turned his attention back to Jeff. "Who beat you up, Jeff?"

Jeff shook his head. "I don't remember. I just want to work on this car here."

Whatever had happened, Dumas suspected, it had been pretty traumatic. Jeff didn't seem to be quite right in the head, which could either have been the result of a concussion or some other type of brain trauma. Could even be psychological. The evidence of the partially disassembled cars, none of which had license plates, made it clear to Dumas that they'd hit pay dirt. He had no doubt that once they ran the VINs, every one of these vehicles would show up as stolen. Which likely was why Walters and Parsons had ended up here: Parsons may have hoped to swap Walters' car for another one.

"I'm going to have a look around," he told Jeff.

"Yeah, go ahead. It's a fun place."

*Undoubtedly*, Dumas thought. He took out his cell phone and went to the front of the Civic, where he photographed the VIN plate. He then made the rounds of the other cars, taking photos of each to record their conditions and VINs. Last, he investigated the workbenches, shelves, and cabinets, but found nothing out of the ordinary for an auto shop. Except that there was no stock of replacement parts.

As he finished his search and began to wonder where Corina was, he thought he heard a door close. He turned quickly to find Jeff still occupied with the Civic. Nobody else was near. "Was anyone else in here?" he asked Jeff.

"Esteban was over there, but he left."

"Just him?"

"As far as I know. But there are usually some other guys around, too." He straightened and looked around. A certain clarity came into his eyes, as though he were becoming focused for the first time that day. Now Dumas wondered if he were suffering only from the effects of a beating or of something even more insidious, like drugs or alcohol. Or both. "Huh. That's funny. I haven't seen them today." He leaned into the engine compartment again.

Dumas pointed to the back. "Where's that door go?"

"Office."

"Anybody in there?"

Jeff shrugged. "Maybe. I haven't been back there today."

Instantly Dumas made for the office. He listened at the door but heard only silence. Standing to one side, his gun drawn, he threw the door open. Nothing happened.

Dumas moved into the office. A blizzard of loose paper covered the floor. A toppled chair and chaotic pile of spilled repair manuals half-concealed a leg protruding from behind the desk. Dumas shuffled through the mess to find Morgan Parsons lying face down, a gaping wound in the back of his head, blood pooling around his body.

Montufar followed Esteban out of the garage, peering around the edge of the huge door to make sure he wasn't waiting for her. He wasn't. Instead, he was making tracks for a smaller building about two hundred feet away, oblivious to the fact that he was being followed. She drew her gun just in case and followed. She had only covered half the distance to the building when he vanished inside. A moment later she heard a car revving, a squeal of tires, and a white Chevy truck barreled around the corner of the building straight toward her.

Pivoting, Montufar leaped to the side of the lane. The truck roared by, its driver apparently intent on escape rather than mayhem. Montufar activated her lapel microphone and relayed, "Suspect outbound in a white pickup." She watched it go.

"I have him," one of the officers reported. "He's not stopping. I'm in pursuit."

Montufar turned her attention to the building from which the truck had come. It was unlikely that anyone was there; after all, Esteban would surely have raised the alarm. Anyone present would have fled at the first sign of the police, unless they were unbelievably cocky or completely dense. Nevertheless, she hurried to it, entering the same way Esteban had.

The building was dimly lit by light coming through the open opposite bay door and occupied by three cars. The vehicles still bore their license plates, so Montufar guessed they were the property of whoever lived or worked here. Presumably the truck driven by the escaping suspect was one of them. Otherwise, the building was largely empty.

Using her cell phone camera, Montufar took photos of the license plates, then circled the perimeter, alert for anything of interest. A few gardening tools hung on one wall, and two partially-full trash cans stood near the open bay door. Just outside, some crushed cigarette butts littered the earth.

A car door closed somewhere behind her. She spun about as an engine roared to life and one of the vehicles, a light gray BMW, accelerated toward the bay door. She jumped out of its unswerving path. *Now I've been almost run over twice in ten minutes*, she thought, but before she could carry her observation further she was stunned to see a pale Phil Walters in the driver's seat. In the passenger's seat, a gun clearly visible in his hand, a thin man of about sixty shot her a look of contempt.

Whoever he was, Montufar thought, he was in serious trouble. She activated her lapel microphone again. "Armed suspect outbound in a gray BMW. Phil Walters is driving. Looks like he's a hostage."

The remaining officers all responded.

Seconds later, she heard a clash of metal, distant shouting, and a single shot.

# Chapter 16

A plate of lukewarm ravioli on the table before him, the blue-eyed man stared at the tines on his still-unused fork. Its form held his attention for a time, although he couldn't say why. An ordinary utensil, neither ornate nor made of silver, it nevertheless seemed to embody elegance, simplicity. Its sleek curvature reminded him of...

*No.*

He stabbed at the ravioli, picked one up, thrust it into his mouth. He wasn't hungry. He seldom was, or perhaps he seldom noticed hunger when it came. The food wasn't particularly good, either, merely something from a can, tasting of metal and manufacturing. But it was a staple of his diet of late. He didn't know why. He just always seemed to lay in a supply of the stuff. Maybe because it was easy to make and easy to swallow.

Deep inside, though, he knew the real reason.

That day, it hadn't come from a can. That day, it had been served by an angel and tasted like heaven. But if she had been an angel, why on that day had he lost his soul?

The blue-eyed man threw the pan across the room. It hit the wall, spattering sauce. As the thick red liquid ran down the wall to pool on the floor, he saw instead blood, innocent blood, spilled by his own hand.

⌒

As Montufar's voice came over the wire, the situation became clearer to Dumas. For an as-yet unfathomable reason, Walters had been in this office with Parsons and a third person, who was now fleeing the scene via Walters' car. Presumably the third person was also responsible for killing Parsons. Dumas figured that he must have escaped with Walters while the detectives were assessing the situation.

After taking a few initial photos with his cell phone camera, Dumas turned to leave, only to find Jeff standing in the doorway. White-faced and wide-eyed, he stared at Parsons' leg, the only part of the body he could see from that vantage point.

"What's going on?" he asked.

"You'd better stay outside," Dumas told him. "A man was killed in here."

"Killed? Another one?"

That was the last thing Dumas expected to hear, even from the distracted Jeff. "What do you mean?"

"Someone else was killed today. I think."

"Who?" Dumas rapped out, then realized he may have frightened his best witness into speechlessness.

But Jeff shook his head. "Doesn't make sense, though. Why would people be killed here? Who is that, anyway?" He moved forward. Dumas put out a warding hand, but Jeff sidestepped him and peered over the desk. His breath caught in a gasp and he began to edge backward toward the door.

"It's okay," Dumas said. "I'll take care of it."

"Oh, no." Jeff slowly sank to his knees. "No, no."

Dumas tried to lift him to his feet, but the man was dead weight, limp and unmovable.

"I don't remember that," Jeff muttered. "I don't want to remember that." He shuddered.

Dumas felt a wave of exasperation engulf him, but it receded at the sheer horror in Jeff's face. Tucking a supporting arm under Jeff's shoulders, he hauled him up, turned him around, and led him out of the office. "Come on," he said encouragingly. "If you're lucky, a woman I know can get you a room at Spring Grove."

⌒

Meanwhile, behind the wheel of a purring BMW, Phil Walters no longer cared that a gun was trained at his head. This would end, he decided, and it would end now. No book was worth getting killed for. It was just a question of how to end it.

He glanced over at his passenger. Duke. What the hell kind of nickname was that, anyway? Did he like the idea of being a John Wayne two-bit evil twin? But whatever the reason, and whatever he was packing, he'd made a mistake by putting Walters in the driver's seat. Being in control of the vehicle gave him far more control over the situation than Duke must have realized, and with police cars converging up ahead to block his path, by God he was going to use it.

He'd let himself get snatched too easily; he saw that now. Once Duke had discovered that they were no longer alone, he'd quietly closed the door and pulled a gun from a hidden holster. "Nose to the wall."

It seemed prudent to cooperate, so Walters did. A moment later, he heard a sickening thud. Out of the corner of his eye he saw Parsons slide down the wall. Not about to stand idly by while he was attacked, Walters turned, ready to fight. Duke stood over Parson's fallen body, something large and metallic in his hand. It was too large to be his gun, but he dropped the object before Walters could identify what it was.

For a moment, fear had overtaken Walters, but he fought it down. "Why did you do that?" he demanded. "He didn't do anything!"

Duke looked down at his handiwork, then shrugged as though he'd lost interest. "I can't take both of you with me. And the idiot deserved it." Waving Walters to the door, he continued, "Now pay attention. We're going out this door, turning left, and exiting through the nearest side door. Make a noise and you'll end up like him. After we leave here we're going to go to the next building and get in the BMW there. You're going to drive. You will drive safely and legally, and follow my instructions to the letter. Understood?"

Although he didn't want to give Duke the satisfaction, Walters nodded. Eventually an escape opportunity would arise; all he had to do was to bide his time.

Duke waved him to the door. "Crack the door and look out. There are two men out there. Don't open the door until they are both turned away. And if you want to stay alive, stay quiet."

Walters did as instructed. He quickly spotted the two men and was surprised to see that one was Eric Dumas. So the police were on the scene. Heartened, he waited until Dumas was examining something on the far side of the garage, then he opened the door and quietly moved out. Along the way they passed the workbench where Esteban had previously been occupied, and he saw the gun lying there. But before he could make a move, Duke swept it up and motioned toward the door.

They left the building, crossed to the next one, and entered. Walters was again surprised, this time to find Corina Montufar examining something near the open bay door. Duke indicated the BWM they were to use. The vehicle was unlocked. He got in, closing the door as quietly as possible, but Montufar's sharp ears picked up the sound. She turned.

Good.

"Go," Duke snapped.

Walters started the engine and pulled out of the garage, hoping more police would be up ahead. Making for the road, they crested a small hill to find three squad cars moving in to block their exit. Walters glanced at Duke, but Duke's attention was taken up by the cruisers, his expression one of disgust rather than fear. "Floor it," he said. "Go around their left flank."

Walters immediately saw was he was trying to do. Two of the squads were moving in from the left, while the other was angled only slightly left. The ground on the left was more level, too, while on the right the land rose sharply. He cut right, barreling up the slope on a collision course with the police.

"Left, you moron!" Duke snapped, but they were committed to the course now. The car tilted drunkenly, throwing Walters against the door. The gun still in his right hand, Duke braced his left palm against Walters' shoulder to keep from falling into him. Their bodies strained against the seat belts. Walters felt like he was being torn in two.

The closer of the squad cars made an almost impossible turn to come alongside the Beemer. Their outside mirrors locked, and the

BMW's was torn off with a piercing shriek. The other squad fell into line behind, ramming its prey. Air bags exploded from concealment. Walters realized he was standing on the brake pedal, with no memory of having depressed it.

The air was full of dust and a burning smell. Someone was cursing, but he didn't understand their words. Something moved in front of him, blocking his path. It took a moment for him to recognize it as the third squad car.

He looked at his passenger. Red-faced, Duke pointed the gun at Walters' forehead and snarled something incomprehensible.

He heard an explosion.

He felt nothing.

Duke's eyes went wide; the gun dropped nervelessly from his hand. Slowly he fell into Walters' side. Walters put the gear in park and set the parking brake as though it were the most natural thing to do. He felt as though he had just run a thousand-mile race and collapsed across the steering wheel. From somewhere, blood seeped onto his shirt sleeve. He stared at the spreading stain, his mind a blank save for one thought:

*Penny's going to have a fit when she sees this.*

⤳

"If this is what Howard County is coming to," Peller said, "I'm not sure I want to come back from vacation."

Dumas and Montufar had called him from the station after they finished up the key paperwork on the day's events. Now he was on speaker phone at Montufar's desk. The rest of the office was quiet, with only a couple other detectives remaining at their desks.

"This is what happens when you take a vacation," Dumas told him. "The place falls apart."

"So Parsons is dead, John a.k.a. Duke Calvert is dead, Calvert's partners in crime have scattered to the four winds, and Jeff Doe is in the psychiatric ward, babbling incoherently. Well. At least our writer friend escaped with only minor injuries. And the car theft business will be a tad less lucrative for a week or two."

"There is that. We also have news on the other matter."

Peller said nothing. Montufar nodded for Dumas to continue.

"We can't prove it yet, but we're pretty sure Orion Speros was driving the truck. Corina found a witness who'd been missed, one Randall Sommers, a relative of the couple that owned the farm. He was out doing chores when the accident occurred and saw the truck leaving the scene. He picked Speros from a group of photographs as the most likely suspect."

Still Peller kept his silence. Dumas wasn't sure what to make of it.

"Rick?" Montufar asked.

"Still here. Just trying to work through all this."

"I'm afraid it gets harder," she told him.

"There's more?"

"This is based on a rat's nest of circumstantial evidence and guesswork, but we don't think it was an accident. We think Speros may have been hired help. Worse, we think the job went wrong. He wasn't after Sandra. Somehow, he mistook her car for the one he really wanted."

"Are you saying..."

They waited, looking into each other's eyes. Dumas thought he saw some fragment of Peller's pain reflected there and was sure Montufar saw the same in him.

"Why do you think that?" Peller finally asked.

Montufar hesitated, so Dumas answered. "Sommers said the driver of the truck looked angry as he sped off. Speros was at ease, even jovial, when I questioned him about Parsons, but he nearly exploded when I brought up Sandra's death. One minute he was as playful as a kitten, the next he was a fire-breathing dragon. It didn't make any sense until Corina told me what Sommers had said."

"I see," Peller replied. "But if you're right, even if we can nail Speros, how do we identify his employer?"

"We'll have to break him," Dumas said, although he didn't relish the prospect.

"From what you've said," Montufar warned him, "he's not likely to break without killing someone else."

"Neither of you is to put yourselves in danger on account of this," Peller said sternly. "I mean that."

"Don't worry, boss," Dumas said. "I'm not letting Corina anywhere near him, and I won't go near him without plenty of backup."

Peller actually laughed at that.

"What?"

"Male protective instincts don't generally register with her."

Montufar smiled at the desktop.

"I think," Dumas said with a grin, "that I can persuade her in this instance."

∿

After relaying Phil Walters' call for aid, Penny Lowell's steps were dogged by the sort of fear she had felt as a child watching B horror movies. Fangy monsters awaited her around every corner, behind every closed door. The text Walters had sent watered the fear Detective Dumas had planted. When she called Dumas, she'd barely been able to relate the message without choking.

For the next hour, the minutes crept by—one hour, two, and still no word. She turned to trivial work in an effort to distract herself—vacuuming, sorting laundry, loading the dishwasher—but every attempt failed. Inevitably, she found herself seized by waking nightmares: Phil lying broken on the ground, Phil shot and dying, Phil crying her name in vain.

Finally the phone rang. Afraid of what she would hear, she hesitated to answer. As the answering machine began to pick up, she snatched up the receiver and faltered, "Hello?"

Dumas' voice came calmly from the ether. "Penny," he said, "Good news. Phil's okay."

The emotion rushing into her voice throttled her.

"Penny?" Dumas asked.

"Yes. I'm here. Thank God." Sudden tears overwhelmed her and she sank into a chair.

"He got a bit shook up, but nothing serious. We sent him to Howard County General just to be safe. Word is he'll be released within an hour. Are you okay to drive? He'd like you to take him home if so."

"I'll be there," she said. "Tell him I'll be there."

"I will. Oh, he wants you to bring him a change of clothes. I guess he's wearing a hospital gown."

Wasting no time, she gathered up fresh clothing for him, drove to the hospital, and hurried to the emergency room, oblivious to the collection of sick and injured awaiting triage and treatment. She was directed to Walters' bedside, where she fought down the urge to throw herself onto him.

He got up, though, and embraced her. "You're a sight for sore eyes," he said into her hair.

"My God, Phil, what happened to you?"

"That's a long story. Right now I just want to go home." He pulled the curtain shut and reached for the items she had brought.

"Where are the clothes you were wearing when you came in?" Penny asked, searching in vain for the usual white bag that held a patient's belongings until he was released. Finding none, she at last ventured out to find a passing nurse. "I'm looking for the clothes Mr. Walters was wearing when he was admitted, but I can't find them. Do you know where they might happen to be?"

"Oh," said the nurse, "oh. We're holding them until the police say we can destroy them."

Bewildered, Penny said, "Destroy them?"

"Yes," the nurse explained. "They were covered in blood. We need to know if the police want them for evidence. They're ruined, either way."

Shaken, Penny returned to the now-dressed Phil. "The nurse says your clothes were covered in blood."

He looked at her, his eyes wide and staring. "Yes. They were."

"But you're all right."

"Yes. Yes, I am." He regarded his clean sleeve intently. "It was his blood."

"His blood? Whose?"

Abruptly he sat down on the bed. "The guy who tried to kill me. He's dead now." He stood again. "Please, Penny. Take me home."

⟿

In Colorado, under Belinda's serene supervision, evening tea had become a comforting tradition. With the children in bed, the adults gathered around the kitchen table, hands cradling warm mugs. Small talk about mundane events of the day gave way to a restful silence.

Tonight a gentle, lulling rain pattered on the roof and windows. The homely sounds of the kettle boiling and cups rattling as Belinda brewed and served the tea enwrapped them all in a pleasant warmth. Unfortunately, Peller knew, sooner or later he would have to disturb the coziness, and it might as well be sooner.

"I realized something the other day about the accident and asked my colleagues back home to check it out." He exhaled heavily, not sure how to continue.

Jason, not looking at him, said, "They found out something."

"Yes. Possibly. Hard evidence is lacking, but they think they know who the other driver was."

Belinda took her husband's hand in her right hand and her father-in-law's in her left.

"This is going to be hard to hear," Peller continued.

Jason nodded, still not looking at him.

"They think it wasn't entirely an accident. The other driver may have been trying to kill someone, although Mom almost certainly wasn't his intended victim. He may have mistaken her car for his real target. There's also a possibility that he was a hired killer. If so, someone else is involved, someone we still don't know anything about."

"Dear God," Belinda whispered, and Jason squeezed his eyes shut.

"But the case has been reopened," Peller went on. "We now know the truck was stolen, and there's no statute of limitations on auto theft. Moreover, if it wasn't an accident, well, the other driver can be charged with voluntary manslaughter or murder."

Jason raised his head at last and looked from his wife to his father. Peller wanted to turn away from the pain in his son's eyes but couldn't. "I don't know how you can stand your job," Jason said. "Any good news you get is always tainted, isn't it?"

Feeling a hundred years old, Peller answered, "That's often the case. Police see the dark side of humanity every day. It can be hard to remember that most people are basically good. Your mother never forgot that, and she never let me forget it, either. I was blessed in having her to come home to at the end of every day."

Belinda's smile warmed him, but Jason looked even more troubled. "What it is, son?"

Shifting in his chair, Jason took a sip of tea before responding. "Dad, did you ever know anyone who looked like you, but with lighter hair?"

Wondering what had prompted the question, Peller nodded. "Jim Cowden. He was a lieutenant on the force when I was a sergeant. People used to confuse us all the time, if they didn't get a good look at us."

"What was he like?"

"Good man. Good cop. We all figured he'd be promoted to chief once Blake Compton retired." He scowled into his tea as though it held the answers to ancient puzzles. "But after Mom died, he went to pieces. He oversaw the investigation, of course, but the detectives working the case said he was in a fog. He couldn't keep details straight, couldn't even remember who was assigned to the case sometimes. One day about two weeks later, he didn't show up for work and didn't call in sick. Same thing the next day. The department sent a couple of officers to check on him. His car was there, but he was gone."

Now Peller tried to resort the pieces of the puzzle. At the time of Sandra's death, he'd been lost in his own pain. Later he'd tried to construct a plausible scenario from the scattered events but was unable, and eventually the incident faded into memory. He couldn't save Cowden from whatever demons had tormented him.

"Nobody ever heard from him again," he continued. "His checking and savings accounts had been closed. He'd withdrawn everything in cash. It was like he'd dropped off the earth. The usual attempts were made to locate him, but he had no next of kin, so finally the powers that be figured that if he wanted to vanish, he could. I don't know if the case was ever closed, but it went stone cold very quickly, and the department turned its attention to things it could do something about. For all we knew he could have been on a beach in the Caymans, or in a monastery in Kathmandu, or six feet under."

Belinda, still holding his hand, squeezed lightly. "What do you think happened?"

Peller thought he knew the what, but the why had eluded him for years. "I think he was reacting to my pain. In his mind it became imperative for him to resolve the case, but it wasn't to be. He drove himself crazy. One day he woke up and realized he had to escape. So he left."

"Did he know Mom?" Jason asked.

"He did. He didn't come to our house often, even though we invited him a number of times. I wouldn't say they were close, but you know how she was. If he had ever needed a friend, she would have been there for him."

Jason rotated his mug in his hands. It was one Belinda had picked up not long after their wedding, cheerfully glazed in a quilt pattern and bearing the quote: "This is the day which the Lord hath made; we will rejoice and be glad in it". He seemed to ponder it for a long while, as though searching the psalm for hidden meanings. Finally he asked, "Did he ever need a friend?"

The question hung between them, a heavy curtain behind which something ominous lurked. Peller wasn't sure he wanted to pull it back, wasn't sure he'd like what he found. But they had been silent too long. Whatever it was, it had to be confronted.

He didn't want to cause his son any more pain. Yet—

Choosing his words carefully, he said, "There were a few rumors. I didn't pay much attention."

"What kind of rumors?"

Peller shook his head. "Jason…"

"Please, Dad."

"Well. I'd heard it said he had a gambling problem. But it was only a rumor, and it had nothing to do with anything, so far as I could see."

"Would he have talked to Mom about it?"

The question made no sense to Peller. "What's this about?"

Jason's eyes wandered around the room as though searching for something but finding nothing. Finally he turned and faced his father. When he spoke, his voice was subdued. "I saw him at the house once, not long before we moved. He was talking to Mom and holding her hands. After he left, she seemed upset. She didn't know I'd seen them. I asked her if something was wrong, but she wouldn't talk to me about it."

Peller couldn't remember too many times when Sandra had been seriously upset, certainly none that he could connect with this story. "It's possible he might have confided in her," he said, doubting it even as he said it. "If he did, I probably wouldn't have heard about it. She would have respected his privacy."

"A gambling problem, though. That wouldn't have rattled her."

Peller had to agree with that. But there had been another rumor, one that could explain it: Cowden, it had been whispered, was a womanizer. Peller had always assumed that his reputation was at best an exaggeration; at worst, a lie. Cowden's success had made him a few enemies along the way, jealous people who would have gleefully watched him fall from the heights. Certainly, he'd never witnessed Cowden in any inappropriate behavior.

"Well, I wouldn't worry about it," he said. "We could speculate until doomsday about Jim Cowden and have no answers. But we don't have to speculate about your mother. We know her. She's worthy of our faith."

Jason took another drink of his tea. "I suppose you're right." He looked pensive for a moment longer, then relief transformed his features. "It's strange, but..." He looked behind him as though expecting to see someone there. "Suddenly I feel like she's right here with us, and the world has turned out right after all. Does that make any sense?"

Peller, too, thought he could feel Sandra by his side, holding his hand, smiling at the two of them. "She always could work magic," he said. "Yes, it makes perfect sense."

# Chapter 17

He wasn't quite sure how he'd ended up in the hospital, but that's where he woke, covered in antiseptic white sheets. It looked like a comfortable room, a modern sort of room designed to feel less like a hospital than a hotel, but it was nevertheless a hospital and he immediately wanted to escape.

He wasn't hurt. At least, he felt no pain, wasn't hooked up to an IV, and wasn't bandaged or stitched so far as he could tell. So what was he doing here?

When the nurse came in pushing a cart with a computer and other paraphernalia on it, he pulled himself up to sitting. Before he could ask her what had happened, she smiled warmly and asked how he was feeling. She was pretty, he thought, that round face and that dark hair peeking out from under her cap. He wondered if she had a man in her life and briefly hoped not.

"I'm okay," he said, returning the smile. "What's your name?"

"Penny. What's yours?"

"Jeff."

"Jeff what?"

With a wink, he replied, "Penny what?"

"Now don't play games with me, Jeff. Do you know where you are?

With a sigh, he leaned back. "It looks like a hospital."

"Spring Grove Hospital Center. Have you heard of it?"

He shook his head. "Why am I here?"

"You're here, Jeff..." She looked at her computer screen. "What's your last name, Jeff?"

"You don't know it?"

"Apparently not." She frowned at the computer as though very concerned that something so vital had gone astray.

He was sure she was putting on an act, but he answered anyway. There wasn't much point in not answering. "Levinson."

"Thank you." She typed it in. "So Jeff, you're here because something happened to you that left you very confused, according to the people who brought you in. But nobody knows what happened. Do you?"

Memory returned like a tidal wave crashing down on him. Orion Speros. Caroline Fisher. Death. He felt her unmoving body weighing him down, felt his own limbs grow sluggish as if they, too, yielded to death.

"Jeff?"

"I'm in a psychiatric hospital. Aren't I?"

"That's right. But don't worry. We're going to help you."

Levinson pulled the blankets closer around him. Shaking his head, he said, "No." He didn't doubt he likely needed help, but he couldn't tell a soul what had happened. Not only would he be incriminating himself, he'd be endangering Calvert's operation.

Unperturbed, the nurse repeated, "No?"

"I can deal with it on my own. I want to leave now."

The nurse shifted her position, revealing a man who hadn't been there a moment before. "I'm afraid," the man said in a husky bass, "you can't leave just yet. The last guy who ran out of a hospital on me got himself killed. I'm not going to let it happen again."

A flush of anger warmed Levinson's chill, but kept his voice steady. "Who are you?"

The man flashed a badge. "Detective Sergeant Eric Dumas, Howard County Police. The fellow I mentioned was a guy named Morgan Parsons. He was killed by your boss, John "Duke" Calvert. And you—" Dumas pulled up a chair, sat, and smiled like they were best buddies, "—are going to tell me everything you know about that farm."

∽

Friday, April eighth. *So little time left*, Peller thought as he finished an everything-topped bagel liberally smeared with vegetable cream cheese. The kids had left for school and Jason was on his way to work, leaving only himself and his daughter-in-law in the house.

Busy at her laptop, Belinda was already looking frustrated. The job market must still be as dreary as ever. Peller picked up his coffee cup and polished off the dregs. Outside, it looked like another nice day, sunny with a light breeze.

Belinda shook her head and pushed back from the table.

"I'd like to walk down to the park again," Peller said. "Care to join me?"

"I'd love to, but I really shouldn't stop working on this."

He gave her what he thought was his most cajoling smile. "It'll keep for an hour."

She glanced at him, gave the screen a disgusted frown, then firmly closed the computer. Standing up, she said, "You're right. Let's go."

Donning jackets, they set out into the bright morning. Belinda drew in a deep breath of the cool air and Peller found himself doing the same. Last night he had felt as though he were trapped in an airtight space, his spirit entombed in memory.

Belinda waved to someone passing in a car. "That's Heather Davis," she said. "She lives a couple doors down. We're both in the church's women's auxiliary." She sighed. "I wish I could convince Jason to come with me more often. Ever since—" she broke off, searching for words, then finally said, "I think he has too much to think about lately. His mom's death, and now this new development."

"And you losing your job," Peller suggested.

"Yes, me losing my job," she agreed. "It's a lot to take in at once."

They reached the park. On the playground, a woman pushed her daughter in a swing; the little girl's blonde ponytail soared out behind her. On the path ahead of them, a young man in sweats was running; on a bench near the pond an elderly black man was absorbed in a book. Peller thought of his neighbor Jerry Souter, the World War II veteran, and wondered how he was doing.

"This trip hasn't been what you expected," Belinda said. "Has it?"

"I'm not sure what I expected."

"Not this, though."

*Not this*, he silently agreed. The previous day's revelations had driven Peller not towards resolution but frustration. With old questions answered, new ones pushed forward to take their place like eager children jostling for a glimpse of the lions at the zoo. Whom had Speros meant to kill? Who had paid him to kill? Why had the job gone so horribly wrong?

"Life tends to surprise us," he said.

"That's for sure. A month ago I certainly hadn't expected to be where I am now. Every day I hit a point where I'm wondering why my resume isn't good enough, why my experience isn't good enough, why I'm not good enough. Some days it happens faster than others."

Peller put his arm around her shoulders. "It's the economy," he said reassuringly. "It's not you."

"I know. But sometimes I can't help feeling that it's me."

They came to the playground. Peller motioned to a bench and they sat. "We like to think we're in control, I guess," he said. "But there are always factors beyond our control. Sandra was in control of her vehicle, but that didn't prevent her death. Why did she have to be there at just that moment? I don't know."

"From what you've told us, it sounds like if it hadn't been her, it would have been someone else."

Peller nodded. Speros had been out to kill someone. Not Sandra, but someone. He would have done it one way or another.

"So maybe she died to save someone else."

The thought startled him. On the face of it, it couldn't be true. It wasn't as though Sandra had known Speros was lying in wait. She'd just been on her way to an event. But even if it was true, even if there was some grand design that required her death, why did it have to be her? Why couldn't some other lamb have been led to the slaughter?

*Would the death of another have been any less tragic?* she asked silently.

*For us*, he replied.

"Now you're brooding," Belinda told him.

Straightening, he smiled at her. "Old habit. Probably an occupational hazard."

"Oh, so all detectives end up brooding their days away?"

Peller laughed. "Sadly, yes. Every last one of us is eventually cooked hard-boiled."

She arched a maternal eyebrow.

"Well, okay, maybe not all of us. Eric Dumas might escape that fate."

"Does it bother you, what I said?"

"No, but I'm bothered by my own reactions, sometimes. What worries me most is what happens if we do find the person responsible."

"You're a good man, Rick. Whatever happens, you'll do the right thing."

The ponytailed girl on the swing suddenly jumped down and pointed upward, chattering excitedly. Peller looked up.

Two great birds were riding the thermals, pirouetting on wingtips in an elaborate dance. Peller wasn't sure what he was seeing, but he thought they might have a raptor look about them. He stood, and watched, and felt his eyes refreshed, his heart lightened.

At his shoulder, Belinda said, "Aren't they beautiful? The hawks start to arrive in March, in April they nest, and in the fall they head south with the youngsters. Some will return, some will not. The wheel turns."

Overhead, the hawks soared away; the little girl chased after them as though she were their human fledgling. Her mother followed, calling her name. Only the wind stirred the swings. Belinda spoke again. "Trust God. Like Sandra said."

He had no other plan. "I will if you will."

"Deal."

"Should we go back?"

Shaking her head, Belinda pointed to the playground. "If I can fit on one of those swings, will you push?"

"You're a little bigger than Susie," he laughed. "It might look strange."

"Nobody's here to see." With a wink, Belinda took his hand and tugged. "Let's give it a try."

It turned out to be more fun than he would have thought.

⌒

Unfortunately, Levinson proved smarter and harder to intimidate than Parsons. Dumas figured the search of the farm would likely uncover useful information, but it would be better to get the story straight from the horse's mouth. Levinson, though, knew the temper of the sea in which he was adrift, and knew better than to navigate it on his own. He called an attorney, one Charles David Kirby III, a stern, sharply-dressed black man who somehow gave the illusion of being able to simultaneously keep one watchful eye on his client and one wary eye on the detective. Dumas was impressed, if miffed.

"It's a foregone conclusion that once we go through the computers and papers at the farm," Dumas was saying, trying to sound congenial, "that your name will come up in more than a few incriminating ways. We already know stolen vehicles were processed there. What else transpired on those premises, I wonder?"

They were still in the hospital room, Levinson still abed, but he looked confident now, as though he hadn't a care in the world. "In my house, most of what transpired involved me and my girlfriend. That would make interesting reading, I guess. What Duke was up to, that was his business."

Dumas had told Levinson of Calvert's death earlier, hoping for a reaction. He'd gotten none. "I'm sure it was your business, too. So what was your role?"

"My client is not answering that question," Kirby said, "or any other that has potential to incriminate him."

Levinson smiled at the ceiling.

Dumas stood and walked to the window. Looking out over the parking lot, he wondered what the team was uncovering. This job might be easier if he had some concrete information to hand. Unfortunately, he had to work without that particular net. Still looking out, he said, "Okay. How about a question that shouldn't incriminate you?"

"Do you have any of those?"

Dumas could hear him grinning. "Oh, sure." Turning, the detective leaned casually on the window sill, arms crossed over his chest. "Who beat you up, and why?"

The smile turned sickly.

"At least help me out to that extent. You might be a crook, but I don't think you're a violent guy. How about we catch the slimeball who did this to you?"

Kirby's expression said he didn't like where this was going, but before he could object, Levinson said, almost whispered, "He's uncatchable, I think."

Dumas came back to the bedside. "You're afraid of him."

Levinson nodded without looking up.

Dumas' stomach did a backflip. Who could induce fear in someone as confident as Levinson? Who would anyone label uncatchable? "Orion Speros?"

The other closed his eyes tight, as though trying to shut out the world.

Dumas sank into his chair, his mind racing. Speros seemed to be in the middle of everything: Sandra's death, the assault on Morgan Parsons, and now the assault on Levinson.

"How do you know Speros?" Dumas asked.

"One moment," Kirby interrupted. "Who is this Orion Speros?"

Eyeing the lawyer, Dumas decided to keep it simple. "A real scary guy with a knack for escaping prosecution."

"You think my client has information about him?"

"That's what I'd like to find out, if you'll let me."

Regarding Dumas without expression, Kirby let the request hang for a full ten seconds before replying, "How badly do you want this Speros?"

"They want him bad," Levinson said, still not looking up. "He killed a cop's wife."

Dumas wanted to slap him. Then he wanted to slap himself for giving Kirby a glimpse of his cards.

"Could I have a moment alone with my client, Sergeant?"

Irritated, Dumas stood and left the room. He knew where this was headed but couldn't see any way out. His mind a roiling mass of disconnected thoughts and emotions, he wandered blindly past the nurse's station and out to the family lounge beyond the ward. Pacing back and forth, a good ten minutes passed before he was settled enough to think clearly. Unfortunately, he could see only one course of action. He pulled out his cell phone and called Captain Morris.

"We're going to need someone from the State's Attorney down here," he told her.

"What's up?"

"Levinson knows about Sandra's death. He confirmed it was Speros."

"God in heaven. He wants to deal?"

"I expect so. He's having a heart-to-heart with his lawyer right now."

"What do you think? Is it worth it?"

Dumas didn't want the weight of that decision on his shoulders, but he sure had an opinion. "No."

Morris didn't answer right away.

He wondered if she needed an explanation, although he thought it was perfectly obvious. How could Levinson possibly have known what Speros had done?

"Calvert's dead," Morris said, "and his operation died with him, whether Levinson goes to jail or not. If he could help us nail Sandra's killer..."

"He's part of it, Whitney. He has to be. We can't give him a get out of jail free card. Not on this."

"He didn't kill Sandra."

"How do you know?"

Morris' voice was taut. "Eric, if Speros was driving the truck..."

"Somebody hired him to do it. Levinson's a likely suspect."

"Why?"

Dumas didn't have an answer for that, but he was certain of it. Levinson must have hired Speros to kill someone—not Sandra, but someone.

When he didn't answer, Morris said, "Okay, Eric. Your concern is noted. I'll get someone down there as soon as possible."

Dumas pocketed his phone and rubbed his aching temples. He knew they had to go through the motions, but it felt like they were about to bargain with the devil. He wished Montufar were here. She was better than he was at working through these sorts of tangles. He almost called her, but he knew she was busy at Calvert's farm and didn't want to interrupt her work there.

*Trust your intuition*, he told himself. *Once Jeff Levinson's tale is told, we'll know where we stand.*

⤳

After their sojourn in the park, Belinda and Peller returned to the house. Re-energized, Belinda settled in on the sofa with her laptop for more job searching. Peller snagged a Louis L'Amour western from Jason's books and leaned back in a recliner that must have set the younger Pellers back a pretty penny. He was deep in Sackett territory when Belinda gave a pleased squeal. Thinking she had found a good opportunity, he looked up and asked, "Hear from somebody?"

"Jason's coming home early!"

It struck Peller that his reason for doing so could be good or bad. "What for?"

"He wants to take us out for dinner."

That was more hopeful than not, Peller thought. "Sounds good. Where are we going?"

"He wants me to pick. Typical." She gave the computer an exasperated look. "Now I have to think about that instead of getting anything useful done."

Grinning, Peller said, "You make it sound like such a chore."

"Trying to please him, the kids, and his father? You have no idea. Fortunately, I went through the same exercise a week ago. My browser remembers what I looked at even if I don't."

Peller watched her typing, amused by her intensity. He couldn't imagine putting that much effort into a restaurant search. Back home, he patronized the same few eateries over and over. But then, he usually was either on his own or, at most, with the same few colleagues.

Then another thought crept up on him. He puzzled over it, not sure what it had to do with anything, but it nagged at him like a small child begging for candy. As much as he tried to ignore it, it pressed itself upon him, refusing to yield.

"I'll leave you to that," he told Belinda. "I need to make a phone call."

〰

After Captain Morris's briefing, the Howard County State's Attorney's office dispatched a lawyer to Spring Grove Hospital Center to confer with Dumas and negotiate with Levinson's attorney. Dumas was concerned about cutting a deal with the attorney, and Captain Morris thought that sidestepping any arrangements was in their interest as well. Considering the evidence they'd gathered so far, Levinson was likely a key player in Calvert's organization. With Calvert dead, locking up Levinson would not only ensure the demise of the ring but would give certain politicians bragging rights come next election. It never hurt to give the powers that be a reason to smile for the cameras.

But convicting Speros of homicide would certainly make a splash. And finally resolving Sandra's death would wash away the bad taste lingering in everyone's mouths.

Lost in these thoughts, she jumped when her phone rang. "Captain Morris," she answered.

"Hi, Whitney. It's Rick."

"I heard a rumor you were on vacation, but I'm finding it hard to believe."

"I haven't been this relaxed in months," Peller told her.

"Glad to hear it. So why spoil the mood by calling me?"

"I'm curious about something. You remember when Jim Cowden disappeared."

It was clear from his voice that the words were a statement, not a question. "What about it?"

"What happened to his things?"

Morris picked up a pen and absently clicked it a few times as she searched her memory. "A couple of his friends on the force arranged for storage in case he returned. Once it was clear he wasn't going to be paying rent, his landlord wanted everything out pronto."

"So everything's still in storage?"

"Beats me. Maybe. As far as I know, nobody claimed any of it. I don't recall any close relatives. He'd been married once, but by the time I knew him he'd been divorced for some years. He never mentioned any children."

"Nothing would have been held as evidence, I suppose."

"Nope. There wasn't any sign of foul play, so there wasn't any cause. Why?"

"I'm wondering if he might have left a computer behind."

"A computer? What's this about, Rick?"

Peller didn't answer immediately. Morris gave him time. She didn't want to worry him, but the thought that his former obsession had taken on a new life and scampered off in some fantastic direction crossed her mind. Eventually she prompted, "So what about this computer?"

"It occurs to me he might have researched potential hideaways before he left. His computer might still have a record of such a search."

Morris tried to recall any details of the incident, but the passage of time had erased most of her memories of the event. Nothing in particular stood out. Cowden had disappeared, all attempts to locate him had failed, and finally they had moved on to the task at hand. "Someone would have checked that," she said, but she didn't feel as confident as she hoped she sounded. "They went through everything they could find. Emails, financial information, everything. Nothing ever turned up."

Peller started to say something, but Morris cut him off. "Besides, Rick, if he wanted to run away, it's really none of our business."

"That depends on what he was running from."

"Meaning?"

"I don't know yet. But I've learned that something happened between him and Sandra a few months before she died. Something that upset her. It may be nothing, but I have a feeling there's some connection."

"He didn't kill her, Rick. Orion Speros killed her." In the silence that followed, she added, "Jeff Levinson let slip that he knows about it."

"Our Jeff Doe?"

"That's him. He started remembering things."

There was a moment of dead air on the line, then Peller continued, "Even so, Jim's disappearance is odd."

The captain suddenly felt a mad urge to run screaming from her office, or perhaps simply to retire. Her best officers seemed to be going nuts, along with the rest of the world.

"Okay, I know how it sounds," Peller continued. "I can't explain it. I just have a feeling that whatever happened between them somehow played into her death, and that's why he vanished."

"For God's sake, Rick, everyone who knew her felt the loss!" Morris exploded. "I hate to be so blunt, but you weren't the only one who was devastated. I couldn't sleep for a week. My husband was about ready to put me on sedatives."

She heard Peller's breathing, steady, measured. She didn't know if it meant he was angry or calm. When he spoke, it was in the subdued voice of a boy who'd been wrongly scolded and felt compelled to point out the obvious to his mother: "But only Jim ran away."

She couldn't argue with that. "Fine. I'll find out if his effects are still in storage. If so, I'll see if a computer is among them. But you have to promise me something in return."

"Name it."

"Actually take a vacation during what's left of your vacation."

He laughed. "I will. Thank you, Whitney."

She said goodbye and hung up, then considered Jim Cowden's unexplained disappearance. At the time they had simply assumed that grief had somehow sparked his flight. But the two events didn't connect properly.

Why would Cowden have felt such grief at the death of another man's wife, even though she was his friend? At the time nobody had questioned it, but now it didn't make any sense at all. Simple grief couldn't account for it. Cowden's disappearance was incomprehensible without some intimate connection to Sandra's death.

After so much time, she wondered whether they could even make the right connections.

# Chapter 18

A cool, clear morning gave way to a cool, cloud-flecked afternoon. Once upon a time, the blue-eyed man would have thought it a good day for yard work, but now he had no yard to speak of, only the wild land surrounding the run-down cabin, and on such days he had no desire to go outside. Sometimes he would sit in the Bentwood rocker on the front porch and stare at nothing, but not to enjoy the weather or the forest or the wildlife. To be honest, he wasn't sure why he sat there, although he suspected he simply didn't wish to hide anymore. Possibly someday someone would come looking for him, and when they did he would be there, rocking, waiting, offering no resistance.

He had thought about this a lot recently. Were he found, it would have to play out in one of two ways. They might come to arrest him, in which case he would have to feign resistance. He would have to fire on them, giving them cause to return fire and kill him. This was the more likely scenario, but he hoped it wouldn't come to that.

The other scenario, the one to be desired, the only one in which he could truly find release, also culminated in his death: his life would have to be taken in revenge by a man he had once called friend. Only so could justice be served. Only so could he atone for his sins.

Something deep within him whispered something about twisted logic.

He barely heard and paid it no mind.

⌇

Mark Fuller, attorney with the Howard County State's Attorney's office, proved an interesting adversary for Charles David Kirby III, Dumas thought. Kirby looked like an aristocrat, but Fuller looked more like an NBA player: tall and fit, with an intensity about him that in another man might have been unfriendly. His skin was ebony-dark, his eyes a deep brown that commanded attention. Dumas thought that juries might find Fuller's arguments persuasive by virtue of the man's sheer stage presence. He introduced himself to Kirby and Levinson as though they were meeting in a sports bar to armchair quarterback a game, although they were actually seated around Levinson's hospital bed.

Fuller got down to business quickly. "Your client is likely facing a host of charges related to auto theft. Frankly, our office is not inclined to negotiate. But presumably you think you have something substantial to offer."

Levinson, now the center of attention, looked relaxed and confident. Dumas reckoned that he probably felt secure in the knowledge that he had a powerful ally in Kirby.

Kirby parried. "Mr. Levinson has knowledge of a serious crime, an unsolved case in which a police officer's wife was killed. He can testify that the woman's death was the result of a willful act and can identify the person responsible. He is willing to provide complete details to the police in exchange for full immunity from prosecution for all crimes he may have committed to date."

Fuller put on a surprised expression. "Full immunity? You're suggesting your client has information about a murder. If he does, then I'd say it's his civic duty to share that information with the police."

"Voluntary manslaughter," Kirby corrected. "Mr. Levinson states that the man in question intended another victim."

Fuller glanced at Dumas, who nodded. Before coming into Levinson's room, they had already gone through the details as known to them, as well as the evidence, suppositions, and hunches that had led them to this point.

"The police are already aware of that."

Kirby didn't rise to the bait, although Levinson looked surprised. "Perhaps, but they lack evidence."

Fuller's eyebrows rose to their full height.

"They would have filed charges were they able," Kirby pointed out. "My client can provide testimony that will secure a conviction in the case."

"Even assuming he can provide sufficient evidence," Fuller asked, "why should we grant full immunity?"

"There is a possibility that his testimony could be self-incriminating."

Dumas felt every muscle in his body clench. He knew this would happen. He desperately wanted to call Fuller off. They didn't need Levinson's testimony. They had gotten this far without him. But he had agreed before coming in here to let Fuller do all the talking, so he restrained himself.

He needn't have worried. Fuller adopted a concerned look and shook his head. "If your client is implicated, we can't offer immunity. Suppose he tells us that he hired the killer? I'm sorry, Mr. Kirby, but we're going to need to know what we're being asked to agree to before we can make a decision."

Kirby nodded. "If you'll agree not to enter any of its contents into evidence without a grant of immunity, I can provide you with a synopsis. There is also another matter. My client can testify that the same person who killed the police officer's wife recently committed a murder, one of which the police are wholly ignorant."

Fuller didn't even blink. "He can lead us to the body?"

"He can provide the general location."

"Who was murdered?"

"A woman named Caroline Fisher. She was Mr. Levinson's girlfriend. It was her murder that caused him the mental distress that put him here."

Fuller looked to Dumas, but he couldn't help. This was the first he'd heard of Caroline Fisher, although he could well imagine that if Speros had killed Levinson's woman, it might have driven him over an emotional cliff.

"One further question," Fuller said. He looked pointedly at Levinson while he asked it. "Is Mr. Levinson looking for revenge?"

Kirby opened his mouth to speak, but Levinson sat forward and said furiously, "Yes, Mr. Levinson is looking for revenge! He's also looking for protection. Orion Speros is insane. He threatened to kill me. He'd do it. I don't want him to ever have a chance to get at me."

His attorney skewered him with an icy stare. Levinson retreated to his pillow.

"I can believe that," Fuller said sympathetically. "Mr. Kirby, once you provide me with that synopsis, we'll consider your offer."

That afternoon in the conference room at headquarters, Montufar, Dumas, Morris, and Fuller assembled to discuss their progress and Levinson's offer.

"We've seized every computer from Calvert's farm," Montufar reported. "They kept extensive records of vehicles and financial transactions."

"That's encouraging," Morris commented.

Montufar shook her head. "Not so much. We enlisted a financial consultant to have a preliminary look. She tells me the records are so cryptic, it could take months to make sense of them."

"Great," Fuller said. "And then we still have figure out how to make it comprehensible to a jury."

Morris clicked her pen a few times. "What about names? Can we at least identify the players?"

"I'm afraid not," Montufar replied. "They used code names for their suppliers and customers. We have nothing concrete on Levinson or anyone else at this point."

"Would Levinson know he couldn't be connected to the operation?" Fuller asked.

Montufar nodded. "Most likely."

"Then why's he asking for immunity?"

"Not because of the farm," Dumas said.

Montufar thought he sounded angry. "Then what?"

"Because of Sandra. He hired Speros. If we take his deal, he gets away with it."

"It's more complicated than that," Fuller said. "According to his attorney, Levinson was approached by someone who wanted to contract a killing. Levinson negotiated the deal and hired Orion Speros for the job. Speros planned and carried out the job. He requested the F250, which Levinson provided. But Levinson swears he was just a middleman."

"Dammit, he killed Sandra!" Dumas snapped, banging his fist on the table. "He's as guilty of her death as Speros is!"

"Be that as it may, without him we might never convict Speros, and we certainly won't find out who hired Levinson."

Montufar watched Dumas chew on his anger. She didn't like this, either, but she knew Fuller had a point. And the captain, apparently, wasn't about to let emotions get in the way of progress. "What can he give us?" she asked before Dumas could say anything more.

"The full story, including the name of the person who contracted the killing and the name of the intended victim. He'll also tell us everything he knows about Calvert's operation, including the names of all key players. Finally, he'll fill us in on the alleged murder of Caroline Fisher, which he says is also the handiwork of Orion Speros."

"Quite a package," Morris said.

"Yes."

Montufar studied Dumas' face. From the darkness in his eyes, she knew he still wasn't going for it. Quietly, she told him, "We at least have to get Speros off the street. I think we have to do this."

"Levinson had a hand in her death, too," he replied, addressing the table. "We can't let him off the hook."

"Sergeant, he's not on the hook," Fuller said. "Yes, he's guilty as sin, but we have no case against him. Or against Speros, for that matter."

"I agree," Morris said. "Run it up the flagpole. Let me know as soon as you have an answer."

Refusing to look at any of them, Dumas rose and hurried out. Montufar called after him, but he didn't stop.

Unwilling to let him go so easily, she pursued through the office area. When she caught up with him, he was at his desk, sunk in his chair, looking at nothing.

She watched him for a few moments, wishing he'd look up and say something, flip a coin, fumble one of the silly magic tricks he'd learned just for their amusement. She knew he was mortally tired of this case, but his thousand-yard stare unnerved her. It seemed almost as though he had unconsciously decided to carry the pain of the reopened investigation for all of them.

"Hey," she finally said. "How about our Chinese place for dinner?"

"*Our* Chinese place?"

If he couldn't laugh anymore, maybe she could manage to laugh for both of them. "Yeah, flatfoot," she said with a heavy fake-mobster sneer, "*our* Chinese place."

He looked up and smiled wearily. "You name it, doll. Go get your glad rags on."

⌒

More than a few things occupied Detective Lieutenant Bill Trengove's mind that afternoon. In addition to the usual assaults and robberies, three apparently connected arsons had occurred in the past month, but as yet he had no suspects. As if that weren't enough, his son had emailed to say he was thinking of dropping out of college to accompany some friends exploring the Australian outback, and his wife was hospitalized following knee surgery. So when Captain Morris called him to her office, he stamped down the corridor, leaned into the doorway, and snapped, "Now what?"

"Maybe this is a bad time?" She didn't look particularly taken aback by his attitude, but he knew why. He always had an attitude. It was just a bit sharper today.

"Like there's ever a good time." He plopped himself into the chair opposite her. "At least let it be something interesting, like a mugger attacking people with live blue crabs." He made a pinching motion.

"Jim Cowden," Morris said.

Trengove stared at her.

"You put his stuff in storage, as I recall."

"Some of it. Andy Newton stashed some of it, too. Don't tell me he's returned and wants it back."

Morris shook her head. "A question came up in relation to his disappearance. Did he have a computer?"

This new development in an old tale was at least interesting. "Honestly, what could possibly come up after so long? Cowden just vanished in a puff of smoke. Everybody forgot about him. End of story."

The captain persisted. "So what about the computer?"

"It's been a few years, Whitney. I haven't rummaged through his stuff even once in all that time. Which is pretty decent of me. He had some nice stuff. What're you after?"

Morris rose, closed the door, and leaned against it. "This is confidential."

"Must be juicy."

"It's actually Rick's request."

*God help us*, Trengove thought, *here we go again*. To be fair, he understood. He didn't know what he'd do if anything happened to his wife Jean, even though the two of them hadn't fused as tightly as Rick and Sandra had. But it had been four years. Sandra wasn't coming back.

"So was there a computer?" Morris asked, patience draining from her voice.

"Yes."

"Could you fetch it in?"

"Is there an investigation? Do you have a warrant?" He looked up at the Captain to gauge her reaction. He couldn't find one.

"I'm asking a favor, Bill. I just want to look for something."

"And if you find it?"

"I'll tell Rick that I found it, then I'll forget about it."

He doubted Peller would be so forgetful. The man's memory verged on the scary. "Jim was my friend. Is my friend. What are you asking me to do, Whitney?"

Morris moved slowly back to her chair and sat. She studied the photo of her husband that she kept on her desk. "I'm not sure. I don't think I'll know until I know what's on that computer."

Trengove stood. "If you want it, get a warrant." He yanked the door open and stomped back to his desk, wondering what was really going on. Even if Peller had gone off the deep end, he didn't think Morris would follow him over the edge like a lemming. Whatever had occurred to Peller, Morris thought it legit.

All the more reason, Trengove figured, to make sure it stayed buried.

The little storefront restaurant was practically deserted this evening. Montufar and Dumas took a table on the opposite side of the dining room from an Asian couple and their two children, where they could almost forget that they weren't alone. The comfortable chatter of the family, punctuated by an occasional child's laugh, soothed Montufar's strained nerves. When the waiter came to take their order, she opted for Kung Pao shrimp; Dumas contrarily asked for sweet and sour pork.

"No General Tso's chicken?" Montufar asked.

Dumas shook his head. "Hey, do you think those people over there know who General Tso was?"

Montufar laughed. "I don't think anyone knows who General Tso was. I looked it up once just out of curiosity, but there were something like six or eight generals with similar names. We have a better idea where Chicken Marengo came from, but we're not in a French restaurant."

"Where did Chicken Marengo come from?" Dumas asked innocently.

Montufar grinned. "A battle that Napoleon won."

"Maybe General Tso won, too."

When the food arrived, Dumas picked at it Western-style as Montufar, suddenly hungry, dug in with chopsticks. They didn't talk much until nearly finished, when Dumas suddenly set down his fork and looked at her, emotion distorting his features. "I don't understand how the Captain can stomach this deal."

Montufar looked up from the last bits of rice on her plate. "Yes, you do," she said gently. "Anyway, it's not a foregone conclusion. A million things could stop it from being approved."

"Levinson killed her, Corina," Dumas exclaimed. "He killed her as surely as if he'd been driving that truck."

There was sudden silence at the table across the room. Montufar felt the Asian family's eyes dart toward them, linger, decide that there was no danger. A pleasant chatter rose again as the elder of the children read the younger's fortune. The father said something teasing, and the mother laughed.

"Eric..." Montufar began, then fell silent. He didn't seem to be listening to her, and she didn't blame him. The anguish in his eyes spoke clearly. "Eric, I know how you feel. We all want to get the guy who did this. But pain and anger won't solve the case. What's that line Ed Harris has in *Apollo 13*? 'Work the problem'?"

"Don't go there, Corina."

"Levinson's not important," she insisted at the risk of angering him further. "He's just the flunky. Speros is the one we want. Speros, or whoever bankrolled the murder."

The doorbell rang and an elderly couple entered. It was time to stop talking like a cop before they frightened the other diners away. "You know what I think?" she asked.

In spite of his mood, a weak smile overtook him. "Every so often, yes."

Montufar momentarily lost her train of thought. She could feel her cheeks absurdly warming, as though she were a schoolgirl noticed by a cute boy. Her reaction didn't escape Dumas' notice. "So tell me," he prompted, with a grin.

She took a deep breath. "What's happened this week is no accident. I think it will end well."

"You mean it was meant to be? Destiny? Karma?"

"I don't know if I believe in destiny, or karma. But I do believe in angels, and that it doesn't matter which side of the grave we're on.

Maybe angels are watching over Rick. Maybe Sandra herself is leading us to resolution."

Montufar half expected Dumas to laugh at her. Instead, he looked thoughtful. "If anybody else said that to me I'd tell them that they were crazy. Over the years I've come to believe that we make our own destiny, but it's not so simple, is it? We try but can't help running into each other at the crossroads. Every collision changes our course. If we collide with an angel, what does that do to our momentum?"

"I don't know," she answered. "But nothing would ever be the same again. Would colliding with an angel change our course, or would it change us?"

"I know," he said rather hesitantly, "you're not quite the same Corina you used to be. You've changed since your brother's injury, and since Leo." He grimaced as mentioned the Fibonacci killer.

She stumbled over her words. "I—I've tried to pretend to myself, I think, that I'm only doing what I am to help my brother. I've actually set foot in a church for the first time in fifteen years." She gave an embarrassed laugh and looked down. "But, really, what I'm doing has less to do with him than with me. I think." She raised her eyes to his again. "Maybe I just need reassurance."

He studied her gravely. "It's not surprising, given what you've been through. Or maybe it's something more. You know, Rick believes in this stuff. His daughter-in-law is probably dragging him to church every Sunday while he's on vacation. And Sandra—if anybody could come back from the grave to do good work, she would."

"I wish I'd known her longer," Montufar said, and meant every word.

Dumas pushed himself back from the table. "Listen to us. Police metaphysicians. We must be going nuts. God, Corina, how did we land in the middle of this?"

She reached out and took his hand. "For one thing, it's our job."

He gazed at her hand on his. "You done with dinner?"

"Yeah."

"Me, too. Let's go to my apartment."

She doubted he meant it in any other way than the most innocent, but she made a show of arching an eyebrow at him.

"Don't give me that," he laughed. "I just want to show you something."

She was intrigued. "Like what?"

"Some memories."

ᕰ

"Be prepared," Dumas said as they mounted the stairs to the second floor of his apartment building.

"Why, haven't you done laundry for three months?" As they reached the landing, a thick miasma of cleaning fluids befogged them. Montufar's first instinct was to pinch her nose shut, but she grimly kept her hands at her side. "And what is that smell, anyway? Did somebody try to clean up the evidence after murdering their roommate?"

Dumas ignored that and explained, "Be prepared for Ozzie."

"Who?"

"You remember."

It took a moment, but she did. "The guy who arranges your love life. How much do you pay him for that?"

He gave her a wry look. "I'd pay him to quit."

Dumas opened the fire door at the top of the stairs, gesturing for silence. They tiptoed out of the stairwell and into the hall, where the reek was even stronger. As they passed Ozzie's door, Montufar whispered, "What does he do? Bathe in formaldehyde?"

As if on cue, the door swung open and Ozzie appeared. "Hey Eric! I had another idea this...oh."

Rolling his eyes, Dumas turned and skewered his neighbor with a hard glare, but Montufar smiled sweetly. "Hey, Ozzie, how've you been?"

Ozzie nearly melted. "I've been great, Ms.—uh, Cora, isn't it?"

"Corina."

"Corina," he corrected himself. "You're not here to talk business again, are you?"

"Well, you know, there's business and then there's business." She winked.

Ozzie grinned. Dumas looked as though he wasn't sure which of them he wanted to strangle first.

"Well, I gotta go," Ozzie said too quickly. "Maybe I'll see you two later?"

"I'm sure you will," Montufar told him.

Ozzie grinned, waved, and hurried back into his apartment. Before closing the door he waved one more time. Dumas stood like a statue of wrath, but Montufar waved back. It briefly crossed her mind to blow a kiss to Ozzie, but there was no point in encouraging him.

Dumas turned to Montufar, his voice aggrieved. "Did you have to say that?"

"Of course. He'll leave you alone now."

"He'll want details."

"Just smile and wink. He'll take it as a full explanation."

Dumas fished his keys out of his pocket and unlocked the door. "Wink and nudge, huh? You're scary sometimes, you know that?"

Montufar shrugged. "So what about these memories?"

"In here."

He unlocked his apartment door and led her through the small foyer into the living room and then to the dining area that adjoined the kitchen. Mercifully, the wicked fog was unable to penetrate the distance. Montufar settled herself at the dinette table.

"Coffee?" Dumas asked.

"Not right now, thanks," she said, and he nodded and vanished into the recesses of the apartment.

Montufar had only been in Dumas' home once, and since then nothing had changed. The sparse living room furniture looked comfortable, albeit nothing fancy, and the television was of modest size. A few nature prints hung on the walls in both living room and dining room, depicting forests and fast-running streams. She found the overall effect restful, calming, a good place to retreat after a day spent chasing bad guys. Maybe she should come here more often.

"I haven't opened this in years," Dumas said, returning with a small box which he set on the table. "I nearly threw it away several times." Opening it, he pulled out a large manila envelope and passed it to Montufar. "Have a look." He sat across from her.

She opened the envelope and pulled out a pile of photographs. She expected to see Dumas' family, but instead she saw wilderness: trees, streams, expanses of barren rock, snow-capped mountains, wild creatures. No trace of human presence marred this pristine world; it might be fresh from its Maker's fingers. "Where is this?" she asked.

"Desolation Wilderness, in the Sierra Nevada."

"You took these?"

"Yep."

"When?"

Dumas got up and dragged his chair around the table to sit beside Montufar. "You could say I was born there."

She shot him a long-suffering look. "Raised by wolves, were you?"

He laughed. "I knew you'd find out eventually. No, actually I went there about six months after Uncle Ethan threw me out. One of my friends from the force gave me crash space for a while, but I couldn't stay there forever. I didn't know what to do. I wasn't even sure I wanted to stay in police work. I wandered off, and this is where I ended up."

Montufar regarded one of the photos, a view from a respectable altitude overlooking a rocky valley studded with pine. She set it aside and took up another, an image of an algae-covered pool surrounded by trees. "How long were you there?"

"Four days. That was the limit of my skills and endurance. It's a true wilderness. You only have what you carry in with you."

The next showed an expanse of fractured gray rock. Downslope, at the edge of a forest, a mule deer seemed to pose for the unseen cameraman. "So you wandered the mountains for half a week snapping photos?"

He looked at the picture in her hand for a long moment, as though wishing he could simply walk into it and lose himself again in the purity of that place. Finally he answered, "Dumping the accumulated garbage of two decades."

Montufar handed him the photo, wondering where this unexpected revelation was going. She had thought she knew Dumas well, but now she caught a glimpse of another man dwelling within the first. He'd brought her here and shown her this for a reason, surely.

"You wouldn't believe the night sky up there. Hundreds of stars. Maybe thousands. I don't know, really, but so many you can't pick out the constellations. Or I can't, anyway. The whole universe spread out before you."

"I'd like to see that someday."

"You should. Then the sun comes up in the morning, driving off the night chill, and all the stars fade out. Watching that one morning, something occurred to me."

He laid the photo gently on the table, seemingly hesitant to go on. Montufar prompted, "What was that?"

"When the sun is up, you don't get your light from the stars." He glanced at her quickly, perhaps needing but not wanting to see her reaction.

Again Montufar was surprised by the depth of his words. Up till now she hadn't thought Dumas to be spiritually inclined. Intelligent, certainly; intuitive, capable of leaps of imagination that defied her more analytic mind, but not a man on a vision quest. It would take her some time to grow accustomed to this new man.

"Crazy?" he asked. "Or just unintelligible?"

"Neither. You've been chasing the sun ever since."

Dumas relaxed visibly. "Pretty much. It's hard to find, though. I certainly don't find it in material things. The rich and famous, pundits and politicians, even the truly wise never seem to me to be more than glimmers in the night sky, and often not even that. But life isn't all cold and dark, is it? In spite of it all, I can feel the sun all around me. You can, too, can't you?"

She did: for her, it was her family and, increasingly, her rediscovered faith. But where was it for him? "Have you found it, then?"

His eyes held hers for a long moment. Then he raised his hand to the thin silver chain encircling her neck. Carefully, he lifted it, revealing the crucifix that had nestled beneath her blouse, to hold it gently between his fingers. "You didn't used to wear this," he said quietly.

"A long time ago I did. But not since you've known me. Not until just recently."

"What made you put it on again?"

Montufar didn't know that she could answer the question, not really, not in any rational way. But it occurred to her that in another of his intuitive leaps, Dumas already knew the answer. "I remembered what it was like, when I was a child, to see the sunlight. I'd almost forgotten."

He placed the crucifix against her skin, ran his index finger along her cheek, and sat back. "I've only ever sensed it. I never actually saw it."

She shook her head. "No. You wouldn't be looking for it if you had no memory of it."

"I suppose you're right. I have seen glimmers of it." He took her hands in his and regarded her steadily. It seemed he wanted to say something more, but either words eluded him or he was afraid to speak.

Montufar thought she knew what he'd say, if only he could. And although she rather wanted him to say it, she wasn't sure she was ready to hear it.

# Chapter 19

Friday evening, Peller enjoyed dinner with his family at a popular local steakhouse and stayed up late with Susie and Andrew, watching Disney films. On Saturday, they took another jaunt into the mountains, where they spent the whole of a jolly day hiking, taking photographs, and throwing snowballs at one another.

That is to say, he was true to his promise to Captain Morris to end his vacation by taking a vacation.

# Chapter 20

Dumas usually slept late on the Saturdays he didn't have to report to work, but not this Saturday. This Saturday descended upon him in a thunderous hammering at his door, while a frenzied voice cried his name.

Instantly he tumbled out of bed, sure that the apocalypse had begun, or at least that the building had caught fire. Shaking off the fog of sleep, he followed the frantic noises to his door only to find Ozzie White trembling with excitement on the threshold. "Breakfast?" Ozzie said breathlessly.

Dumas looked behind Ozzie. There was no smoke in the hallway, no fire alarm, no sirens; everything was peaceful.

Except Ozzie. "Breakfast?" Dumas said.

"You want me to make breakfast for you and Corina?"

Dumas could see himself slamming the door in Ozzie's face and going back to bed, but he couldn't bring himself to do it. "What are you talking about?"

"She's still here, isn't she?"

"No, Ozzie. She's a respectable lady and she went home, although at an admittedly unrespectable hour." What time was it, anyway? He felt like he'd had all of ten minutes' sleep.

Ozzie was crestfallen. "Oh Eric, how could you let her get away?"

Dumas opened the door wide and motioned. "Since I'm up, why don't you come in and make breakfast anyway? After that rude awakening, I'd probably break everything in the kitchen."

Shuffling in, Ozzie gave Dumas a look of deep disappointment as he passed by. "I guess I might as well. What did you do to drive her off?"

Dumas didn't quite slam the door, but it was a close thing. "I didn't drive her off. I work with the woman, Ozzie. I see her five days a week, about forty-eight weeks a year, once vacations are taken into account. I even have dinner with her every now and then. We're close colleagues and good friends."

"Is that all?"

Dumas followed Ozzie into the kitchen and leaned against the counter as his neighbor rummaged in the refrigerator and cabinets for ingredients. He didn't care to answer the question, in part because he wasn't sure of the answer. No, actually, he was sure. There certainly was more to their relationship, but they seemed to be fumbling towards an understanding of what it was. It couldn't be put into words yet.

"I do a mean cinnamon pancake," Ozzie said, setting out eggs and milk. "So, work. Is that all?"

"You just aren't going to let it go, are you?"

The other grinned over his shoulder. "Nope. It's my mission in life to get you some action."

"Why?"

Ozzie pulled a whisk from the drawer with a flourish and began beating eggs with great gusto. "Because you deserve it!" he exclaimed. "You're a good guy, Eric. You care about people. That's why you're a cop, right?" He stopped beating and skewered Dumas with a critical look. "But you aren't close to anyone. Whatever happened to you, I guess it wasn't pretty, but you need to move past it."

Ozzie's shrewdness took Dumas by surprise. He had no idea his flighty neighbor could see into other people's souls. Taking a seat at the table, he puzzled over the contradiction.

Ozzie resumed his work. "Do you love her?"

Dumas hedged. "I'm still working on that one."

"It's not that complicated. What do you feel when you see her?"

"Can we talk about something else?"

Before Ozzie could reply, Dumas' cell phone went off so loud it nearly knocked him from his chair. He snatched up the device and answered irritably.

There was a moment of dead air, then an old voice said, "Eric?"

"Speaking," he said. "Who's calling?"

"Please don't hang up, Eric. It's Uncle Ethan."

Dumas felt his hand start to shake, but something in his uncle's voice kept him from closing the connection. "How did you get my number?"

"I called your police department and told them it was a family emergency. I'm sorry, it was the only way I could think to get in touch."

Dumas made a mental note to find out who had fallen for that deception.

The tired voice crackled over the line. "I suppose you got my letter."

"I'm sorry, Uncle, but I've built a life for myself, and I'm not dropping it in the trash for you or anyone else."

Silence replied. Dumas was about to hang up when Uncle Ethan spoke. "I know that, and I know what I said in my letter sounds like I don't know it. It's just that when I heard about you on the news...I guess I was desperate to have you back again."

"Why?"

"You're all I have left."

Dumas frowned at the phone. That made no sense at all. He realized Ozzie had gone still and was looking at him, alarmed, so he turned to face the opposite wall. "What about Aunt Maggie? What about Jen and Karen?"

"Maggie isn't herself anymore," Ethan said, his voice almost a whimper. "I don't know where Jen went. She ran off with her boyfriend shortly after Phillip was killed. Karen got married and moved to Chicago, but she never calls or writes or emails or texts or probably even thinks about us anymore."

Although not surprised by these tidings, Dumas found he didn't want to think about them. None of this had anything to do with him anymore.

"I guess you see death all the time."

"Not all the time," Dumas replied automatically.

Uncle Ethan didn't seem to have heard. "You see it, but you don't know it. Not true death. True death isn't the death of the body.

It's the death of the soul. It's such complete separation from those you love that you don't even know where to look for them."

Dumas's mind drained of thought. He neither understood what was happening nor knew how to respond.

His uncle didn't seem to have anything more to say, either. The line went dead.

Ozzie brought Dumas a plate piled with syrupy hotcakes and slid it in front of him. "You really should tell her," he said quietly.

Dumas looked up, uncomprehending. "I'm sorry?"

"Corina. Tell her."

First Ozzie's revelation, then Uncle Ethan's unanticipated call. It was too much to process. Dumas picked up his fork and cut into his breakfast. "Ozzie, you really are the most irritating, meddlesome fool I've ever met."

Ozzie grinned widely. "You're just saying that because it's true." He turned back to the stove. "More pancakes?"

As a rule, Captain Morris didn't make social visits to her underlings' homes, but on the morning of Saturday, April ninth, she made an exception and called on Detective Sergeant Andy Newton, who along with Bill Trengove had taken in Jim Cowden's possessions for safekeeping. She knew that Newton didn't have what she was after, but maybe he could prevail upon Trengove to make Cowden's computer available for a search.

She pulled up in front of Newton's Ellicott City rowhouse at ten o'clock. The gray sky looked like rain but so far hadn't delivered as much as a drop. Wearing a denim skirt and a lavender long-sleeved blouse, she rang the bell and waited. Newton's wife Charity answered the door, still in her robe and slippers. The two women knew each other by sight, although they hadn't met more than a couple of times and had only exchanged pleasantries.

"Whitney, what are you doing here?"

"I need to ask Andy for a favor. Is he home?"

"Sure, come on in. I'll get him."

Morris waited in a living room that held a huge television and an arrangement of enough old but serviceable modular sofa pieces to hold two adults, four kids, and a litter of Labrador puppies. It looked immensely comfortable. Morris wondered how many tubs of popcorn it had seen in its lifetime.

A minute later, Newton entered, wearing jeans and a paint-splotched t-shirt. Standing six foot three, he had a lanky frame that masked considerable strength. His long face always looked a bit surprised and often threw suspects off-guard during interrogations.

Now he looked like a gloomy scarecrow. "What's wrong?"

"Nothing, I just came to ask a favor."

Newton relaxed. "Thank God. For a minute I thought it was business, and I have two rooms to paint today." He motioned at his shirt.

"It is business, in a way, but unofficial. I understand you helped Bill Trengove stash Jim Cowden's belongings for safekeeping."

His eyebrows rose. "He's back?"

"No, nothing like that. A question about his computer was raised, and I was hoping to have a look at it."

"I don't have his computer. Bill has that."

"I know. I talked to him about it already, but he isn't inclined to let me look at it. I thought maybe you could prevail upon him."

Newton's eyebrows shot up even further. Morris thought of a startled owl.

She shrugged and said in what she hoped was a casual voice, "It's unofficial, you see. I don't have a warrant, and I can't order him to turn the computer over to me."

"Ah. Yeah, I can see his point."

That, Morris thought, was unfortunate. "You don't think Jim was hiding something, do you?"

Newton shifted uncomfortably. "You probably heard the rumors. But no, I don't. Anyway, he's got the same right to privacy as the rest of us, and the computer was already searched, wasn't it?"

"True enough. Nothing came up that explained his disappear-ance. But that's not what interests me right now."

"What does?"

"I can't say. Again, this is unofficial. The last thing I'd want is to spark rumors."

Newton looked as though he wanted to escape back to his painting project and leave Morris and her disquieting questions far behind. "Understood. If we knew what you were after, could Bill and I could conduct the search?"

"Maybe, but unfortunately I can't give you that information."

Silently, Newton gazed at her until she began to feel uncomfortable. Finally, he stood. "I'm sorry, Captain, but I can't in good conscience agree to this."

"Even if it helps us catch Sandra Peller's killer?"

Newton opened his mouth, closed it, sat back down. "What's Jim got to do with that?"

"Probably nothing, at least not directly. Please, Andy. I don't want to tar and feather Jim's good name, but if he left behind some clue as to why Sandra died, I have to find it."

The sergeant said nothing, just shook his head and refused to look Morris in the eye.

"All right. If you change your mind, let me know." She let herself out, got in her car, and drove down the street. Pulling into a donut shop, she bought a cup of coffee and pondered the matter. It wasn't surprising that Trengove and Newton would refuse to cooperate, but somehow it disturbed her. She couldn't help but wonder if they knew something about Cowden that they weren't telling.

The car parked at the end of his street where no car had any business being parked was the first hint that all was not right with the world. He saw it well before he passed it. He also saw that it was occupied by two men who were eyeballing his house, and at least one of them had binoculars.

The situation reeked of cops. Orion Speros drove carefully by, his speed exactly the legal limit, as though unaware of the unmarked car's presence. If the surveillance team noticed him, they would surely pursue him. Who would fail to recognize Orion Speros?

But the car remained idle at the curb.

It seemed to Speros that there were two reasons why the police would be staking out his place. The first completely innocent explanation was that Detective Sergeant Eric Dumas suspected his involvement in the death of the Peller woman. If Speros were in Dumas' place, he'd certainly have suspected the same thing. He'd let his emotions get the better of him for a moment, all but broadcasting his guilt. But he also knew suspicion wasn't enough to get a conviction, and he didn't think the police were so stupid as to believe that watching his house would do any good.

The more likely possibility—no, the damn near certain possibility—was that Jeff Levinson had cut a deal with the cops. Speros was surprised that Levinson could be so stupid, but killing his slut, yeah, that had been over the top. She'd deserved it, though, her and those screeching vocal cords. If she'd only shut up like he'd told her to, she'd still be alive. No great loss, he thought, but possibly she was more than a bed partner to Levinson.

But so what? Crossing Orion Speros was the act of a fool. Everyone knew that.

As he turned north, making for Jeff Levinson's place, something else occurred to him. Levinson couldn't talk to the police without risking the entire stolen vehicle operation. When "the man" found out—and he would—he'd dispose of Levinson in his own pitiless way. That guy was a reptile. Speros had only seen him once, very briefly, but he had immediately disliked him. Although both men were capable of killing, hot human blood ran through Speros' veins. The heart of Levinson's boss was frozen.

So if Levinson had talked to the police, Speros reasoned, it had to be to strike a deal, and that meant the farm had already been compromised. It wouldn't be safe to go there. Speros wondered what had happened, whether everyone at the farm had been arrested, whether anyone had escaped. He decided to drop by Esteban's house. If anyone managed to avoid capture, it would be Esteban. He was easy to talk to: up-front, never scared, with a strong instinct for self-preservation. Speros thought that Esteban could almost have been his brother, had he not been so boring.

Doing a u-turn in the middle of the road, Speros set course for his new destination.

Montufar arrived at her brother's house mid-afternoon, and their younger sister Ella let her in. She smiled radiantly when she saw Montufar, but as they turned to enter the living room a shadow crossed her face. "You okay?" Montufar asked.

Ella shrugged and nodded. "Yeah." It was clear she was as worried as Montufar, but it was characteristic of her—always in good spirits when the family gathered, but underneath always worried about something. It wasn't hard to guess what had her worried now. "Father Owen's here," she told Montufar. "Have you met him?"

"Yes, once," Montufar answered, trying not to let her secret slip and hoping that Father Owen would be the soul of discretion.

"Corina!" Eduardo called, waving her over. He was seated on the sofa between Father Owen and his wife Sylvia, who was holding his hand. Montufar thought it looked less like a gesture of affection than an effort to keep him with her. "This makes it perfect! Look who's here. Father Owen is our..." He peered at the priest for a second. "From our church."

Father Owen rose and shook Montufar's hand as though meeting her for the first time, but didn't say anything, possibly so as not to speak a falsehood. His eyes were kind, though, and it was clear that he remembered her. "Hello, Father," she greeted him, then turned her attention on Eduardo. "How are you feeling today?"

"Better every day. Come, sit." Turning to Father Owen, he said, "Corina is a...hmm. Police lady. She solves crimes."

"Oh, a detective," Father Owen said with a smile.

"Yes. Detective." Eduardo beamed at his sister.

"She must be good at it. You're obviously very proud of her."

"Absolutely the best. She catches most of the crooks in the county all by herself."

Ella laughed and nodded. "Not most of them, all of them."

Montufar felt herself starting to blush. "Oh, stop it, you two. I'm just one of a team."

"Modest, too," Father Owen said with a secret smile. "Eduardo was filling me in on his medical adventures. It sounds like he's making good progress. I have to admit, though—" he scrutinized Eduardo—"I'm a bit concerned about the trouble you seem to be having finding the right word. Like just now, when you couldn't come up with the word 'detective'. Has your doctor said anything about that?"

Eduardo waved his concern away. "It's nothing."

"Is that the doctor's assessment or yours?"

He shrugged and looked at Sylvia. "Can Father Owen stay for dinner?"

"As far as I'm concerned, he can stay for breakfast, too," Sylvia said. "We have plenty." Smiling, she looked around her husband to the priest.

"That's very kind of you," he said. "But it doesn't answer the question, you know."

With a sigh, Eduardo looked heavenward. "He hasn't mentioned it, and I haven't talked to him about it. What could he do about it, anyway? It'll get better. Just takes time."

Father Owen set a supportive hand on Eduardo's shoulder. "I know that Sylvia is concerned, too. Are you worried about what the doctor might say?"

Eduardo looked around at his sisters. "I have to be strong. For my family."

Montufar slid forward and looked him in the eye. She knew she should probably let Father Owen handle it, but her brother's obstinacy was beginning to irritate her. "Eduardo, there's a difference between strong and stupid. Talk to your doctor."

Ella looked mortified, but Eduardo just smiled affectionately. "Little sister," he said, "you always did have me pegged. But please don't worry. I'm fine. Trust God to keep us safe."

"Trusting God doesn't mean behaving recklessly," Father Owen said gravely. "Eduardo, I'm afraid I have to agree with Corina. I'll be happy to go with you when you talk to the doctor, if you want."

Eduardo frowned into his lap and stroked Sylvia's hand. "What is for dinner, anyway?" he asked.

Esteban Narvaez thought of himself as a family man even though, strictly speaking, he had no family anymore. He had grown up in a crowded neighborhood in northern Hermosillo, surrounded by brothers and sisters and cousins. Swept along by a flash flood of youthful ambition, at nineteen years of age he had emigrated to the U.S., legally documented, and set his sights on Hollywood.

Reality punched him in the gut almost immediately. It turned out that "United States" wasn't spelled with dollar signs after all. Work had been hard to find and once found paid poorly. He got crash space with other Mexican expatriates, often illegal immigrants whose stigma rubbed off on him in spite of his documentation. He moved northward, then eastward, then further eastward, always searching for those dollar signs but never finding them, until in time he came to be destitute in Baltimore, again sharing crash space with illegals.

The trouble was, he had few skills. The only doors that opened for people like him led to menial jobs. Despairing of ever escaping this trap of his own devising, he almost didn't act when a friend referred him to Jeff Levinson. But he did act, if reluctantly and without hope, and to his surprise Levinson gave him a chance.

When Narvaez realized the nature of Levinson's business, he wanted to run the other way. But he couldn't. He'd finally found those dollar signs and craved them with the intensity of an addict. The irony wasn't lost on him: a legal immigrant wed to a criminal enterprise. But Narvaez managed to convince himself it was a necessary evil, and with luck a temporary one. Once he had enough cash, he would find a proper job.

In the meantime, Narvaez rented a nice apartment in Ellicot City, assembled a nice wardrobe, bought some nice furniture and gadgetry, and tried to become at least a semblance of a family man again by living with first one woman, then another, then a third. But he couldn't talk to them about his work, and sooner or later that want of openness gnawed away trust. His present relationship already corroding, he now he had to tell Danna that he was out of work without telling her why. He dreaded that revelation, but come Monday she would learn of it one way or the other.

For the moment, Danna was padding around the apartment in jeans and a tight sweater, looking beautiful, tidying the place while he sat on the sofa with his laptop, searching for news about the raid. He didn't know what had happened after his narrow escape. He had no idea what had become of Levinson or "the man" or anyone else, and it rattled him. He expected the cops to pound on the door at any moment.

Danna passed by, scowling. "Feet off the coffee table."

He obeyed without looking up.

"You could put that thing away and help me."

"You need help?"

"Well, look at this place."

Narvaez didn't want to look, didn't need to look. "It's fine. Sit down and read or something. You're making me nervous."

A sudden pounding at the door jolted them. Narvaez leaped up from the couch, knowing that he had nowhere to run but ready for the worst. Danna yelped, "What the hell?"

Narvaez closed his laptop and waited for the police to announce themselves.

"Esteban!" a voice called. "Esteban, open up! We have to talk!"

"Oh, Christ," he muttered. "Not him."

Recovered from the shock, Danna glared at Narvaez. "Another one of your low-life friends?"

"Get in the bedroom and stay there."

"Don't you talk to me like that!"

He took her by the shoulders and spoke firmly. "Go in the bedroom and don't come out for anything. This man is trouble."

"But—"

"Go!" He pushed her toward the hall.

She looked as if she wanted to argue, then changed her mind and bolted from the room. He heard the far door close.

The clamor at the door began again, and a voice bellowed, "Come on, Esteban! Open up!"

Collecting himself, Esteban Narvaez walked to the door and opened it to admit Orion Speros. "What the hell, Orion?" he said. He hoped that Speros' appearance at his home was a mere annoyance rather than a distinct danger.

Speros waded into the room. In the wake of his passage Narvaez found it difficult to breathe, as though all the air had been consumed by an unseen force. Speros dropped onto the sofa and waved expansively. "I like coming here, my friend. You're such a gracious host."

"You're scaring the little woman," Narvaez said.

"Me? Oh come on, Esteban, am I really that scary?" Speros grinned toothily.

Narvaez didn't think Speros had any reason to harm him. Their relationship had always been simple: Narvaez never lied to Speros, therefore Speros never doubted Narvaez or his loyalty. But he also knew that Speros didn't have that kind of affinity with everyone. "You know what you are, Orion. I don't have to tell you."

Speros grinned again. "Your honesty is refreshing. That's another reason I like coming here." He leaned back and put his feet up on the table. "So tell me, what happened up at the farm?"

"I wish I knew." With a glance down the hall, Narvaez lowered his voice. "The cops raided us."

Speros' features assumed a soberness that didn't fool Narvaez. He knew the man wasn't at all concerned about the fate of the business. "The operation is dead?"

"As far as I know. I ran for it as soon as I realized what was going on. I had a cop on my tail and only got out because he made a wrong turn and ended up in a ditch."

Speros laughed at that, then feigned seriousness again. "Was Jeff arrested?"

"I don't know. I haven't heard a thing from anyone since then."

The news seemed to set Speros back. He was uncharacteristically lost in thought for a few moments. Finally he said, "I need to find him, Stevie. Could you do me a favor?"

"If I can."

"Assuming the cops don't have him, he'll probably get in touch with you sooner or later. If he does, find out where he is, then give me a buzz. Don't let him know I'm looking for him. Will you do that?"

"Why?"

Speros spread his hands, a gesture that made him look like he was holding the entire world in his arms. "I have business with him, okay?"

"He's on your list, isn't he?"

Speros rose and crossed to the apartment door in a few huge strides. "Now, Stevie, don't start rumors." He opened the door, then looked back over his shoulder. "But just between the birds, you, and me, if Jeff is lucky the cops will shoot him dead while he's trying to escape." He winked and carefully closed the door behind him.

Narvaez didn't like it. Levinson had helped him when he was at his lowest. But it wasn't smart to cross Speros. He shouldn't have gotten involved in any of this. He should have stayed poor. No, he should have stayed in Mexico. But it was too late for misgivings.

Narvaez walked back to the bedroom and opened the door. Danna was sitting on the edge of the bed, her face lost somewhere between irate and terrified. "Who was that?" she demanded.

"Like you said," he told her with a shrug. "One of my lowlife friends."

# Chapter 21

Sunday evening, Captain Morris was at home loading the dishwasher with the help of her husband Daniel when Fuller called with the news. She took the call standing in the middle of the kitchen.

"It's been one hell of a weekend here," Fuller told her. "But we've reached a plea agreement with Kirby."

"How much did you have to give up?"

"Full immunity in the death of Sandra Peller and reduced charges in connection with Calvert's operation."

Morris moved to the counter and leaned against it. "And what did we get in return?"

Fuller didn't reply at first. Just when Morris was about to prompt him, he said, "The full story."

"That's good. Tell me."

"No, Whitney. It's not good."

"What do you mean?"

Fuller told her. As she listened, she began to feel as though she were dragged by the hair into a dark cave from which there was no escape. Although she didn't see him approach, Daniel's hand was suddenly on her shoulder. "Is everything all right?" he asked quietly.

Putting her hand on his, she said to Fuller, "We'll need to go over this with my team."

"You want to get them on a conference call?"

"It'll keep until tomorrow. Rick deserves to be in on this, although I wish I could spare him. He's already been through hell. He doesn't need a knife in the back, too."

"I can be there first thing in the morning," Fuller said.

"May as well get it over with as early as possible," Morris agreed.

She gently set her cell phone on the counter and stared at it as though it had come from an alien world.

"What is it?" Daniel asked.

"You wouldn't think catching a killer could be a bad thing," she said.

And then she said nothing further.

∽

Leaving was harder than Peller had expected. Part of him wanted to stay forever. He wanted to spend every afternoon with his grandchildren; to spend every evening sharing tea and conversation over cards with Jason and Belinda. Another part wanted to get back to work, to discover whatever Montufar and Dumas had dredged up from the waters of the past, assemble the fragments, and at long last understand why Sandra had died.

His leavetaking had been tearful on all sides, and Susie and Andrew had begged him to return soon. He promised to visit again, possibly over the summer, even if only for a weekend. During the flight, he stared out the window at blankets of clouds, slept fitfully, and thought he could feel Sandra in his arms.

Once he dreamed he saw her walking away, walking into the Greenway building. She looked back at him, smiling, filling him with warmth.

He woke, knowing that although she was gone, she was yet beside him.

∽

The red morning sky heralded either rain or a beautiful spring day depending on the adage one preferred. Either way it was Monday, four days before tax day, not the most cheerful of times even without the event Captain Morris was dreading: the revelation of Jeff Levinson's testimony and the detailed questioning to which the team must subject him.

She arrived at Northern District Headquarters early, ran through her email, dispatched a few replies, and jotted down a few notes based on what she knew so far. All too soon, Peller, Montufar, and Dumas arrived and fell into intense conversation, no doubt regarding the events of the previous week. Morris watched them through her open door, not wanting to disturb them but painfully aware of time ticking onward. With a heavy sigh, she picked up the phone and called Peller's desk.

"Good morning, Captain," he said, sounding cheerful. "I guess vacation's over."

"Afraid so. Could I see the three of you in my office?"

"We'll be right there."

And so they were, Peller ready to take on the world, Dumas smiling, and Montufar exuding an air of contentment, as though something broken had been repaired.

"Good to have you back," Morris told Peller.

"Good to be back," he replied, "although I could have stayed forever."

"I know Corina and Eric kept you in the loop. I got word over the weekend that a deal was worked out with Levinson. He and his attorney will be here for a preliminary interview in about fifteen minutes."

Dumas' smile abandoned him. "He's not getting off the hook, is he?"

"Not entirely, but with respect to Sandra's death, yes."

"What's he giving us?" Peller asked, his face unreadable.

Morris picked up her pen and studied it. How much should she tell him, and how much should come from Levinson's mouth? If she could absent herself from this process, she would be sorely tempted to do so. But she couldn't.

Peller must have sensed her reluctance, for worry distorted his features. "Captain?"

"Levinson was a middleman. He hired Speros on behalf of someone else. He'll give us the full story, insofar as he knows it."

Montufar leaned forward. Placing a hand on Peller's shoulder, she said, "You already know what he's going to say."

"Yes. Rick, Corina, Eric, this is going to be ugly. I can't think of a worse ending to this tale than the one Levinson's going to tell us. I don't know how to prepare you for it. All I can say is, brace yourselves and do your best to keep it professional."

Peller stood and walked to the window. His back to the rest of them, he gazed out at the world for a long time. None of them spoke, but Morris noticed Montufar take Dumas' hand in hers.

When Peller finally turned to face them, he seemed to be at ease. "It's all right, Captain. Sandra would tell us to trust God. I don't know about anyone else, but I think I can do that now. I've learned a lot this past week from my family and from Sandra herself."

Morris raised an eyebrow at that, wondering how he meant the last part.

"She's not gone, Captain. She's here." He tapped his chest. "I'm never apart from her."

There was nothing Morris could say, nor was there time for more. Mark Fuller appeared in the doorway, a laptop bag slung over his shoulder. "Sorry for intruding," he said. "Mr. Kirby and Mr. Levinson are getting settled in the conference room. We can start whenever you're ready."

Morris rose. "As ready as I'll ever be," she said. "Come on, let's get this over with."

⌇

Discretion never struck anyone as Orion Speros' middle name, but he could be discreet when necessary. Now was such a time. With his house under surveillance, he paid a surprise visit to a female friend with whom he'd had an on-again, off-again relationship for several years. As their affair had been off-again for a few months, she wasn't particularly thrilled at his appearance, but he promised to make it worth her while. Dazzling visions of new clothing, jewelry, and dinners at upscale restaurants filling her mind, she decided that he wasn't that bad after all.

With safe lodging arranged, he pondered how to find Jeff Levinson. Given what Narvaez had told him, Levinson was almost certainly in police custody. Adding up the charges he'd likely be facing, serious jail time was in his future. Balanced against that was the sum of his knowledge of various criminal operations. When he factored in the surveillance of his house, Speros didn't like the resulting equation.

If a deal was in the making, the cops would need to interrogate Levinson, and unless they did that at a detention facility, they'd have to transport him. Speros feared it might be a long shot, but odds aside it was the only hope he had of catching his quarry. He decided to conduct his own stakeout, right in front of his adversaries. If Levinson came into or went out from Northern District Headquarters in the next few days, Orion Speros would hand-deliver him his fate.

In the conference room, a video camera focused on a well-dressed Jeff Levinson. He was flanked by an even sharper Charles David Kirby III, who smiled at the gathered detectives and attorney Mark Fuller, who looked like he'd had a long weekend wrestling hyenas. Levinson contented himself with a smile, saying nothing, waiting for Kirby to wave the starter's flag.

Peller felt a curious calm. He barely noticed Levinson's smile. But he could tell that Dumas was on edge, and from the way Montufar shot furtive glances at Dumas, Peller knew she was worried about him. That was interesting, he thought. Although the three of them were friends as well as colleagues, he'd never observed her lavishing quite that much concern on Dumas. Or himself, for that matter.

"We've prepared a written statement," Kirby said, passing a sheaf of paper in a transparent cover to Fuller, "that covers all aspects of Mr. Levinson's agreed testimony. We hope minimal questioning will be required, but are prepared to answer whatever questions you may have."

Fuller took the statement but didn't look at it. Setting it aside, he nodded to Morris.

"Mr. Levinson admits to being part of an organization that bought stolen vehicles and sold them either whole or as parts," Morris began. She sounded cold, Peller thought, intentionally so, as though suppressing anger.

"He does," Kirby replied. "It's all in the statement."

"He admits to being one of the chief operators of that business, the other, the late John Calvert, being the owner, and claims full knowledge of the business's operations."

"Again, it's in the statement."

"How many people were killed by operatives of this business?"

Kirby's eyes widened slightly. "None whatsoever."

"What about this Caroline Fisher?"

With a nod to his client, Kirby leaned back.

"Caroline Fisher was killed by Orion Speros," Levinson said. "He never worked for Duke."

"But Calvert's operatives disposed of the body."

"They buried her somewhere in a field. As far as I know, nothing like that had ever happened, but we'd planned for it. Duke didn't want police on site, ever."

"Why did Speros kill Fisher?"

Levinson's smile slipped away, replaced by a terrible sadness. "I don't know. He attacked me, but he didn't mean to kill me. Killing Caroline doesn't make any sense."

Montufar, arms crossed on the table, asked, "How do you know he didn't mean to kill you?"

Levinson's eyes widened, but he said in a matter-of-fact voice, "I'm still alive. If Orion means to kill you, you die."

"Why," Morris asked, "was he angry with you?"

"That gets into the death of Sandra Peller." Levinson glanced nervously at Peller. Maybe he hadn't expected to come face-to-face with the victim's husband. "Orion found out that the woman he'd killed was a cop's wife. He doesn't like to cross the police. He's always been careful to stay on their good side."

"And you were the one who hired him for that job."

"Yes."

"But not to kill Sandra Peller."

"No, that was a mistake," Levinson said quickly, now looking at Peller as though pleading for forgiveness. "Orion planned the job to look like an accident. He just needed a description of the target car, and where and when to expect it. We were given the information, but it was bad. The car, when it showed up, was the wrong one. Or…"

Levinson glanced at Peller again. Peller met his eyes, waiting.

"Or what?" Morris prompted.

Levinson folded his hands on the table and stared at them. "Had the wrong driver. The right car, but the wrong driver."

Peller went cold. Montufar and Dumas simultaneously snapped, "*What?*" Half rising and planting his fists on the table, Dumas seemed to be trembling with rage. "What do you mean, the wrong driver?"

"The mark was…" Levinson squeezed his eyes shut as though in pain.

"Who?" Dumas demanded.

The other looked up at him. "Look, all I had was a name. I didn't know it was a policeman!"

Peller felt as though the room and everyone in had shrunk to a single point. "Someone hired you to kill me? Why?"

"I don't know. The client didn't say and I didn't ask. That information wasn't necessary for the job. But believe me, had I known he wanted to kill a police officer…"

"It's a little late for contrition," Dumas said, his eyes boring a hole into Levinson.

"All right," Morris said, motioning Dumas to sit down. "What happened in the aftermath?"

"Orion was furious. I'd never seen him that angry. The client vanished, which was a good thing for him, otherwise Orion would have killed him."

"Why was Speros so angry?"

"Because the woman—Sandra Peller—shouldn't have died."

Dumas started to rise again, but Montufar touched his arm. "Speros couldn't care less about that."

Levinson shook his head. "You're wrong. He'll happily kill anyone he thinks deserves it, and he'll take on a contract, but he does have a few standards. He's very careful about limiting his—damage, shall we say—to the target."

"Then why did he kill Caroline Fisher?" Montufar asked. "You seem to think he only intended to send you a message."

"I don't know. Maybe that was part of the message. He never liked her."

Morris regarded her subordinates in turn. The tension in the room ratcheted up. Then she said, her voice cold and hard, "The client. Who was it?"

"A man named Jim Cowden," Levinson answered. "I don't know much about him. I'd never met him before."

The name hit Peller in the gut, knocking the wind from him. "That's—no, that's insane."

Befuddled, Levinson asked, "You know him?"

Dumas sprang up again and made to grab Levinson. "You pathetic little liar! What the hell are you trying to do?"

"Sit down, Eric," Morris snapped. Montufar put a shaking hand on his arm and drew him back to his chair.

"Why would I lie?" Levinson asked. "Who the hell is this Cowden, anyway?"

Attorney Fuller spoke up. "Jim Cowden was a highly respected Howard County detective. Everyone in this room considered him a friend."

Levinson paled. He turned to Kirby for help, but for once his attorney shrugged, at a loss for words. Peller knew what must be going through Levinson's mind: he was trapped in a nightmare. His only hope was that the deal his lawyer had struck would be able to hold up under the assault of this new revelation.

But it would. It must. Peller turned to Morris, saying, "You knew all of this already."

"Mr. Fuller and I discussed the key points yesterday," she said. "But we need to hear it from Mr. Levinson."

"Then the deal is secure."

Morris stared at Levinson with undisguised loathing, but she nodded nevertheless.

"All right," Peller said, turning his attention back to Levinson. *Forget everything but your job*, he told himself. "You have no idea why Jim wanted me dead."

"None."

"Did he say anything that might even have hinted at a reason?"

"Nothing."

"What did he say?"

"Just that he wanted a man out of his way."

"Were those his exact words?"

"Pretty much. He didn't want to give me any details until I could arrange that. After that, he gave us what Orion wanted—your name and a description of you and your car. That was it."

"Did you know him?"

"No."

Montufar frowned. "How did he come into contact with you?"

"He said a friend referred him to me as someone who could arrange what he wanted." Levinson pondered that for a moment, then added, "Maybe he had an informant who knew about me?"

Peller thought that likely, but it wasn't important. "And the day it happened?"

"Orion asked Cowden about your routine. He wanted to know if there was any chance of ambushing you in open country. Cowden said he could find out. He eventually came back with your travel plans for that day, and Orion told him to watch your movements so he could time the hit. They were talking to each other on their cellphones the whole morning. I don't know what went wrong. Cowden screwed it up somehow."

Peller ran a hand over his face. "I know what happened."

"Rick," Morris began, but he waved her to silence.

"Sandra was going to an agricultural expo at the county fairgrounds. I planned to go with her, but I had to be somewhere else in the afternoon, so we were going to drive there separately. I probably mentioned it to Jim. We often talked about our weekend plans. When the day came, I wasn't feeling well, so I stayed home. Sandra took my car for some reason I don't recall anymore." Peller felt more empty than he had in a long time. Belinda's words crept into his consciousness: *Maybe she died to save someone else.*

Captain Morris rose. "Mr. Kirby, we're going to continue this shortly, but I want a few minutes alone with my team. Please wait here."

Kirby, impassive, nodded.

Morris put a hand on Peller's shoulder. "Come on, Rick. Let's get out of here for a while."

Peller rose and followed, feeling more robotic than human.

Penny Lowell eventually coaxed most of the story from Phil Walters, but it came out in tangles, like a skein of yarn that had been mauled by a cat. She wondered if he remembered all of the details or the even the right sequence of events. She peppered his narrative with questions, but when his tone edged toward irritation she backed off. She understood. He wouldn't want to think too hard about what he'd been through, not yet. It would take time. Meanwhile, she fussed over him as though he were a sick child until her adrenaline rush finally wore off on Saturday and she collapsed on the sofa.

By Sunday she could almost believe that nothing unusual had happened. Walters, though, seemed pensive. He said little and spent considerable time at the window, looking out on the neighborhood. Lowell took Monday off to be with him but wasn't so much with him as in the same room as him. His silence began to irritate her. Mid-afternoon, she took his hand and told him they were going outside to resume their yard work. He followed without comment and set to work.

Half an hour later, he shoved his spade into the earth and stared at it as though it were an ancient artifact he'd just dug up. "That's it," he said.

"What?"

"My next project."

She waited and, when he didn't continue, shoved her own trowel into the soil. "I'm not a mind reader, Phil."

"I'm going to write about Morgan Parsons, Duke Calvert, and the auto theft industry."

Lowell digested the news. Last week, the prospect of crime reporting offered intrigue and excitement. Mortal danger had soured her on it. "Maybe you should go after something safer."

He looked at her, his expression blank. "Safer?"

"Like a war." The words came out before she could catch them. She'd always been supportive of his plans and wasn't sure how he'd take her sudden lack of enthusiasm.

"You're scared."

"Not today. I'd rather not be tomorrow."

Walters shuffled to her on his knees and took her in his arms. "Don't worry. The key people in this story are already dead or in police custody. It won't be dangerous. Not anymore."

"You could have died, too," she protested. "Anyway, why would you trade the Fibonacci story for something as mundane as this? You could make a lot of money on a book about the Fibonacci killer."

Walters gazed up at the treetops above them. "Nobody will ever get that story. Not really. And this isn't mundane. Calvert had quite an operation. But I guess my real motivation is Parsons."

"Parsons? He's just another hood."

"Yes, but he's a tragic figure, too. He was dead long before Calvert killed him. I think I'd like to understand what happened to him. Criminals are made, not born. There but for the grace of God go I. You know?"

Penny wasn't sure she understood, but there was no point trying to stop him. She'd never wanted to stop him before, and she didn't want to start now, even though a book about the Fibonacci murders would sell far better, she was certain, than any of his other work had.

But why couldn't he be interested in writing about something less dangerous? Something like, say, gardening?

# Chapter 22

Early Tuesday morning, she did something she'd never done before or had ever expected to do. Something that felt like betraying family.

Detective Lieutenant Bill Trengove, wrapped in a navy blue robe, answered the door. At this hour his eyes were bleary, and he stared at her as though at first he didn't recognize her. "Whitney? What's wrong?"

"I'm sorry to wake you, Bill. I have a warrant to search all items in your possession previously belonging to Jim Cowden."

Trengove straightened. "You're serious."

"One thousand percent."

"If it were anyone but you, I'd ask which judge you slept with."

Morris wasn't about to rise to the bait. She waited, silent, not sure whether to hate herself for doing this or hate Trengove for making it necessary.

"What grounds could you possibly have had?"

"I can't comment on an ongoing investigation. Are you going to let me in, or do I have to cite you for failure to comply?"

Trengove ran his hand through hair. "Damn it, Whitney. Fine, come in." He opened the door wide.

She spent nearly an hour inspecting Cowden's effects, then another hour searching the computer. When her search was complete, she left Trengove's house without a goodbye or thank you.

She knew where Jim Cowden had gone.

She had no clue why he had gone there.

Also among the bleary-eyed that morning, Father Owen snagged a fast-food breakfast and ate it while driving to Eduardo Montufar's home. Once there, he helped Corina's brother to the car and drove him up Interstate 95 into Baltimore, surrounded by rush hour traffic. Eduardo's favorite time of the year—baseball season—was now underway, and he chattered happily about the Orioles' win in their home opener. Father Owen wasn't a baseball fan himself, but he was impressed by Eduardo's encyclopedic knowledge of the game.

Downtown, Father Owen navigated to the University of Maryland Medical Center's underground parking garage, circled down to the lowest level, and eventually found a parking place. From there it was a one block walk east through the city noise to the doctors' offices and a half hour wait before they seated themselves in an exam room.

The doctor, a tall young man with almond-shaped eyes hinting at Asian ancestry, seemed to Father Owen to be barely old enough to be out of med school. "Good to see you, Eduardo," he said with a broad smile. "How are we doing these days?"

"Better and better!" Eduardo told him.

"Wonderful. Excellent." The doctor turned his attention to Father Owen. "I don't believe we've met."

"This is Father Owen, my pastor. Father, this is Doctor Byoun, my neurologist."

"Pleased to meet you," Father Owen said.

"Likewise. Thank you for helping Eduardo this morning. We have to remind him he's not ready for the Indy 500 yet."

"Next week, maybe," Eduardo said with a laugh.

Father Owen waited patiently through the review of lab work, the questions and answers, and the brief exam, noting that two or three times Eduardo seemed at a loss for a word. But neither doctor nor patient broached the subject.

As the consultation ended, Father Owen said, "We're concerned that Eduardo has been having difficulty with finding words lately."

"Yes, I've noticed the same thing," Dr. Byoun agreed. "Loss of verbal memory is not uncommon following a concussion. In Eduardo's case, it's modest enough that I don't think it's cause for worry. In fact, stress can make post-concussion symptoms worse, so it's best not to worry over it." Turning to Eduardo, he continued, "You and everyone around you should take things one day and a time and not get frustrated if it takes a while to get back to normal. Keep up with the physical therapy and keep talking. Eventually your brain will sort itself out."

Afterwards, as they rode the elevator down to street level, Eduardo nudged Father Owen. "Told you so," he said with a grin. "After all, I can still remember all the Mass responses correctly!"

Father Owen laughed. "Yes, you can. Faith is my business. I never should have doubted you."

"Let's go home and tell Corina the good news, huh?"

Captain Morris gathered Peller, Montufar, and Dumas into her office. None of the trio could make any sense of her opening words. "Centerville," she said, sinking into her chair. "West Virginia."

The three exchanged glances. "Never heard of it," Peller said. "What about it?"

"Almost heaven?" Dumas cracked, only to receive a stern look from the captain. "Never mind. What's Centerville?"

"It's the town that swallowed up Detective Lieutenant Jim Cowden. His web browser remembered the details of a pretty extensive search he made of small towns in Appalachia during the week prior to his disappearance. Towards the end of that search, Centerville became the chief focus. I have no doubt that he was looking for a place to hide and that he picked that town."

"So we can have him picked up and shipped home," Dumas said.

Morris nodded but looked to Peller, waiting for his reaction. She had a feeling she knew what it would be and hoped she was wrong.

"No," Peller said. "This is my job."

"Not your jurisdiction," Dumas said.

"And not smart," Montufar added. "If anything goes wrong, you know how it will look."

"Nothing will go wrong."

"Rick," Morris said wearily. "You should sit this one out. Trust me on this."

Peller looked exhausted by the ordeal. Hopefully, he looked around the room at his fellow officers. "Levinson might be lying."

"Rick—" began Morris, only to be cut off by simultaneous protests from the others in the room.

"Or not," Peller said hastily. "Either way, Jim was my friend. If it's true, I have to hear it from his own mouth."

She could order him to stand down, but Morris didn't want to pull rank on him, not after everything that had happened. Had their roles been reversed, she probably would have felt the same as he did. "You'll need backup," she said, again knowing what his response would be.

"No."

"Rick," Montufar began, but he shook his head and she fell silent.

"You've all done an amazing job. I can't ever repay you. But this isn't something you can do for me, and I won't put you in danger on account of it."

"He wanted to kill you," Dumas said, suddenly irritated. "What's to stop him from plugging you two seconds after you knock on his door?"

Frowning at nothing, Peller said, "Sandra."

Morris wondered if he had finally given way under the strain. "Sandra?"

"Or maybe nothing. It doesn't matter." He stood. "Email me the directions, Whitney. I'll take it from there."

She leaned back. Had she known the lay of the land, she never would have reopened this case. But the box had been opened, the evil had escaped into the world, and like Pandora the only counter she had was hope. Still, she thought, this was Rick, and if only for that reason, hope might be justified.

"You be careful," she said.

He nodded and walked slowly back to his desk.

⟿

Part of the deal, in spite of the charges outstanding against him, was that Levinson was released on twenty-five thousand dollars bond. It irritated him to have to part with such a sum, but at least he had it. With the help of his attorney, he posted bail mid-morning and by lunchtime was a free man, lounging in the passenger seat of Charles David Kirby III's black Lincoln Navigator.

"What did you decide?" Kirby asked once they were on their way.

"I've arranged to stay with a friend for a couple of weeks. There's no going back to the farm. Orion will know if I go there."

"You trust this friend?"

"We were in high school together. He's a teacher now."

Kirby glanced at him with some skepticism. "Is he married?"

"Divorced. Twice. He's got his own place, though, with enough room for an old friend in trouble."

"Where at?"

Levinson grinned, knowing that Kirby wouldn't like the answer. "Cumberland."

"Cumberland! And how do you propose to get there?"

"I pay you enough, man. You can drive me."

"That's a two-hour drive. I don't have time to be your chauffeur."

Leaning his seat back and closing his eyes, Levinson replied, "Add the gas to my bill. I'm going to take a nap now. Wake me when we're almost there so I can give you directions."

He took a last peek at Kirby. The attorney wasn't visibly fuming, but he looked irked. Levinson smiled inwardly. The man had done an incredible job, but he was far too smug. Bringing him down a peg felt good.

⤚

Keeping at least two cars between himself and the Navigator at all times, Orion Speros followed in the spotty sunlight, westward to Frederick, westward to Hagerstown, westward still through the Sidling Hill road cut where lay exposed an ancient river underlain by massive folds of rock, all the way out to Cumberland. He followed through the city up its northern flank along Valley Road, then down a side street sparsely populated by small ranch homes. The Navigator stopped at a tan and black house. Speros turned a corner, parked on the street, and waited.

From that position he couldn't see the Navigator, but he didn't need to. The lawyer certainly wouldn't stay more than a few minutes. Levinson must have come here to hide, and that SUV was anything but unobtrusive.

Fortune had been with Speros so far. As he'd hoped, Levinson had been questioned at Northern District Headquarters, but he'd been transported to another facility. At the time, getting to him looked well-nigh impossible, what with cops surrounding him. Then came the call from Esteban Narvaez: Levinson had arranged bail and was looking for a place to stay. Esteban didn't have room for him and wouldn't have let him stay there anyway, knowing what was after him, but the information was all Speros needed. He merely had to wait and watch until Levinson emerged.

And the rest, he thought with a grin, was history.

Speros considered a fast strike, giving Levinson no time to get comfortable, but he didn't like it. For one thing, it would be more fun to attack when Levinson felt secure. For another, Speros didn't want collateral damage. Whoever he was staying with needed to be in the clear. That meant ambushing Levinson either when he went out or when he was home alone.

Speros felt a rumble in his stomach and realized that he hadn't eaten for six hours. Putting his truck in gear, he made for downtown. No rush, he thought. Once he had a good meal inside him, planning would prove easier.

The drive to Centerville took over six and a half hours, during which Peller had too much time to think. At first, he puzzled over Jim Cowden's involvement in Sandra's death. An exemplary member of the force, Cowden had been a friend and mentor to him, had taken a personal interest in Peller's professional development. Short of mental illness, Peller couldn't see any way Cowden could have wanted him dead. Jason's recollection of Cowden's visit to Sandra haunted him, too. Something indeed had been wrong, very wrong, at that point, but whatever it had been seemed irretrievably lost, buried beneath the sediments of time.

Puzzlement soon gave way to anger, for there was little doubt that Cowden was ultimately responsible for Sandra's death. Whatever had led him down that path, whether illness or evil, he deserved death himself. For Sandra, for the suffering he had caused her family and her friends, justice demanded an accounting.

But was Peller the one to call him to account? Would doing so settle the score, mete out justice, or would it devolve into mere revenge, thereby perpetuating the tragedy?

The sun played hide and seek with the clouds as he drove through the mountains. He couldn't hold to either anger or logic for long. Wandering through the past, replaying bits and pieces of it, his mind soon detoured to his meeting with Sandra, their early days together, their wedding, and fixed upon a day when he had come home from work to find June, Sandra's one-time roommate, collapsed on the sofa in the living room of their apartment, eyes red from crying, a plastic bag half full of crumpled tissues at her feet.

Water was running in the kitchen sink, and there was a clink of glass against metal.

"What's wrong?" Peller asked.

June didn't look at him. "I'll be okay," she sniffed.

Sandra brought a glass of ice water from the kitchen and sat next to her. "Here you go."

June took the glass and sipped at its contents. Peller waited, not sure if his presence was wanted or needed.

"Pete," June finally said. "He wrecked my car."

Alarmed, Peller sat on the other side of her. "Is he okay?"

"Yeah, but the car's totaled."

"I didn't hear any accidents reported today."

"Not in town. Up by Wrights Corners."

"What was he doing up there?"

Her head slowly turned toward him, her eyes dull. "Good question. Bad answer: his ex-girlfriend lives there."

Peller exhaled heavily. June and Pete had been together for over a year, and Sandra had often expressed the hope that they would marry. They seemed happy together. June had never been shy about talking about her problems, but she'd never once said a negative thing about Pete. In spite of how it looked, he wondered if maybe June was jumping to conclusions. He started to say so, but Sandra flashed him a look of warning.

June reached for a box of tissues on the coffee table. "They had a bad breakup two years ago. Why would he go sneaking back to her after all this time?"

Sandra put an arm around her friend's shoulders. "Did you ask him?"

"Of course not." She blew her nose and tossed the tissue into the plastic bag. "He'd just get mad at me."

"But June..."

"Oh God, Sandra, take off those rose colored glasses for once! If you found out Rick had been visiting an old girlfriend, what would you think?"

Sandra said nothing, but neither did she pull away. She looked pityingly at her friend, then questioningly at her husband.

"How do you know he was visiting her?" Peller asked.

June shot him an exasperated look.

"Well, did he say that's where he was?"

"Come on, Rick, not you, too. You're a cop. You can figure it out."

"Cops have to develop a chain of evidence. How things look is very often not how they are. There could be a hundred reasons why Pete was in Wrights Corners. And even if he did visit his old flame, that doesn't automatically mean he did anything wrong."

June glared at him for a moment, then slumped. "Yeah, yeah, okay."

"If you don't want to ask him, I'll do it for you."

"Oh, that'll be even better."

Patting her gently on the shoulder, Sandra said, "Rick can do it without it sounding like it came from you. He's good at that sort of thing."

"Whatever." She reached for another tissue. "And what if it wasn't innocent? You think he'll tell you?"

"No," Peller admitted. "But I know him fairly well. If he lies to me, I'll think I'll know it."

"Great." She blew her nose again and tossed the tissue into the bag. "Marvelous. And if you find out he was fooling around? Would you tell me, Rick? Or would keep your mouth shut out of pity for me? Or to protect him?"

Peller didn't want to deal with that possibility. "Let's not hang him before the trial."

"But what if he was?"

"Do you love him?" Sandra asked quietly.

"More than anything in the world. You know that."

"Then forgive him."

She made it sound so simple, Peller thought, but it wasn't, was it? From the look on June's face, he knew she was thinking the same thing: how could anyone forgive betrayal?

Sandra seemed to know his thoughts. Looking at him instead of June, she said, "Seventy times seven. That's what Jesus says. You know that." She turned to June. "Seventy times seven."

Peller looked at his shoes, embarrassed.

June closed her eyes. "You know how much I hate math," she said.

"I don't like it, Jeff."

"You think I'm crazy about it?"

"How did you ever end up in this mess?" It was Wednesday morning, April thirteenth. Ryan Tasker, busy buttering a piece of sourdough toast, didn't look up. His frown of concentration seemed more for the food he was preparing than for his friend.

Levinson took a sip of coffee, pondering the question. It wasn't a question he'd asked himself too often, but he had to admit that he probably should have. Being the number two man in a criminal enterprise, that wasn't what he'd expected of life back when he and Tasker had been in school. He should have realized far earlier that in due course the piper would call in the debt.

"Okay, I should know better than to ask," Tasker said, finishing with the knife. He set it on his plate with a clank and sank his teeth into the toast.

"Let's just say that my fate was tied in knots by women."

"Bless their hearts. Seems that's always how it goes."

"Doesn't matter, though, does it? Here I am, me and my death mark. The only way it ends is in death."

Tasker shifted uncomfortably. He was a short, bespectacled, balding man, pale of complexion, wearing a bit more weight around the middle than when Levinson had last seen him six years before. The subject of death, Levinson recalled, had always disturbed him.

"I don't intend it to be mine, you know."

"But it could well be anyway."

"I just have to make sure I don't underestimate Speros."

Tasker set down his toast and finally looked Levinson in the eye. "From what you've said, nobody does, yet he always wins."

"He's real good at throwing you off your guard." Levinson looked around the kitchen at the white appliances and the window opening on the back yard where a couple of squirrels chased each other. "I need to turn the tables. Throw *him* off guard for once."

"Tricky," Tasker said, turning his attention to his food again. "He's a polar bear."

"Beg pardon?"

"A polar bear. They're known for being unstoppable. I heard about a guy up north somewhere who woke up one morning to find a polar bear climbing through the window to get at him. He unloaded his shotgun into the bear's face, point-blank, three times before the bear gave up and went in search of an easier breakfast."

Levinson couldn't help but laugh.

"You'll have to ambush him. That's the only way you can win."

He didn't laugh at that. "I'm in enough trouble without a first degree murder charge hanging over me."

"Self defense. Speros is trying to kill you. What choice do you have?"

"You a lawyer now?"

Tasker finished eating his toast.

"Ambush," Levinson mused.

"Just one thing, if you please."

"What?"

"Not in my house."

Levinson grinned.

Tasker did not.

# Chapter 23

Evening closed in, and with it a flotilla of altocumulus clouds blanketed the sky. At the small restaurant called Aunt Nellie's Kitchen, situated on the northeast edge of town, Aunt Nellie herself, a.k.a. Eleanor Pryce, was tending the cash register and chatting with a regular paying his bill when the stranger came through the door. Looking haggard, the man waited patiently while the customer took his time about paying, then stepped to the counter.

"What can I do for you?" Pryce asked.

"I need to ask a favor." He pulled a photo from his jacket pocket and handed it to her. "Do you happen to know if this man lives around here?"

Looking at the photo, Pryce narrowed her eyes. "Who wants to know?"

"He's an old friend of mine. My name is Rick Peller. I'm with the Howard County police department in Maryland. This fellow used to work with me, but he moved away a few years ago and I lost contact with him."

She turned narrow eyes on Peller. Aged seventy-three, she had smoky eyes, a smoky voice, and smoke-gray hair. She could have been made of mountain fog, although her presence was entirely substantial. "And you just happened to be in the neighborhood, I suppose?"

"Not really, no. I think he's living around here somewhere. I just don't know where."

"Long way to come for a social visit."

Peller smiled at her. "Nobody pulls the wool over your eyes, do they?"

"Not if I can help it, young man. Is he in trouble?"

"I don't know. Maybe. But I'm not here in an official capacity. I'm out of my jurisdiction, you know. I just need to talk to him. He really is an old friend."

Pryce studied the photo again. "Don't know much about him," she said. "Not even his name. He comes to town sometimes, but doesn't hang about. Seems he was a lot happier when this was taken." She handed the photo back.

"You think he's unhappy now?"

She pinched her lips tight for a moment and looked through Peller. "It's his eyes. I think they've seen something no man should see."

"Do you know where he lives?"

"Nope. Maybe Chester Reece would, though I doubt it."

"Where would I find Mr. Reece?"

"He owns the Shell gas station and garage half a mile up the road from here. He'll be closed up by now. You'll have to catch him in the morning."

"Thank you, ma'am. I really appreciate your help." Peller pocketed the photo. He looked around the restaurant. "I could do with a meal. Anywhere I should sit?"

"Take your pick. The waitress'll be right out."

With a nod, Peller went to a table by the front window and settled in. Pryce watched him while he ordered, noting how tired he looked, then went into the kitchen, wondering if he was telling the truth and what the town's mystery man had done to draw him here.

No matter where he went, Orion Speros couldn't reasonably hide from anyone who might be looking for him, a fact he reveled in. On the morning of Thursday, April fourteenth, he was drawing attention to himself in the dining room of the Bruce House Inn, a brick B-and-B situated atop a hill at the corner of Fayette and Smallwood streets, one of the oldest houses in one of the oldest parts of the city of Cumberland. A beautiful, light-filled room with a large fireplace, he fancied that his presence added something to it. Of course, it did: he was Orion!

Flaunting his Orion-sized appetite, he kept the staff busy while he chatted up an elderly couple who were staying the week in the western mountains of Maryland and a young couple celebrating their first anniversary. He regaled them with stories of his exploits in the Himalayas (all fabricated) and Antarctica (likewise). They ate it up with their eggs and bacon and Belgian waffles. Later they would agree they had never known anyone as full of life as Mr. Speros.

Mr. Speros, though, had death on his mind as he left the inn and ventured northward to Jeff Levinson's hideout. By now Levinson should have started to settle in, secure in the knowledge that his nemesis had been left behind in Howard County. He would be vulnerable. Now a bit of recon was in order to ascertain when Levinson's friend left for work.

Driving slowly past the house, Speros carefully noted the lack of activity in the neighborhood. The driveway was empty, but there was a one-car garage with its door closed. No movement was evident in the windows, no lights shining from within. He needed to get closer.

If there was a drawback to being Orion, it was that sneaking around was impossible. He'd be obvious snooping at the windows, both to anyone inside and to any neighbors who happened to be looking. He was prepared to deal with that, though. Parking around the corner from his target, he donned a dark green cap sporting a white lightning bolt and the word "Janson," grabbed a tool belt lying on the passenger seat, and got out of the truck. Around his neck he hung a lanyard from which dangled an ID card identifying him as Paul Whitmore, an employee of Janson Utilities, a certified Columbia Gas contractor.

The morning air was cool, the sky dotted with cumulus clouds. He took a small gadget from the tool belt and made a show of waving it around several storm drains, then approached the house directly across the street from the one where Levinson was staying. He rang the bell and waited.

The door was opened by a young man, a short, overweight fellow who looked about college age. He eyed Speros suspiciously, but didn't seem alarmed.

"Good morning. We're doing some safety inspections in the area today. Any chance I can have a look at your gas meter?"

"You with the gas company?"

Speros held up his fake ID. "I'm a contractor."

The man studied it for a moment as though not sure that the photo matched the man. Speros had to admit it wasn't the best picture.

"Yeah, okay. It's in the garage." Opening the door wide, he motioned Speros in and led him through a cluttered living room into a cluttered kitchen overflowing with unwashed dishes, through a small laundry room piled high with unwashed clothing, and out to a very cluttered garage.

"Looks like you could use a wife," Speros said, grinning.

"Why? Here's the meter."

The water heater was tucked in a corner of the garage, with the gas meter nearby. "None of my business, I guess," Speros said as he made a show of inspecting the equipment. The other man hovered nearby, pretending to know exactly what Speros was doing although he clearly had no clue.

Finishing the mock inspection, Speros nodded. "Looks good. By the by, is your neighbor across the way at work? I rang his bell, but nobody answered."

"No clue, man. I don't usually see anyone on this street."

"Now that I can believe."

"Actually, I think he does usually leave around seven-thirty. I sometimes see his car pulling out."

"Keeps it in the driveway, does he?"

"No, the garage."

"I suppose that's where his meter is, too."

The man shrugged. "Maybe. Never been there."

"No problem. I'll try again. If he doesn't answer, I might see if there's a side or back door into the garage. If so, I'll have a quick peek. Better safe than sorry."

"I guess."

Speros thanked his unwitting host and left. He took his time approaching the target house, careful to move in from the side rather than the front. There was indeed a back door to the garage, but as he came up to it, he heard voices inside, then the sound of the garage door sliding up and a car engine coming to life. He moved to the corner of the house and waited while the car backed out of the garage. Peering carefully around the corner, he saw a dark red Firebird pull away with two people inside.

Just his luck.

Once the car was gone, he strode back to his truck and rushed to catch up. Likely they had gone toward the city, so that's the way he went, and soon he saw them a few cars ahead of him. Following at a discreet distance, he tailed them downtown, onto the interstate, and westward towards Frostburg.

Did Levinson suspect Speros was in the neighborhood? Was he running again? Speros doubted it, but the thought bothered him. He'd almost lost Levinson this time. He wouldn't let that happen again. On the plus side, the farther west they went, the farther they got from civilization, which as far as Speros was concerned was just about perfect.

"Seen him around," Chester Reece told Peller after studying the photograph. He was sitting on a stool behind the gas station counter, a Shell Oil cap on his head, his graying mustache twitching slightly as he pondered. "Don't know his name, though. Nobody knows his name."

"Do you ever talk to him?"

"He fills up his tank and I take his money."

"That's it?"

"That's it."

Peller shook his head. "That's not how I remember him. He used to be a friendly guy."

Reece said nothing, nor did his expression.

"You wouldn't know where he lives, I suppose."

"Not sure I should say."

This time Peller waited, curious to see if Reece would volunteer anything further. Sometimes silence was the best prompt; it made people uncomfortable. Reece, though, wasn't moved to speak, so the two men simply watched each other, each waiting for the other to blink.

"I really am his friend," Peller finally said. "I just want to talk to him."

"He don't talk. But okay, I think he must live up State Road 91 east of town. I seen his car come down from there one day. No reason for him to be up there otherwise."

Peller doubted he'd get much more, so he thanked Reece and left. He drove to the junction with the indicated road, turned east, and followed it upward from the river. Alongside the road, a small run cut between two mountains, splashing over a series of rock steps as it came down from higher ground. Before long, he noticed an unpaved track that slipped southward into the trees, wending its way up an undulating slope. He couldn't see where it led, but it seemed properly anonymous, the sort of road you could pass by a thousand times without remembering. He turned onto it and drove slowly upward, winding through trees, bouncing over ruts where runoff had cut into the track. The forest engulfed him, and in a few minutes he felt as though he'd been driving this road forever without passing any sign of human presence.

Then he saw something above him, partly hidden in the trees: a rundown cabin, a structure that might have been weathering there for two centuries. He stopped and killed the engine, gazing upward from behind the steering wheel, not wanting to move, not wanting to find out what hid behind those decaying timbers.

With a start, he realized someone was there on the front porch, seated in a rocking chair, rocking slowly back and forth, back and forth.

The distance was still too great, the view partially blocked by leaves fluttering in whispers of wind, to see who it was. He sat in the car for nearly ten minutes, heart thumping, before he stirred. Slowly, quietly, he opened the door, forced himself out of the car, and just as quietly shut the door.

The figure in the rocker gave no sign of awareness.

Peller wanted to hide in the trees. He wanted to find a way upslope concealed by the foliage, but the tangle of undergrowth looked too thick. He would be heard crashing through it, no matter how carefully he moved. The road was the only way up.

He started walking.

Coming around a slight curve in the road, Peller finally had a clear view of the cabin and its occupant, who also had a clear view of him. He could see now that it was a man in the chair, a thin, old man, a man aged beyond his years, a man who seemed almost on the verge of tears.

The man stopped rocking.

He looked familiar to Peller, yet a stranger, as though he were looking at an old, broken version of himself. For a long time the two watched each other, not moving, not speaking.

Peller tried to find his voice. "Jim?" he whispered.

The other man's face was a palette smeared with grief and joy, exhaustion and relief.

"Jim?" Peller said, louder now, loud enough for the other to hear.

The man didn't reply, but it looked to Peller as though he nodded, almost imperceptibly.

A tidal wave of anger crashed down upon Peller. Once his friend, this man basking in the spring warmth, sitting here rocking as though he hadn't a care in the world—this was the man who had sought to kill Peller, who had instead killed Sandra, who had nearly destroyed his life. Peller touched the .38 concealed under his jacket at his right hip. He could have drawn the weapon in an instant, could have shot Cowden dead where he sat.

He wanted to.

Cowden seemed to tense, as though expecting Peller to signal the direction they should go.

Peller drew a long breath and reminded himself that there were yet links missing from the chain. Easing his hand away from the weapon, he took a few more cautious steps and spoke words he didn't feel: "It's good to see you again, Jim."

Drawing ever closer, he now could see tears tracking down Cowden's face, could see his lips moving as though to speak, but no sound came out. Cowden's blue eyes blinked away the moisture, and he pushed himself out of the chair. Standing now, he raised a hand, not to wave but to signal his old friend to stop.

Peller stopped.

Cowden turned away and went into the cabin while Peller waited. After a time he returned, a shotgun in his hand, held upright—not as a threat, it seemed, but Peller stiffened at the sight.

Cowden sank into the rocker again, cradling the gun in his lap. Again his lips moved as though trying to form words. At first none came out, but then something did.

"I'm sorry."

Peller at first took it as a confession, and his anger threatened to rise again. "For what?"

"I was always weak."

"Tell me, Jim."

"She seduced me. All I could think of was her."

*You liar!* Peller thought, but he felt suddenly numb, as though the air around him had in an instant turned bitter cold. Could he have been so wrong about her?

Shaking with rage and grief, he heard another voice, Sandra's voice.

*Hear him out.*

He didn't want to listen. He didn't want it to be her, didn't want any of this to be real.

*My love. Please. For your own sake, you must hear him out.*

Her voice was so real, her presence so strong, he could do nothing but wait.

"If you were out of the way..." Cowden's voice caught in his throat. He moaned like a wounded animal, then raised the gun and took aim at Peller, hands shaking. "It wasn't supposed to be her!"

Peller nearly reached for his gun. He longed to feel its weight in his hand, to empty every last round into Cowden, for Sandra, for Jason, for everyone who had known her, for himself. Most especially for himself. Rage held him in its grip, yet Sandra's words rang in his brain and he could feel her hand on his, holding him back. In that moment of hesitation, his own reason insisted that this wasn't as it seemed, that Sandra was right and that even now he was missing something vital.

Cowden couldn't steady his weapon. It wavered up and down, back and forth, as tears flooded his eyes once more. "It wasn't her," he said. "You can't kill an angel. I was the one who died that day."

He pumped a round into the chamber and fired. The miniature explosion echoed through the woods and between the mountains, but the shot flew so wide that Peller didn't as much as flinch.

"I'm sorry," Cowden cried. "I'm so sorry, Sandra!"

He pumped the weapon again, fired again, missed again. And a third time. And a fourth. Peller watched, paralyzed, as Cowden dug in his left pants pocket and extracted several more shells, then fumbled to reload. Cowden could have killed Peller at any moment if only he could have shot straight, but he seemed powerless to hit his mark.

And then Peller understood. Cowden wasn't trying to kill him. He wasn't firing wildly, wasn't unable to control his aim. He was going out of his way to miss. Peller's anger melted away before the pitiful display. A great weariness overtook him.

He understood. He understood everything. He wanted nothing more than to lie down and sleep for a thousand years.

Another shot reverberated around him.

"Put the gun down, Jim," he said. "It's over."

"It's not over!" Cowden screamed. "One of us must die! Where's your gun, Rick? Defend yourself!" He fired again, fired at nothing, hit nothing.

"I'm not going to kill you."

"Yes you are! You hate me! You must hate me!"

"What's left to hate? Look at yourself. You already tried, judged, and sentenced yourself. All that you have left is your execution, and you've already done that, too."

Cowden stared at him, mouth agape, eyes blind with terror.

"Jim. Put the gun down."

The shotgun slipped from Cowden's hands and crashed to the porch.

Peller slowly approached until he stood at the foot of the steps while Cowden, head cradled in his hands, wept.

"You hate me," he repeated.

Peller drew a long breath and slowly released it. He felt Sandra at his side and knew her heart overflowed with pity.

"No, Jim," he said. "I forgive you."

Still bent over, face buried, Cowden shook his head. "You can't," he said.

"Please," he said.

"Please don't," he whimpered.

# Chapter 24

Peller returned home on Sunday. On Monday, April eighteenth, he reported for work as usual and convened a meeting with Captain Morris, Montufar, and Dumas. In the conference room with the door shut, the first words he spoke, addressed to the tabletop as much as to his colleagues, were a repeat of what he'd told Cowden: "It's over."

They waited.

"Jim shot and killed himself Thursday evening, probably just about sunset."

"Did you speak with him before that?" Morris asked.

"Yes. The short version is, he tried to provoke death by cop, but it didn't work. Afterwards, I had to drive back to town to get help. He didn't have a phone, and cell service up there is very spotty. They dispatched a squad and an ambulance to collect him for emergency hospitalization and psychiatric evaluation, but we were too late. We searched his place and I spent a couple of days talking to people around town who'd crossed paths with him. I had to do a lot of reading between the lines. He didn't talk to people in town and left little by way of explanation, but I think I know what happened."

He leaned back and stretched his legs under the table. He felt exhausted, and not just from the drive. But somehow he also felt a degree of lightness, as though he'd set down a burden he'd been carrying for four years.

Nobody prompted him; he continued on his own.

"Rumor had it that Jim was a womanizer and had a gambling problem. There was probably some truth to the former, if not the latter. His marriage didn't last long, which may say something. In any case, he definitely fell under Sandra's spell."

Montufar frowned. "But she didn't encourage it, certainly."

"No, I don't believe she did, but you all know how easy it was to love her. I think Jim knew he was in trouble, maybe from the first time he met her. He was the only person I ever knew who would refuse her invitations to a get-together. He came to our house a few times, but often he would make excuses. Sandra never pressed him on it as far as I know, but neither did she give up on him.

"Eventually, he must have become infatuated with her. My son remembers a visit he paid to Sandra not long before she died. Jason saw Jim holding Sandra's hands. After he left she was upset but wouldn't tell Jason why. I think Jim must have told her how he felt about her, maybe even asked her to leave me. Whatever passed between them, Jim was already lost at that point. After that, it must have been a slow descent into madness."

Dumas picked up a pen and studied it, rotating it between his fingers. "He must have been mad, thinking that your death would bring Sandra into his arms. That never would have happened."

"No," Peller agreed, "but desperation seldom makes for good logic. And he was desperate. Sandra consumed him. She was all he could think about. One of his informants put him in touch with Jeff Levinson and Levinson hired Orion Speros to take me out. But the day I was supposed to be on that road, I wasn't feeling well. I stayed home, and Sandra took my car. She died in my place."

Peller noticed that Morris seemed to be watching him like a concerned mother. "And then," she said, "he had to personally take charge of the investigation to keep the spotlight from finding any of the participants."

"Exactly. Driven to distraction by obsession, then driven mad by a twist of fate that killed the object of his obsession, chained by the need to avoid exposure, he ran away as soon as the case was sufficiently obscured. But he couldn't run from Sandra and what he'd done to her. All he could do was wait for me to find him and kill him. And then that went wrong, too, because I didn't kill him. But Jim Cowden didn't die when he shot himself. He died four years ago, when Orion Speros slammed his truck into Sandra."

Montufar nodded. "Spiritually, he died well before even that."

"True death," Dumas mused.

Morris shifted her gaze to him. "Sorry?"

"Something someone said to me recently. True death. Not the death of the body. The death of the soul."

"Maybe so," Peller said. "In any case, it's over. Jim judged and sentenced himself."

"And you?" Morris asked.

"I think," Peller said, "I can finally make peace with the past." He smiled a peaceful smile. The others couldn't have known it, but he was smiling at Sandra. She was there, with him, with all of them, and always would be.

"But we still need to deal with Levinson and Speros," Dumas told him. "They have to face a reckoning, too."

"Speaking of which," Montufar asked, "do we know where they are?"

⟨⟩

Initially, it looked like a tragic accident: on Friday, April fifteenth, a rental car and a pickup truck collided on the Maple Street bridge in Friendsville, the westernmost town in Maryland along Interstate 68, spilling both vehicles into the Youghiogheny River. The driver of the car was dead before he hit the water, while the driver of the truck clung to life for a time. Flown by medivac helicopter to a hospital in Cumberland, he slipped away the day after the accident without regaining consciousness.

The rental car driver, police learned, had obtained the car the day before at a cut-rate place in Frostburg, where the agent said he'd been dropped off by a friend. Later that day, he checked in under an alias at the Riverside Hotel in Friendsville on the west bank of the river. Meanwhile, the driver of the truck—a big, exuberant man impossible to mistake—had also arrived in town on Thursday and took a room at the Yough Valley Motel on the other side of the river. He, too, had used an alias.

As there were no eyewitnesses to the crash, the exact circumstances would probably always remain a mystery. But when such details as could be determined finally arrived in Howard County a few days later, the detectives of the Criminal Investigations Division had little doubt: Jeff Levinson and Orion Speros had indeed been called to their reckoning, and justice had won out.

Thank you for reading! Please leave a short, honest review wherever you bought this book. I greatly appreciate it, and it will help others discover my books.

# Further Reading

Rick Peller, Corina Montufar, and Eric Dumas return in more Howard County Mystery novels, available in print and ebook through your favorite bookseller:

### The Fibonacci Murders (HCM #1)

"I start with zero. Nobody dies today." The strange note delivered to Rick Peller proves to be a warning shot. He, Corina Montufar, and Eric Dumas are soon pursuing a cunning killer basing murders on the Fibonacci series, a mathematical sequence in which each number is the sum of the preceding two. And the only thing Peller knows for sure is that the series never ends.

### Ice on the Bay (HCM #3)

A veterinary technician vanishes without a trace. A arson in an exclusive area bears the marks of an arsonist currently serving a prison term. A murder victim leaves behind an address book full of suspects. While temperatures plummet, cold cases collide with new crimes, and somewhere a killer with blood as icy as the waters of the Chesapeake watches and waits.

### A Day for Bones (HCM #4)

A catastrophic flood in Ellicott City unearths a human skeleton. Did a colonial settler wash out of his grave? Or is it murder? As Rick Peller and his team investigate, the descendants of James Ferring, a local business icon from a bygone era, become the focus, and Peller is sure they're hiding something.

# About the Author

Dale E. Lehman is an award-winning writer, veteran software developer, amateur astronomer, and bonsai artist in training. He principally writes mysteries, science fiction, and humor. In addition to his novels, his writing has appeared in *Sky & Telescope* and on Medium.com. He owns and operates the imprint Red Tales. He and his late wife Kathleen have five children, six grandchildren, and two feisty cats. At any given time, Dale is at work on several novels and short stories.

Visit https://www.DaleELehman.com to find out more about Dale's books.